Between Worlds

Jacqueline E. Smith

Wind Trail Publishing

Between Worlds

Wind Trail Publishing
PO Box 830851
Richardson, TX 75083-0851
www.WindTrailPublishing.com

Second Paperback Edition, February 2020

ISBN-13: 978-0-9896734-2-6
ISBN-10: 0989673421

Library of Congress Cataloguing-in-Publication Data
Smith, Jacqueline E.
Cemetery Tours / Jacqueline E. Smith
Library of Congress Control Number: 2014941075

Cover Design by Wind Trail Publishing

Printed in the United States of America.

For all my loved ones, in this world and the next.

CHAPTER ONE

"Welcome to The Sally Stone Show. I'm your host, Sally Stone, here to talk with only the most interesting folks around.

"Our first guest is a young man who claims that he can see and speak to the spirits of the dead. He made local headlines three months ago after being held hostage by serial killer Chastity Cannon, now known in most media outlets as The Angel of Death. He was then saved, thanks to a daring rescue by his neighbor and Luke Rainer, star of the ghost hunting hit, Cemetery Tours. Now, here to talk to us today about his extraordinary sixth sense, please welcome Mr. Michael Sinclair."

Sally: Michael, thank you for being here with us.

Michael: Thanks. I - I mean... you're welcome.

Sally: So tell me, how did you become friends with a superstar like Luke Rainer? I must confess I'm a little jealous. I'd love it if Luke Rainer were my best friend.

Michael: Actually, my best friend is my roommate, Brink. And Kate. But Luke's a good friend, too. I mean, he did help save my life. Um... was that the question?

Sally: Close enough. Let's talk about the ghost thing. Is it true?

Michael: Uh... yeah...

Sally: You seem hesitant.

Michael: Sorry. I'm not really used to talking about it.

Sally: That reminds me, how did you manage to keep something like this a secret for so long? I mean seeing ghosts? That's kind of a big deal.

Michael: I guess I kept it the way most people keep secrets. I never talked about it.

Sally: Well, now that it's out there, I'm guessing there are a lot of people who want you to talk about it.

Michael: Yeah. It's kind of crazy.

1

Sally: How are you coping with the attention? Has your life changed very much?

Michael: Not really. It was a little hectic a few months ago, but overall, life is pretty much back to normal.

That was a lie - one of many Michael had told to Sally Stone, the late-night talk show host and self-proclaimed speaker for all things new, hot, and interesting.

Life had never been normal, but at least it wasn't downright chaotic. Well, it *hadn't* been before that incident with Chastity Cannon had left him with a broken collarbone, a gunshot wound, ugly bruises the size of baseballs, and a swarm of reporters tracking his every move and demanding to know whether or not her allegations were true.

Could he actually *see* ghosts?

Fortunately, the bruises were gone, the gunshot wound had healed, and the collarbone was pretty much back to the way it was before. Though it did hurt whenever it was about to rain.

A seventh sense. Lucky me.

Unfortunately, the aftereffects of being outed as a "medium," a "psychic," and something called a "ghost-talker," still lingered. For example, instead of turning on the television to find an actor telling a funny story about something that happened on the set of his latest movie or a new author explaining the inspiration behind her latest bestseller, he was suddenly face-to-face with his own image, looking very much out of place and stammering like a total idiot.

"Well, at least you're cute," Kate had offered up in consolation after the interview aired on TV. But Michael was pretty sure she was just trying to make him feel better because he definitely wouldn't call the nervous guy on the television screen any sort of attractive.

His hair, which usually fell in dark, messy locks around his face, had been styled back so that he looked like he was on his way to Prom in the 1950s. Then the makeup crew had added so much eyeliner that his brown eyes looked even darker (and somehow a lot more sinister) than they normally did. The

2

foundation they'd used did do a good job concealing how queasy-green and pale he'd been, but it had been a totally different color than the rest of his skin, so he'd ended up looking like a rock-star pumpkin with a lot of hair gel. The dark suit he was wearing only accentuated the orange color of his skin. But maybe, just maybe, his awkward appearance would distract from how blatantly uncomfortable he had been during the interview.

He wished Sally Stone had asked Luke to be her guest instead. After all, Luke was the celebrity. He was used to speaking in front of large audiences. And he and Kate were the ones who'd actually done something heroic that night in the field. Michael had just been the damsel in distress.

But he could talk to ghosts. That made him the "interesting" one.

Kate had told him he wasn't giving himself enough credit. After all, he had saved her life. The bullet he'd taken had actually been intended for her, but he'd pushed her out of the way. The thing was no one had actually asked him about that. They just wanted to talk about the ghosts.

At first, Michael wished the reporters and talk show hosts would ask him about something else: where he'd gone to school, what he liked to do in his spare time, how he felt about global warming, anything. But considering the way his life had been going lately, he'd definitely rather talk about the dead people wandering around his living room. They were a lot less of a bummer.

In the three months since the "incident," he'd lost his job at the library. They told him that because of city budget cuts, they couldn't afford to keep menial jobs like shelving books, but he was the only one who'd been let go. He suspected that due to procedural regulations, the library director couldn't fire him because a few paranoid people were afraid that he'd bring a ghost to work. So instead, they blamed it on budget cuts.

Now, Michael spent what few spare moments he had trying to find a new job. It wasn't an easy task. Most potential employers knew his story, and those who didn't usually heard about him from someone else. Before, Michael would have thought that a pseudo-celebrity status might help him get hired. But that was definitely not the case. If anything, it seemed to be preventing it.

Being in the public eye also meant that people everywhere suddenly knew who he was. Instead of being just another guy shopping for paper towels and peanut butter at the grocery store, he was Michael Sinclair, American Medium. Strangers, both living and dead, approached him daily, asking if he would contact someone for them. He tried to accommodate the dead as much as he could, but their living loved ones were a little more complicated. Contrary to popular belief, he wasn't a medium, at least not the kind that could summon spirits who had already moved on. Perhaps there were people out there who could, but he wasn't one of them. The only ghosts he could access were the ones still hanging around in this world or realm or whatever word Luke would use to describe it.

On top of all of that, Kate's parents were putting forth every effort to make sure their daughter had nothing more to do with him. Not that there was very much they *could* do. After all, Kate was a grown woman who was capable of making her own decisions, and she and Gavin still lived right across the landing from Michael. But it was still bothersome.

That was why, whenever interviewers like Sally Stone asked him if his life had changed very much in the past three months, his answer was always, "No."

As annoying as all of that was, he had to admit that some good had come out of being forced into the public eye. For example, he no longer lived in fear of someone discovering his secret. He hadn't quite realized just how tremendous a burden something like that could be on a person until that burden had been lifted. Without having to live in a constant state of awareness of everything he said and did, now, he was able to just live.

The best thing was that he could finally talk to his mother, Dianne, about everything. After growing up with a brother who suffered from a variety of mental illnesses, Michael had tried his hardest to be strong for his mother, to give her some sense of normalcy. Every decision he'd made throughout his life had, in some way, been made out of his desire to protect her, and he'd tried to explain that the evening he'd been released from the hospital... The same day the story about his ghost-talk broke.

"So, this is your big secret, huh?" she'd asked once she helped him settle back into his apartment. "Were you ever going to tell me?"

"Probably not," he admitted.

To his surprise, she smiled. She had that knowing look in her eye that all mothers seemed to get when having a heart-to-heart with their children.

"You know, I've always known," she told him.

He wasn't sure if it was the effects of his pain medication or the shock of his mother's confession, but Michael was suddenly very dizzy.

"How?"

"You couldn't have been more than four years old. You had been playing outside for hours, so I looked out to make sure you were all right. There you were, in the middle of the yard, talking to yourself. But you weren't talking to yourself. Your eyes were fixed on something taller than you. You looked like you were listening very intently to whatever they were saying. When you finally came in for dinner, I asked you who you'd been talking to. You said that her name was Ruth, that she thought my garden was lovely. You also told me that her favorite flowers were the pink tulips, and that she loved to drink iced tea and catch lightning bugs after the sun went down."

Michael was surprised to see tears shimmering in his mother's eyes.

"Growing up, our next-door neighbor was an older woman named Ruth Rawlings," she continued. "All of my grandparents died when I was little, so she was the closest thing to a grandmother I had. I even called her Grandma Ruth. She had the most beautiful garden, and she would always let me come over and help her tend the flowers. Whenever it got hot, she'd make up a huge pitcher of iced tea, and at night, your uncle and I would run around the garden and catch fireflies." Dianne reached out and took Michael's hand. "There was no way you could have known all of that unless she'd really been there."

"Why didn't you say anything?" Michael asked.

"I guess I figured if you wanted me to know, you'd eventually tell me. Though I must admit, I didn't think I'd hear about it on the local news."

Michael hadn't either. But in a weird way, he was sort of relieved that he hadn't had to be the one to tell her. He wouldn't have known how to begin a conversation like that.

"So, that crazy girl who shot me? She did it because I can talk to ghosts."

Yeah, he was definitely better off when somebody else did the talking. He'd never been very good at it. He hadn't even been the one to tell Kate about the ghosts. That had been all Luke's doing. So technically, all of this was Luke's fault.

No, that wasn't fair. Luke had saved his life. He couldn't blame him for this mess. Well, he guessed he *could* if he really wanted to. After all, if it hadn't been for Luke tricking Kate into talking Michael into going on that stupid ghost hunt in the first place, then they never even would have met Chastity Cannon. But that seemed a little convoluted, even to him.

Besides, he had to give Luke some credit. He'd thought that after word got out about his ability, Luke would become more insistent than ever that he make a guest appearance on *Cemetery Tours*, the hit paranormal investigation series that Luke hosted on The Discovery Channel. But after all the fuss had died down, Luke had returned to L.A. to begin work on the next season, with only a simple, "Remember, you're always welcome on the show, Mikey." No pressure. No blackmail. He hadn't even played the I-saved-your-life-so-now-you-owe-me card.

As much as Michael hated to admit it, he was sort of starting to like Luke. And *Cemetery Tours* was actually a pretty decent show. Kate had come over and forced him to watch a few episodes while he was still recovering and he had to say the crew

6

caught some pretty compelling evidence. Michael even found himself almost taking Luke seriously, and that was hard to do when the latter was running around chasing disembodied footsteps in preppy clothes that might have been cool in the sixth grade but just looked ridiculous now. He'd asked Kate why, if Luke was so rich and successful, he couldn't afford better clothes. She had just laughed.

Kate.

Thinking about her reminded Michael of how little he'd seen her since his recovery. He'd thought about asking her out to dinner, but he couldn't figure out how to make it sound like he was asking her as just a friend, not as a date. Not that he would mind if it turned into a date. He just didn't want to pressure her for anything, especially if she wasn't ready. He knew it might take some time, but that was all right.

She was worth the wait.

CHAPTER TWO

It was beginning to look a lot like autumn. About time, too. It was already the second week of October. Then again, Octobers in Dallas seldom looked the way that Octobers were supposed to look. They also seldom felt it. Today was the first day of the season that the weather had been cool enough for Kate to wear jeans and a sweater. However, she'd lived in Texas long enough to know that it wouldn't last. She'd be back in shorts and flip-flops soon, maybe even as early as later that afternoon. In Texas, you really never knew.

But at least for the moment, she could enjoy the clear sky, the cool breeze, and the brightly colored leaves falling like rain from the trees and dancing their way around the marble headstones of Saint Paul's Cemetery. Even though her Color Anomia made it difficult to describe the vibrant shades of the sky and the trees, it was a beautiful and peaceful setting; quiet and still. Kate knew that the calm atmosphere meant she was alone. There were no ghosts waiting for her in the graveyard. Not that she'd expected to encounter one, or anything unusual. Michael had told her that most ghosts didn't spend too much time floating around cemeteries.

Clutching a bouquet of fall-colored roses, she wove her way through the headstones until she reached the newer section of the graveyard, where the more recent burials had taken place. Finally, she came to a stop in front of a rather new headstone resting beneath the shade of a small ash tree.

Trevor Joseph Hanson
Beloved Son and Friend
April 24, 1986- January 6, 2013

"Hi Trevor," Kate whispered as she knelt down and placed the flowers against the cool, clean marble.

In the past three months, Gavin had told her everything about her late fiancé, from his favorite movie (*Top Gun*) to the time they'd gotten lost in the London underground. Although she still had no recollection of their time together, she finally felt like she knew the man she'd been engaged to marry before a horrific car crash claimed his life and robbed her of her memories of him.

"How are you?" she asked. She knew that he had moved on, to Heaven, Nirvana, or whatever came next, but she truly believed that wherever he was, he could still hear her. "I hope you're okay. I hope that wherever you are, you're happy."

As she spoke, a soft breeze swept past her, toying with loose strands of hair, and she couldn't help but feel that it was his way of telling her that he was all of those things and more. She smiled and wiped a stray tear away from her eye.

"I wish I had known more about you while you were still here. I wish I had known what to say to you. I... wish I knew what to say right now. These last few months have been surreal. This entire *year* has been surreal. Between you and me, I'm kind of glad it's almost over. Maybe next year will be a little less... confusing.

"I am excited about the holidays, though. Halloween is going to be a lot of fun. By the way, I saw that picture from last Halloween, the one where you're Han Solo and I'm Princess Leia. I have no idea how you managed to talk me into that one. Gavin said that I agreed willingly, but I'm pretty sure I lost a bet.

"Gavin is great, by the way. He has a job now, working as a video editor for a company that shoots events like graduations and weddings. He really likes it, but some of the hours are weird. I used to think that I was the night owl of the family, but he'll stay up until two in the morning working on a project. I guess now that he's feeling better, he can do that sort of thing."

Even though the past few months had left her drained, both physically and emotionally, she was grateful for the good things, especially Gavin's health. Not knowing the source of his frequent illness and exhaustion had been worse for her than recovering from the car accident. She could handle that herself. But she hadn't had a clue how to take care of her brother, especially when his doctors seemed equally baffled. They'd all been completely helpless.

That is, until Michael came along. Thanks to him, Trevor had finally been able to tell Kate everything that her family had tried to keep secret from her. She understood that they had been trying to protect her, but that didn't make up for the intense betrayal she felt at being kept in the dark. After she woke up from her coma, she'd had a hundred questions, and she had trusted her family to answer those questions honestly. Instead, they'd taken advantage of her memory loss and rewritten her past in an attempt to spare her from further heartache. In doing so, they'd angered Trevor to the point of draining Gavin of his strength and energy, leaving him ill and exhausted for months.

Now that Trevor had moved on, Gavin had made a full recovery. But the damage done to Kate's relationship with her parents had persisted.

Kate tried to remind herself that her parents had acted with her best interests at heart, but the way they had been behaving ever since she'd confronted them about Trevor was making it very difficult for her to forget their past transgressions.

Instead of giving her time to adjust to her new reality, her parents were demanding she seek immediate counseling, that she move out of her apartment, and that she cut off contact from Michael completely. How they had the audacity to blame him for everything after they were the ones who had lied to her... the thought made her blood boil.

"I guess I'm not really telling you anything you don't know," Kate said to Trevor. "I know you're watching over us. Maybe you can send us a little heavenly guidance. I know I could use it."

"Kate?"

Kate was so startled by the voice that she jumped half a foot in the air. She whirled around to see a short, plump woman she didn't recognize standing a few yards away, and staring at her with wide, bewildered eyes.

"Is... is it really you?" the woman asked, reaching out to her. Although she had no memory of the woman's face, Kate knew who she must be.

"Mrs. Hanson?" she asked.

The woman choked back a sob.

"You remember?"

"No," Kate replied. "But I've... I've heard about you. And Trevor."

"Oh, sweetie..." Mrs. Hanson dropped her purse and the bouquet of flowers she was holding and embraced Kate. Though Kate knew that technically, the woman wasn't a stranger, it was still awkward and uncomfortable to be hugged so tightly by someone she couldn't remember ever meeting. "Oh, Kate... I thought I was never going to see you again."

"I'm sorry that it took so long," Kate murmured into her shoulder.

After a few more moments, Mrs. Hanson released her and held her at arm's length.

"Look at you. You look so beautiful," she said. "How are you? Are you good? I mean... are you all right after... after everything that happened?"

"Yeah, I am. I had a check-up last week. Everything is still good. Healthy as can be."

"But you still don't remember."

"No," Kate replied. "My brother has been answering as many questions as he can, but I know there will always be more."

"Well, I know I'm practically a stranger to you now, but know that you can ask me anything you want to know. You're always welcome at our house. We wanted you in our lives so badly, Kate. It broke our hearts the day your mother told us we'd never see you again. You were all of Trevor that we had left. And even if you weren't, we still loved you like you were our own. It was just devastating to think that you didn't even know us... didn't even know him..."

11

Kate offered her a slight smile.

"I think he felt the same way," she said.

Mrs. Hanson looked at her.

"Who told you about him?"

That was a very long story, one that Kate wasn't sure she was ready to share. So to keep matters simple, she replied, "My brother. He'd kept a photo album full of pictures of us. I've looked through it so many times, I've basically memorized them. But they're all new memories. None of the originals."

"Maybe one day you'll get them back," Mrs. Hanson said.

"Maybe," Kate replied.

She would never admit it to Trevor's mother, but she wasn't sure she wanted them back. After Gavin had first told her about Trevor, she thought that sad memories would be better than no memories at all. But Gavin's stories had left her with a strange sense of mourning for Trevor and everything that had been lost with him. She couldn't imagine the heartache she would feel if she actually *remembered*.

"So, tell me about your life now. Are you... seeing anyone new?" Mrs. Hanson asked.

Kate could tell it was a difficult question for her to ask. Truth be told, it was a difficult question to answer as well.

Was she seeing anyone? If "seeing anyone" meant being in a nice, normal, steady relationship with a guy who took her out on dates to dinner and to the movies, then no, she wasn't seeing anyone. But if "seeing anyone" meant having had a brief almost-relationship with her cute new neighbor who could see ghosts and who had actually played a big role in revealing that she was being haunted by the spirit of her former fiancé, then maybe.

It was just that ever since Michael had become an overnight paranormal sensation, she really hadn't been able to spend that much time with him. Alone, anyway. She knew it was due, in part, to his busy schedule. Whenever he wasn't giving an interview or appearing on a late-night talk show, he was dealing with calls, emails, and letters from people who wanted him to contact their loved ones for them. No matter how many times he explained that his gift didn't work that way, that he couldn't just summon ghosts with his mind, it seemed someone had missed the memo.

But even when they did get a moment alone together, they kept things strictly platonic. No holding hands, no kissing, never anything more than a brief, friendly hug. Kate knew that he'd been doing his best to give her time to get used to the idea of Trevor, and to grieve for him, but she couldn't help but feel he could at least be a *little* flirty.

Of course, it was Michael she was dealing with. It had taken Luke outright telling Kate that Michael liked her for him to finally come out and admit it. But she guessed that was part of his charm.

"Sort of," she told Mrs. Hanson. "It's kind of a weird situation. We were dating when I found out about Trevor. He thought I might need some time to adjust, to get over him. We're still friends and we still see each other, but we haven't really picked things up again."

"Do you want to?" Mrs. Hanson asked.

"Yeah, I do," Kate replied honestly. "I was actually thinking about asking him if he'd be my date to a party next week."

"So why don't you?"

"I don't know. He's busy. And... and I'm still not sure it would be right." Normally, this was the kind of conversation she'd have with her mother. But since Terri Avery wanted her daughter to have nothing more to do with Michael Sinclair, she probably wasn't the one to consult on the matter.

"Because of Trevor?" Mrs. Hanson asked gently. "Oh, sweetheart, you can't feel that way. Trevor loved you so much. All he ever wanted was for you to be happy. If you want to honor him, do so by living a wonderful and vibrant life. That's the kind of life he wanted you to live. And if this boy makes you happy, then you need to go and get him."

"Really?"

Mrs. Hanson nodded. "If there's one thing I've learned from all of this, it's that our time here is too precious to not be spent with the ones we love."

Truer words were never spoken, Kate thought. She shouldn't have to have anyone reminding her of that, especially after everything she, and the people she loved, had been through.

Before she left the cemetery, Kate embraced Mrs. Hanson one last time, and promised to come over for dinner sometime in the next few weeks. Then, with one quick, "See you later," to Trevor, she walked back to her car.

When she got home, she made the familiar climb up the stairs to the second landing. Ever since she and Michael had decided to keep things platonic, at least for the time being, she had made a point of bypassing his door, but today, she didn't even hesitate. Knowing that he'd be home, she tucked a stray lock of hair behind her ear and knocked on his door. He answered a few moments later.

"Hey." He was obviously surprised to see her.

"Hey," she replied. "What's up?"

"Not a lot. Just the usual. Looking for a job and trying to keep an eighteen-year-old ghost entertained."

Kate grinned. "How is Brink?"

"Oh, you know. Whiny. Impatient. Plaid. Brink."

"Well, that being said, do you think he'd mind if I stole you next Friday night for a party that one of our clients is throwing?"

"You want me to go with you?"

"Yeah. That is, if you want to. I think it'll be a lot of fun. The lady who's hosting is literally dripping-with-diamonds rich and she throws all these extravagant parties throughout the year. We decorate for all of them. This is going to be the first one I've ever been to. Well, technically, I've been to several but this is the first one I'll have been to since the accident, so it'll be the first one that I remember... I'm sorry, I know I'm rambling."

She didn't know why she was nervous. It was Michael. She knew he liked her. He'd taken a bullet for her. But for some reason, asking a guy out was always a nerve-wracking experience. Granted, she hadn't been all that anxious the first time she'd asked him to a party, but that was just a friendly invitation to Gavin's birthday. She wasn't asking him to be her *date*.

"No, it's okay. I'd love to go," Michael told her, looking genuinely happy for what seemed like the first time in months.

"Really? Great." Kate smiled. "It's a Halloween party, so of course, everyone's expected to come in costume, but not cheap, ten-dollar costumes. Karen expects actual *costumes*. I think I'm going to borrow a dress from one of Gavin's friends. He used to work in a theater, so he has a lot of friends with costumes. If you want, I can ask if one of the guys has something you can wear."

"That would be great since I have no idea where I'd find a legitimate costume," Michael confessed.

"Do you have any preferences? Knight? Zombie? Jedi-Master?"

"Just nothing with lace," Michael grinned.

"Are you sure? You'd make such a cute fop," Kate teased.

"Oh, thanks." Michael grinned.

"You're welcome." Then, not wanting to overstay her welcome (not that she thought Michael would actually ask her to leave), she said, "Well, I guess I'd better be getting home. It's my turn to make dinner tonight and Gavin gets grouchy if he doesn't feed."

Michael laughed. "Tell him I said hello."

"I will. Tell Brink the same."

"You should come over and see him sometime. I think he misses you."

Kate looked up at Michael and smiled.

"I miss him, too."

CHAPTER THREE

"So you're trying to tell me that you are actually going to walk out of this apartment and allow yourself to be seen... in public... by actual *people*... looking like *that*?!" Brink asked, staring over Michael's shoulder into his friend's reflection in the bathroom mirror.

"That's a lot of smack talk coming from the guy who once admitted to having a mullet," Michael rebuked.

"Hey, the mullet was *in* back in those days. That monstrosity you've got on hasn't been in style since like, the 1500s."

"Brink, it's a Halloween party. We're supposed to be in costume. Besides, I think this is more like 1700s."

"Whatever. You couldn't have picked anything a little less... frou-frou?"

Michael didn't know what Brink was griping about. He didn't think he looked half bad, actually. The outfit Kate had borrowed for him was a pirate costume with brown pants, a flowing white shirt, a brown leather vest, and a red sash that tied around his waist. The guy who had loaned it to him had even thrown in a prop sword and pistol. He kind of felt like Jack Sparrow in *Pirates of the Caribbean*. Of course, he couldn't admit that to Brink. Not unless he wanted to be teased and taunted for the rest of his life.

"I didn't pick it. I borrowed it."

"Well, I guess that makes it a little better. But you still look ridiculous."

"I'll try not to let your opinion ruin my evening," Michael remarked.

"So what's Kate gonna wear?"

"I don't know."

16

"You think it'll be something sexy? Maybe she'll be like, a tavern wench. You know, with the short, skimpy skirt and the corset and -"

"I think she's a little more wholesome than that," Michael interrupted Brink before he could fantasize further. Though he couldn't deny, he was a little curious himself.

"I don't know. I mean, if this is a date, she might try something a little... risqué." Brink smirked and wriggled his eyebrows before his expression fell serious again. "This is a date, right?"

"I don't know."

"It's got to be a date. I mean, she asked you to a party with things like sexy costumes and alcohol! How is that not a date?"

"Brink, I know this might come as a shock to you, but this isn't a frat party. This is a work party. There won't be any Spin the Bottle games or Beer Pong." Brink looked like he couldn't figure out what they were supposed to do at such a party, but before he could question him, someone knocked on the front door. "Okay, that's Kate. Please behave."

"When do I not?" Brink asked innocently.

Michael ignored him. When he reached the entry hall, he paused just for a moment, took a deep breath, and opened the door.

Although he'd always known Kate was beautiful and had seen her in an array of outfits, nothing could have prepared him for how gorgeous she looked standing there in the glow of his porch light. She was wearing an exquisite blue gown, adorned with intricate gold embroidery and a glittering gold and sapphire headpiece. Her hair was knotted up with a few blonde strands falling into her eyes. All in all, she was the most beautiful girl Michael had ever seen.

"Trick or treat," she greeted him.

"Wow. I - I mean..." He cleared his throat. "You look... wow..."

"Holy sh - "

17

"Thanks," Kate grinned, interrupting Brink's rather inappropriate commentary. "You look pretty wow too."

"Um... thanks." That was the right response, right? At the moment, he was having a difficult time remembering his own name. "I... uh... I'm almost ready if you'd like to... um... if you'd like to come in."

"All right," Kate replied. "Just so you know, there's no hurry. It's more of a come and go type thing. It's not so much of a party as it is her giving people the opportunity to see her house and all her cool Halloween decorations. But there will be food, which, if you ask me, is the most important part."

"Oh, yeah. Absolutely. Food is the best." As soon as the words were out of his mouth, Michael wanted to kick himself.

Please, for one night, can you not make a complete idiot of yourself? Can't you at least try to be cool?

Fortunately, Kate just laughed.

Ten minutes later, they were in her car, on their way to the party. Michael had offered to drive, but Kate had explained that the woman's house was in such a rich and exclusive neighborhood that she'd had to give her license plate number to the security guard ahead of time. Michael hadn't even known that people that rich actually existed. They were very real, however, as the mansions, all alight with their big glass doors and dazzling crystal chandeliers, stood to testify. Michael could only stare, mouth agape, as they drove through the neighborhood of three and four-story houses, all of which looked like they belonged in Beverly Hills, not North Dallas.

Karen's house turned out to be the most extravagant of all. A three-story white mansion near the end of the street, it reminded Michael of a palace he might have seen in a storybook. In front of the lavish front doors, which were made of crystal and decorated with intricate and glittering gold, orange, and umber wreathes, stood four men in red jackets.

"She has valets?" Michael asked, incredulous.

"I told you. She is really rich," Kate replied, pulling up to the walkway and handing her keys over to one of the valets as she climbed out of the car.

Two greeters opened the front doors for them before either had the chance to knock or ring the doorbell. There in the entry hall, a spirited woman dressed in a black evening gown, adorned with pearls and shimmering diamonds, stood in the entry way, chatting loudly with a group of guests.

"That's Karen Borden, our hostess" Kate explained.

"She seems very friendly," Michael observed.

"Oh, yes," Kate confirmed. "She has a story for everyone. But she's a real sweet lady, very genuine. And there's nothing she loves more than a good party."

It was only after they made it past the entry hall that Michael finally got a good look at the house's interior. It actually seemed more like a museum than somebody's home. The living room was a wonder in and of itself, even without all the decorations, artifacts, and antiques. The back wall consisted entirely of windows, revealing a lavish backyard complete with a large swimming pool and several trees, all illuminated with orange, yellow, and purple lights.

The living room itself was so full of people that Michael had a hard time taking in all of its grandeur, but he could see enough. Although the everyday furnishings were beautiful, elegant, and obviously expensive, they paled in comparison to the exquisite decorations that Kate and her crew had assembled. They weren't your stereotypical Halloween decorations, like spider webs or skeletons. Instead, golden candelabras, brass Jack-O-Lanterns, and wreathes and garlands of sparkling gold and orange leaves, acorns, pinecones, and pumpkins adorned the walls, mantle, and tabletops.

"So, what do you think?" Kate asked.

"I'm sort of afraid to touch anything," Michael confessed. Kate laughed. "So did you guys put up all the decorations?"

19

"Yep. Val even made some of the wreathes. When she's not decorating, she loves doing crafts and making her own decorations."

"That's incredible." Michael marveled as a young woman dressed in an outlandish and sparkling witch's outfit approached them.

"Well hello, darling," Valerie Banks greeted Kate with a warm embrace.

"Your ears must have been burning," Kate told her.

"Burning? Is it because I'm a witch?" Val asked dramatically.

"I was just telling Michael all about your decorations."

"Michael?" Val asked, turning dark eyes toward him. "Well, well, well. It *is* you! I barely recognized you in your little pirate costume. How are you?"

"I'm good, thanks. How are you?"

"Thriving, darling! Can't you tell?" She threw her hands up in the air, just like a witch out of a kid's movie.

Kate snickered.

"You should have been an actress," she told her boss.

"Trust me, sweetie, you wouldn't say that if you could remember my performance as Dancer #4 in *Hairspray*."

"Ah."

"So, what exactly are you supposed to be?" she asked Kate.

"I'm a princess, duh," Kate replied playfully.

"And Michael's the pirate who captured you and whisked you away to a deserted tropical island under a full Atlantic moon?"

"Or my cabana boy. I haven't decided yet." Kate grinned up at Michael, and linked her arm through his.

"He's got too many layers on to be a cabana boy." Valerie winked. Michael could feel his ears and cheeks getting pinker by the second. "Aw, look, I made him blush! Kate, he is just too cute."

Again, Kate smiled up at him.

"He is kind of cute, isn't he?" She nudged his shoulder with hers.

Valerie watched them wistfully.

"Well, I guess I should let you kids enjoy your evening together," she said.

"Val, you don't have to run off," Kate told her.

"It's all right. Rumor has it Karen's very single nephew is running around somewhere and I'm going to see if I can accidentally bump into him. Can't have the two of you cramping my style." Val flashed them an impish grin.

"We wouldn't dream of it," Kate replied, embracing her friend.

After Val disappeared, Kate led Michael over to the buffet table, which was fit to overflow with a veritable smorgasbord of fancy finger foods: cocktail shrimp and dipping sauce, fruit and cheese platters, sausages, crackers, and rolls. The dessert platters looked even more tantalizing: five different kinds of cookies, brownies, fudge, cupcakes with orange and purple icing, and enough candy to satisfy every trick-or-treater in the neighborhood. Michael hadn't thought he was all that hungry before, but now, standing in front of the greatest buffet ever assembled, his stomach began to growl.

"Shall we?" Kate asked.

After they'd loaded their plates, they made their way into the dining area, which had been cleared out to make way for the makeshift bar and its tenders. Michael couldn't help but gawk at the people around them as he and Kate meandered through the crowd. There was a couple completely decked out in Steampunk garb, a woman who must have paid a fortune for her extravagant Elizabethan gown, and a man who looked like he'd stepped right out of *Bram Stoker's Dracula*.

"What can I get for you?" The bartender's voice distracted Michael from the extravagant costumes around him.

"Champagne, please," Kate said.

Michael watched her in awe. It was like she wasn't even intimidated by the glittering mansion or the high society company, like she was used to sipping champagne and hobnobbing at fancy parties.

"And for you, sir?" the bartender, dressed in a full out tux, asked Michael.

"Champagne," he responded automatically. In a feeble attempt to act like he actually belonged there, he'd blurted out the first thing to come to mind. He didn't even like champagne.

Unfortunately, it was too late to reject the crystal glass of bubbling liquid.

After they ate, Kate took Michael on a tour of the house. The bedrooms, in particular, were a sight to behold. Each room had a color theme, a king-sized bed, and a collection of antiques placed strategically around the perimeter. One room, the blue room, had a dozen antique brooches, all covered in glittering rhinestones, on display.

The white room, however, was by far the most mesmerizing. With sheer white curtains, lush white bedding, lacquered white dressers, and an old white and gold rocking horse in the corner of the room, Michael almost missed the woman, also dressed in white, hovering around the antique horse. She must have been used to strangers taking tours of the room, because she didn't even look up at them.

"Pretty neat, huh?" Kate asked.

"It's unbelievable," Michael agreed, choosing not to acknowledge the ghost. "And Karen is okay with people looking around her house?"

"Oh, she loves it. That's why she had Val decorate all these rooms."

"Wait, I thought you guys just decorated for parties."

"We do, but Karen keeps Val on call year-round to help her decorate her rooms. Any time Val is out and sees something she thinks Karen would like, she just picks it up. She'll go around to estate sales for fun sometimes, and she almost always comes back with some sort of nifty antique for Karen."

The tour ended with Kate introducing Michael to Karen herself. Michael wasn't sure what to say. He'd never met a really wealthy person before. Well, except for Luke. But Karen was different. She was elegant, sophisticated, and high-society. Luke was still wearing the same cologne that guys were supposed to stop wearing after high school.

As it turned out, Michael didn't need to know what to say. Karen was talkative and enthusiastic enough for all three of them.

"Oh, this is the boy who can see ghosts! Oh, it's so wonderful to meet you," she gushed after Kate introduced them.

"Um, thanks. You too," Michael replied.

"Kate didn't tell me she would be bringing you. Of course, I know all about how you saved her life in that field. What a heroic thing to do!"

"Actually, she was the one who saved my life," Michael said.

Kate smiled and took his hand. She looked like she was going to say something, but Karen had already moved on.

"I have a question for you, and I hope you don't mind me asking, but did you see our ghost?" she asked.

Michael was a little surprised, not only that she knew she had a ghost, but that she talked about her like she was some sort of beloved family pet.

"You know about her?"

"She's a her? Oh, good Lord. And here we've been calling her Casper all these years. I hope she's not offended."

"She didn't seem to be," Michael told her.

"Good. She can be kind of a pill at times. I swear, she likes to hide things. One day, I was looking all over for a strand of pearls that John brought me back from India and I kid you not, I found them in the white room, underneath the music box that plays 'Memory' from *Cats*."

"Oh." Michael glanced down at Kate, unsure of what else to say. This was the first time someone had gone out of their way to describe a ghost to him.

"I am just so glad you came this evening. Did you enjoy yourself?"

"Oh, yeah. Your house is amazing."

23

"Well, thank you. You know, I owe it all to my wonderful decorating crew." Karen wrapped an affectionate arm around Kate's shoulders.

After they bade Karen goodnight, Kate said a quick "Bye, see you Monday," to Val. Then she and Michael walked hand in hand out into the cool October night.

CHAPTER FOUR

Kate didn't really know how she expected the night to end. They'd never officially agreed that it was a date, and she wasn't sure how to bring it up. She knew for a fact Michael wouldn't say anything. He was even more awkward than she was. But he had held her hand. That had to count for something, right?

Well, whether it did or not, Kate was going to at least try to get something out of him. It didn't have to be some huge declaration of love. It didn't even have to be a kiss. She just wanted to know where they stood.

"I'm really glad you came tonight," she offered once they'd made it to his doorstep at the top of the stairs.

"I'm glad you invited me."

"Me too," Kate said, hoping she wasn't about to make him uncomfortable. "I miss you. I mean, I know I see you all the time, but I miss spending time with you."

To her sheer relief, Michael blushed and smiled down at the ground, before raising his eyes to meet hers. "I miss you, too. I've wanted to talk to you for ages, to ask if you wanted to have dinner, see a movie, maybe. But..."

"I know. You've been busy," she told him.

"It's not just that," he admitted. "I wasn't sure if you... you know..."

She knew what he was going to say. He wasn't sure if she was ready to date again, or if she even still wanted to date him. Furthermore, he wasn't sure if he'd given her enough time to get over the shock of Trevor's death.

"I ran into Trevor's mom the other day. At the cemetery," she told him. Michael's expression was unreadable, so she kept

25

talking. "I've been a few times... to pay my respects, to talk to him. The last time I was there, so was she."

"Did you recognize her?"

"No, but I knew who she was as soon as she said my name. We talked a little. It was good, you know? To finally meet her. It brought me a lot of peace. And I think - well, I hope - that maybe life will start... I don't know... getting back to where it was before," she said, tucking a loose strand of hair behind her ear.

"You mean...?" Michael trailed off.

To answer his question, Kate took a step closer to him, stood up on her tip toes, and rested her arms around his neck. She felt his hand slip around her waist and she closed her eyes. She could feel his breath on her cheek when –

"Oh! I hope I'm not interrupting anything!"

Kate leapt away from Michael and whirled around.

"Gavin!" she snapped.

Her older brother was sprinting up the stairs, a cheeky grin on his stupid face.

"Hey, Michael. Hey, Sis. Nice dress."

"Shut up. What are you doing out so late?" Kate asked.

"Went out for drinks with some people from work. Are you guys just getting home from that party?"

"No, we went out for pizza and a movie dressed like this," Kate replied dryly.

"You never know. You used to go all out for those *Harry Potter* midnight premieres. You even stitched that lion thing onto your graduation robe from high school. Did she ever tell you how much of a nerd she is, Michael?"

Kate groaned. Thanks to her drunken, loud-mouthed brother, her chances of spending a magical moment with Michael were all but obliterated. Maybe she should go out and get another ghost to drain the energy out of him. It might make him less chatty.

"Okay Gav, you need to go take an aspirin and lie down. I don't want you to have another one of those episodes like you supposedly had after your first frat party. What was it again? You woke up in a stranger's bathtub wearing nothing but a pair of someone else's pants?"

"She's trying to embarrass me," Gavin told Michael. "Good news for her is that I am not that drunk. Bad news for you is that she is that big a nerd."

"Get lost, please!" Kate snapped.

"Fine. But facts are facts, Kate," he drawled. "I expect you won't be long out here. See you, Michael."

"Bye, Gavin," Michael replied.

"Please, just don't even acknowledge him," Kate said, turning to watch Gavin as he gave one last wave before disappearing into the apartment he shared with Kate. "I'm sorry, he is such a dumbass when he's drunk."

"Alcohol does that to people." Michael shrugged.

Kate smiled, thankful that he was an understanding kind of guy. She couldn't imagine most other guys would want to get within ten miles of her after an encounter like that.

But then, Michael wasn't most other guys.

"Well, I guess I should go ahead and say goodnight. I'm already in for hell from Gavin, and I can guarantee you, he's probably watching us from the peep hole," Kate said. She wished that wasn't true, but she knew her brother. He was an obnoxious drunk. "Again, I am really sorry."

"Kate, I have an invisible roommate who takes every opportunity to spy, eavesdrop, and comment on my entire life. Trust me, you don't have to apologize."

Kate laughed.

"Okay, good," she said, rising up and kissing him lightly on the cheek. Then, she took his hands in hers and gave them a light squeeze. "I'll see you soon."

"Good night, Kate. Thanks for a fun night."

"Thanks for being my cabana boy." She winked. And with that, she headed across the landing and into her apartment.

The next morning was proof enough for Kate that karma was a joke and life wasn't fair. She awoke cranky, groggy, and still tired, while Gavin seemed totally fine and alert, even after his night of alcoholic indulgence. Wasn't *he* supposed to be the one that was miserable and hungover? She'd only had one glass of champagne and wasn't even close to being drunk the night before. She guessed she just hadn't slept all that well.

She'd just helped herself to a bowl of cereal when Gavin joined her at their tiny kitchen table.

"So, I hate to be the one who ruins your morning - "

"You mean like you ruined my date last night?" Kate grumbled, interrupting her brother.

"Oh, come on. I didn't ruin anything. Michael is crazy about you and you know it. I was just giving you a hard time. That's what older brothers do."

"Well, I'm still mad."

"Oh, I'm shocked. Always holding a grudge. That's what little sisters do."

Kate rolled her eyes.

"So what's going to ruin my morning?" she asked.

"I got a text from Mom," Gavin began gingerly. He knew how Kate would react as soon as their mother was mentioned.

"Joy," Kate remarked. "What did she want?"

"She's stopping by later and she wanted me to make sure that you don't go running off before she gets a chance to talk to you." Kate opened her mouth to object, but Gavin cut her off. "Kate, you've been ignoring her for weeks. You need to give her a break. She's your mother, for Christ's sake."

"I'm ignoring her because all I ever hear is how I need to move back home with her, how I need to be more careful because I might trip on a rose petal and break my brain, and how Michael is this dangerous little monster who is going to ruin my life and somehow impair my recovery even more than he already has, despite the fact that that's exactly what she and Dad have been trying to do since the day I woke up from the coma." Kate wasn't sure how well all that had translated aloud, but it made perfect

28

sense in her head. Oh well. Gavin knew her well enough to expect these long-winded speeches every now and then. Even if he hadn't gotten all of it, she was pretty sure he'd understood the gist.

Gavin didn't even try to sort through her messy string of thoughts.

"Be that as it may, I still think you need to hear her out."

Kate was disinclined to agree, but she knew she wasn't going to win.

"Why did you tell me?" she asked. "I mean, if you thought I was just going to run off once I knew she was coming, why would you tell me?"

"Because if the last year has taught me anything, it's that lying to you is not a good idea," he answered. Then he stood up, ruffled her already-tousled hair, and disappeared into the living room.

Never one to be late for an engagement, Terri Avery arrived at two o'clock on the dot. Kate had seriously considered sneaking out and seeking refuge at the mall or something, but after what Gavin had said to her earlier, she decided to stay. Kate knew her mother was desperate to repair the rift between them, and although Kate was still upset, she missed her mother. She used to talk to her about everything, and although she knew she could talk to Gavin or Michael or Val, it just wasn't the same as talking to her mom.

Even so, Kate wasn't looking forward to whatever her mother had to say to her that afternoon. She couldn't know for sure, but she was willing to bet a decent amount that it would have to do with Michael. She'd probably seen him on TV. Or maybe she'd heard from some obscure acquaintance that Kate had taken him as her date to Karen's party.

That was why, when Terri arrived, Kate busied herself applying lip gloss in the bathroom so that Gavin would answer the door.

"Hey, Mom," she heard Gavin greet their mother.

"Hello, sweetheart. Oh, you're looking so good. I'm so happy you're better."

Kate scowled. Even though she had tried to explain to her mother that it was all thanks to Michael that Gavin was better, Terri wouldn't hear it. As far as she was concerned, ghosts didn't make people sick and Michael Sinclair had done nothing to help either one of her children. But Kate couldn't think about that now. If she did, she'd get angry all over again and she wouldn't make it through the afternoon without yelling.

"So, where's Kate? She is around, isn't she?" Terri asked.

"Yeah, she's here. Kate!" Gavin yelled. "What's taking so long?"

"Just fixing my hair," Kate called back. Then, taking a deep breath, she emerged from the bathroom and walked into the living room. Terri smiled at her, but it was a tense, forced smile. Whatever she had come to talk about, she clearly wasn't looking forward to the conversation.

After the standard hugs, hellos, and how are yous, Gavin asked if anyone wanted anything to drink. Of course, that was probably his way of slipping away from the impending conversation while things were still civil.

Terri filled Kate in on what she and Rex, Kate's father, had been up to in the last few weeks. Kate knew now that before her accident, her parents had been planning on getting a divorce but had reconciled after they found out about Kate's retrograde amnesia. Kate had wondered if they would drop the charade now that she knew the truth, but it seemed that Rex and Terri Avery had truly resolved their differences. Kate was happy to hear that things were going well for her parents, but she knew Terri hadn't made the trip over to the Riverview Apartment complex to talk about their renewed relationship.

Just when she was beginning to think her mother would never cut to the chase, Terri looked her in the eye and said, "I got a call from Arlene Hanson the other day."

Oh no, Kate thought.

30

Terri continued, "She said that she ran into you at the cemetery where her son is buried."

"*Her son* has a name," Kate snapped. She knew she should have stopped there, but her touchy temper was already getting the better of her. "It's Trevor. I'm sure you remember it considering I used to be engaged to him."

Terri chose to ignore that. "Kate, what were you doing at that cemetery?"

"I was visiting him."

"Visiting him?" Terri sounded like she didn't quite understand. Kate wasn't sure why. Terri made several trips to the cemetery where her parents were buried every year. Surely, she knew what it meant to visit someone you loved at their final resting place. "Why would you do something like that?"

"Gee, Mom, I don't know," Kate retaliated. "Maybe I wanted to pay my respects to the man I was supposed to marry?"

"A man you don't even remember?"

"I *do* remember him, just not the way most people remember someone they loved."

"Kate, please, I don't want to fight about this," Terri begged. She sounded so desperate that Kate fought the snarky comment that lingered at the tip of her tongue and listened quietly. "I know you don't see the harm in what you're doing, in trying to remember him, or in paying your respects. But if something happens, if something that you do triggers something and you remember... You remember just how much you lost when he died... Honey, I'm not sure you could bear it. And I'm just so afraid..." Terri closed her eyes. Kate realized she was trying not to cry. "I'm so afraid... that you'll want to join him."

"Mom..." Kate whispered. She knew her mother had been trying to protect her, but she hadn't known that her mother had been trying to protect her from *that*.

"I'm sorry, I'm sorry." Terri wiped her eyes. "I know I'm being silly and overprotective. But Kate, I still don't think you understand how very close we came to losing you. You brush it off like it was no big deal because you walked away from it, but baby, it *was* a big deal. It was the very worst thing that has ever happened to our family, and I never, ever want anything like that to happen again. I wouldn't wish it on my worst enemy. So please, understand that when I say I worry about you, it's not because I want to keep you from knowing the man you loved. I just *can't* lose you again."

"Mom, you won't." Kate embraced her mother.

"I'm so sorry," Terri wept into her daughter's shoulder.

"I'm sorry, too," Kate whispered, fighting back tears herself. "And please know you don't have to worry about me. I'm not going anywhere. I promise."

CHAPTER FIVE

Although Michael had dated in the past, he still wasn't clear on what the protocol was for calling after a date-that-may-or-may-not-have-been-a-real-date. He was pretty sure that it had been a date, but not sure enough to send the awkward *So, I had a good time the other night* text. Deep down, he knew he didn't need to worry. It was Kate. After all they'd been through together, he shouldn't have to think twice about texting her, or asking her if she wanted to have dinner sometime that week.

Before he had the opportunity, however, she asked him.

They agreed on dinner Tuesday night. As if that wasn't enough to make his week, he also received a job offer from an insurance company on Tuesday afternoon. It wasn't exactly his ideal career, but under his circumstances, he couldn't afford to be picky. After all, it wasn't a bad job. It came with all the benefits, vacation time, and a decent salary. And at that particular point in his life, he'd take any kind of salary he could get.

Still, as grateful as he was for the job and as elated as he was about his date with Kate, he was hesitant to believe in his good fortune. There had to be some kind of catch. His luck could not have just miraculously improved. If he'd learned anything in the past twenty-seven years, it was that destiny liked to screw with him. Something was going to happen that would ruin his entire week. He just knew it.

Once again, however, fate seemed to contradict him when Kate surprised him by saying she'd had a long talk with her mother, and while their relationship was still recovering, they'd promised that instead of fighting and jumping to conclusions, they were going to be open, honest, and attentive to whatever the other had to say.

"Does that mean she's okay with you still seeing me?" Michael asked. It sounded far too good to be true.

"Well, I wouldn't go so far as 'okay,' but she's not going to fight with me about it anymore." Kate grinned.

"So, she still doesn't like me?"

"Not really," Kate replied. "Which, she should know, only makes you that much more appealing to me. Knowing she doesn't approve of a guy I like really brings out the rebel in me."

"Wow. I've never been the kind of guy that moms warn their daughters about. I've always thought I was the kind that moms wanted their daughters to date. You know... dweeby."

Kate threw her head back and laughed. "Don't worry. You're only a little dweeby."

"Oh, good. Thank you." Michael laughed too.

After dinner, they drove to a park a few blocks down from their apartment complex and walked around. It was a wonderful evening, cool and breezy, and the sky was alight with the vibrant oranges, magentas, and yellows of the setting October sun. Several families and couples were taking advantage of the beautiful dusk. Kids played on the swing set and climbed on the jungle gym, a jogger dressed in a black jacket ran alongside her golden retriever, and a group of teenagers kicked a soccer ball across the field a few yards away.

As they walked, Kate casually took Michael's hand and laced her fingers through his. She told him about their latest client, a woman with a passion for antiques and vintage books. He told her about his job offer. She was thrilled for him. It was nice, he realized, just talking about normal, everyday things. No ghosts. No grieving loved ones. Just a peaceful, sunset walk around the park with a beautiful girl.

The girl.

Then he realized something. Throughout their entire relationship, Kate had always been the one to take his hand. She'd been the first to kiss him. She'd also been the one who'd risked her life to save him. She'd even been the one to ask him out again after he'd ended things so that she could come to terms with the loss of Trevor. Now, looking at her in the soft purple glow of twilight, Michael realized that he'd been a coward. She deserved more than anything he'd ever given her. She deserved someone who would take her hand, kiss her, and tell her how much he cared about her, without her having to tell him that it was okay to do so.

"What are you thinking about?" Kate asked, gazing up at him.

"What?" he asked. He hadn't realized that, in thinking about her, he'd accidentally tuned out.

"You look so serious. Is everything okay?"

"Yeah. Yeah, everything's fine," he told her. Then, without hesitating or asking permission, he pulled her into his arms, leaned down, and kissed her. After he pulled away, he whispered, "I'm sorry."

"Why?" she asked.

"I should have done that a long time ago."

Kate smiled.

"Well, I think you've made up for it." Then, she wrapped her arms around his shoulders and leaned in to accept another kiss.

When they returned to their apartment complex an hour later, Michael was on a high. Finally, *finally*, everything seemed to be going his way. He felt like he could do anything in the world, and that nothing, absolutely nothing, could go wrong.

That feeling evaporated about half a second after he pulled into his driveway.

"Hey, is that - ?" Kate asked, staring at the same black Ferrari that had caught Michael's eye and ruined his good mood.

Before Michael could answer her, the Ferrari's door swung open to reveal a young man with sandy blond hair and a broad, cheeky grin.

Luke Rainer.

"Are you kidding me?" Michael groaned as Kate leapt out of the car to embrace him.

"Luke!" she squealed as he wrapped his arms around her waist and lifted her right up off the ground. "I didn't know you were in town!"

"Well, I just got in yesterday. Thought I'd drop by and surprise you." He grinned. "Hey, Mikey!"

Michael tried not to grimace as he climbed out of his car.

He helped rescue you. Kate doesn't like him like that. He is not here to ruin your life.

"Hi, Luke," Michael greeted him.

"How's the battle wound?" Luke asked, shaking his hand.

"Which one?" Michael asked wryly.

Luke laughed.

"At least you sound like you're back to your old self. How's he doing, Kate? Is he okay?"

"Oh yeah. He's fine." She grinned up at Michael.

"And how about Gavin? How's he doing?"

"Great," Kate replied. "How's filming for the new season going? I loved the first few episodes. I even got Michael to watch them."

"Really?" Luke grinned, looking smug as hell. "Well what do you know? We might just make a *Cemetery Tours* fan of you yet."

Not likely, Michael thought.

Aloud, he said, "We'll see."

Out of the corner of his eye, he noticed Kate had begun to shiver. He had been caught so off guard by Luke's unexpected (and rather unappreciated) appearance, he hadn't noticed how cold and windy it had suddenly become.

Wrapping an arm around her shoulders, he said, "You know, it's getting kind of chilly. Do you, uh, want to go up to my apartment and hang out there?" He couldn't believe he was actually inviting Luke Rainer, the guy he'd been trying to keep out of his life for years, up to his apartment to hang out like they were friends or something.

Then again, Luke had gone out of his way to save his life. That was more than he could say for most of his other friends.

"Why Mikey, I'd be honored." Luke grinned. "You two don't mind, do you? I mean, I wouldn't want to interrupt a date or anything."

"Oh, it's too late for that," Michael told him.

"Ah, well, I wouldn't worry too much. Kate had her shot with me and she still chose you." Luke winked.

Kate laughed and wrapped her arms around Michael's waist. Michael had to admit, he'd never even considered that.

Maybe Luke wasn't all that bad after all.

Up in his apartment, Michael told Kate and Luke to make themselves at home while he fetched them something to drink. As always, Brink felt compelled to express his flat-out astonishment that Michael was actually having guests over; even more so that he was having *Luke Rainer* over.

"What's he doing here, anyway? Isn't he supposed to be off filming old tombstones or something?" Brink asked.

"He said he was in town and decided to stop by," Michael muttered softly.

"And here he is on your date. Nice." Brink smirked.

Michael glared at him. It was like talking to a skinny, teenaged Luke.

Michael could feel Brink trailing him as he made his way back into the living room where Luke was filling Kate in on all of the team's latest adventures. After handing them their drinks, Michael took a seat on the couch next to Kate. She took a sip of her soda and casually snuggled up next to him while Luke continued to talk.

Michael was honestly beginning to believe that Luke really had just dropped in to catch up when out of the blue, he asked, "So, have either of you ever heard of Stanton Hall Manor?"

"No," Michael answered.

"Maybe," Kate replied. "I think it was featured on a documentary I saw about historic mansions in New England."

"It probably was. It's one of the most extravagant manors in Maine. Hell, it's one of the most extravagant manors in the nation. It also happens to be one of the most haunted."

Oh no... Michael already knew where this was going.

"Cool," Kate grinned. "Are you guys going to investigate it?"

"Well, that's the plan. However, there are some... conditions."

"What kind of conditions?" Michael asked.

"The person who owns Stanton Hall is a woman named Carolyn Drake. She inherited it from her uncle after he died. I've been trying to get her to let us investigate ever since the show premiered, but she's always turned me down. She's hoping to convert it into some kind of luxury bed and breakfast and she's always thought that if we tell the world that it's haunted, no one would want to stay there."

"That's strange. I'd think being on *Cemetery Tours* would make more people want to visit. I mean, look at the Stanley Hotel. That place is so haunted that it inspired Stephen King to write *The Shining* and now everyone wants to stay there," Kate said.

"Well, Carolyn's problem is that she doesn't actually believe that it's haunted. If she doesn't believe it's haunted, then she doesn't have a whole lot of incentive to let us come investigate, and so on and so forth. But then, just as we're in the midst of shooting for this season, I get an email from her. She said that she would agree to let the team film..." He paused and looked Michael in the eye. "But only if you come with us, Mikey."

"And there it is. The catch," Brink commented.

Michael was still trying to register what Luke had just said.

"Wait, what?" he asked.

"I don't know. She didn't explain it to me. All she said was that she'd agree to let us come and investigate, but only if we brought you with us."

"That just doesn't make sense," Michael said.

"Maybe she wants you to come along because she wants to show folks that it isn't haunted," Kate said. "Maybe if you get there and you don't see anything, then that will prove once and for all that there are no ghosts."

"Oh, come on. Everyone knows that place is haunted. Carolyn Drake is just a crazy old fruit loop." Luke crossed his arms and slumped back against his chair. "Don't tell her I said that."

"Wouldn't dream of it," Michael said.

"So, what do you think?" Luke asked. "Will you come with us?"

Michael didn't know how to respond. For the first time, Luke was asking him to be part of the show at the request of somebody else. Not just a request. Michael had to go or the episode wasn't happening. That was a lot of pressure.

"Luke," he began. "I know this means a lot to you, but I can't just drop everything and go."

"Why not?" Luke asked. "You're already 'out,' so it's not like you can use that as an excuse anymore. You don't have a job to worry about - "

"Actually, I do," Michael corrected him. "I got an offer this afternoon and I'm going to take it. I have to take it."

"Why? Are you the new Captain of the Enterprise? Because if the job is anything less cool than that, you still have no excuse to turn this down."

"It's for an insurance company. I'd be - "

"Are you *kidding* me?" Luke interrupted him, exasperated. "I am here, offering you a gig on *the* most popular paranormal show on television, just like I have a *thousand* times in the past, and you're turning it down to sell *insurance*?"

Okay, yeah, when he put it like that, of course it sounded like a lousy excuse. But what Luke didn't understand was that the gig on *Cemetery Tours* was a one-time thing. Michael would still need a permanent job after it was over, and he didn't know if he'd be lucky enough to find another company willing to take on the ghost-talker.

"I'm sorry, Mikey, but this time, I *really* don't understand you," Luke continued. "You are so hell-bent on being normal and doing what you think everyone wants you to do that you'd pass up an opportunity that anybody else would jump at. Don't you think so, Kate?"

"*I* want to go," she agreed.

"You're invited," Luke told her. "But of course, if Mikey doesn't go, then no one gets to."

Oh, great. Michael knew exactly what Luke was doing, and Luke knew it too. It had been one thing when not going meant that Luke couldn't go. But knowing that it also meant Kate couldn't go was a whole different scenario. Michael had no problem saying no to Luke. But saying no to Kate? Impossible. That was how Luke had conned him into going to that stupid graveyard. He'd tricked Kate into asking Michael, knowing that Michael wouldn't be able to turn her down.

Sure enough, as soon as the words were out of Luke's mouth, Kate turned wide, pleading eyes up at Michael.

Luke just smiled. He had Michael exactly where he wanted him.

Meanwhile, Brink snickered from the sidelines. "Well, it looks like you're going to Maine."

CHAPTER SIX

The following Monday, both Kate and Gavin were awake at five in the morning, making their final preparations before they went to meet Michael to carpool over to the airport. Their flight to Maine was scheduled for seven thirty, so they wanted to be sure to get their bags checked and themselves through security with plenty of time to spare.

"Gav, did you remember to pack the extra dental floss?" Kate asked, rummaging through her bag of nighttime essentials.

"I did, dear sister, for the hundredth time," Gavin replied. "And even if I didn't, it's not like we're going to some desolate wasteland where convenience stores don't exist. I can almost guarantee that Maine has plenty of places that will serve to enable your obsessive control issues."

Kate narrowed her eyes. It was far too early for Gavin's snarky attitude.

"May I remind *you* just how lucky you are to be going on this trip and that if you tick me off, even in the slightest, I can tell Luke to uninvite you?" Kate asked.

"Aw, come on, you wouldn't do that. We're gonna have fun! Besides, my boss thinks working with the crew of an internationally acclaimed television show will be a great learning experience."

"Yeah, whatever. I still can't believe you wanted to go so bad. Weren't you the one who, not even four months ago, was telling me how ridiculous *Cemetery Tours* was and how fake it was and how you couldn't believe anyone with a brain could possibly take it seriously?"

"You are never going to let me live that down, are you?"

41

"Nope," Kate replied, zipping her nighttime bag into her suitcase.

Ten minutes later, rolling suitcases and backpacks in hand, Kate and Gavin locked up their apartment and walked across the landing to grab Michael. Then, the three of them loaded themselves and their luggage into Kate's Land Rover and drove to the airport, where Luke was waiting for them with their boarding passes.

"This is going to be so much fun! I'm so excited," Kate exclaimed once she had her boarding pass in hand.

"I agree, Beautiful. I've been waiting for this opportunity for a long time," Luke told her. "Gavin, good to see you, man."

"Good to see you, too." Gavin grinned, shaking Luke's hand with enthusiasm.

It was weird for Kate to see her brother actually happy to see Luke. Back when Luke had first shown up, Gavin hadn't wanted Kate to have anything to do with him. But thanks to Michael and Trevor, he'd had a change of heart.

"Mikey, are you ready for this?" Luke flashed Michael a broad grin.

Michael looked at Luke as though he'd just asked him a trick question, but to tell the truth, Kate had a feeling he actually was looking forward to being on the show. Or at least to the trip itself. She had spent the evening before at Michael's apartment, helping him get his things together (and making out on the couch, but mostly helping him pack), and he'd really seemed to have a good time. He'd been smiling and laughing and talking about all the lobster he was going to eat.

But Kate knew there was no way he was ever going to admit any of that to Luke.

Sure enough, he pursed his lips and replied, "Sure."

Kate smirked and took Michael's hand as Luke led the way to baggage check. It was kind of cool to be traveling with not just one, but two celebrities. Out of the corner of her eye, Kate noticed people gawking and whispering as they passed by, but for once, she wasn't sure if they were gaping at Luke or at Michael. While

42

they were waiting in line to pass through security, two girls let an entire row of people cut in front of them just so they could get their pictures taken with Luke. Then, another girl approached them in the terminal and asked for Michael's autograph without even giving Luke a second glance.

Michael looked to Kate as if to ask, *Does she really want my autograph?*

But the girl seemed very insistent.

"I'm really into ghosts," she explained as Michael signed the back of an old receipt for her. "I think it's so cool that you can see them."

Luke scoffed as she sprinted back down the terminal.

"If she's so 'into ghosts,' how come she doesn't watch *Cemetery Tours*? I mean, obviously she doesn't or else she would have recognized me. Right?"

"Luke, you're not jealous, are you?" Kate grinned.

"Me? Never. I just think she was putting the moves on your boyfriend and you need to keep an eye on him."

Kate threw her head back and laughed. "I think I trust him enough to handle a teenager asking for his autograph."

"Well, I don't," Luke pouted.

Kate patted his shoulder. Then looked up at Gavin. "Do you remember that time we were in Austin and that girl asked if you were Kurt Cobain?"

This time, Gavin was the one who laughed.

"Wait, seriously?" Michael asked.

"Yeah. We were at this music festival with a few of our cousins and this one girl, completely wasted, stumbled into Kate and then looked up at me and goes, 'Hey Kurt! It sure smells like teen spirit, huh?'" Gavin snickered.

"Then she spilled her beer down my shirt," Kate added.

"I thought you were going to punch her. You were so angry," Gavin reminisced.

"I'm still angry. I loved that shirt, and now it has a gross beer stain on it."

They made it to their gate with plenty of time to spare, so they decided to grab a bite to eat at the Chili's-To-Go. While they were eating, Luke whipped out his brand-new iPhone and handed it to their waiter.

"Would you mind taking a picture for us?" he asked. "I like to document the journey. And the fans love it."

Kate recalled all the pictures she'd seen posted on his Twitter feed, but never in her wildest dreams had she ever imagined she'd be *in* one.

"What's the caption going to be?" she asked as soon as Luke had his iPhone back.

"'Hanging out with a few special guest stars on our way to dream location.'" Luke replied. "You know, Mikey, you should really think about getting yourself a Twitter."

"No thanks. I'm really not interested in people having more access to me than they already do," Michael said.

"But it's good to share yourself with the world. Yeah, you'll get your creepers and your stalkers, but it's a nice way to connect with the fans and let them know you care."

Kate wasn't going to say anything, since she was technically one of those creepers who liked to follow a bunch of celebrities, but she knew there was no way Michael would ever make a Twitter account. He was rarely even on Facebook.

"I'll think about it," Michael replied.

Yeah, that was a definite no.

"Ladies and gentlemen, the Captain has turned off the fasten seat belt sign, however we recommend that you keep your seat belt fastened while you're seated. Now, sit back, relax, and enjoy your flight to Portland, Maine."

Michael intended to do just that. That was probably the one good thing that would come from this whole experience. He'd always enjoyed airplane rides. Maybe it was because he hadn't had the chance to travel that much growing up. Whatever the reason, being inside a plane was always a very relaxing, very therapeutic experience.

Best of all, there were rarely ever ghosts.

Kate, on the other hand, didn't seem to be enjoying the ride at all.

"It's just a little turbulence. I am okay. I am okay," she muttered to herself.

"Are you all right?" Michael asked, taking her hand.

"She's a nervous flyer," Gavin explained from her other side. "When we were little, she was so bad that whenever we flew anywhere, Mom would drug her."

"That is so not true," Kate snapped.

"Oh yeah? Remember your special allergy medicine?"

Kate gasped. "She told me that was so my nose and ears wouldn't get stuffy on the plane!"

"And it would knock you out for six hours," Gavin quipped.

It was sort of hard not to laugh at the shocked expression on Kate's face, so Michael turned his attention to the world outside his window. Watching the clouds pass by beneath him, Michael felt his eyelids growing heavy. He was just about to drop off to sleep when –

"Man, this flight is *boring*. Don't planes get movies nowadays?"

Michael's eyes snapped open, and he whipped his head around and found himself staring not into Kate's lovely hazel eyes, but into the bright blue and obnoxiously alert eyes of Eugene Brinkley. Who, to Michael's horror and sheer embarrassment, had decided to sit himself right on top of Kate's legs.

"*Brink!*" he hissed, causing Kate to flinch.

"What's wrong?" she asked, looking panicked.

"Nothing, it's just..." Okay, seriously? How was he supposed to explain to his anxiety-stricken girlfriend that his invisible roommate had followed them onto the plane and was currently sitting *on her lap*? "Um... someone decided to follow us."

"Oh, come on. You can use my name. It's not like anyone else on this plane is going to know who you're talking about."

"Brink?" Kate whispered. "Is that why it's suddenly freezing in here?"

"Wait a minute, you brought a ghost with you?" Gavin asked, leaning in across his sister and, funnily enough, straight into Brink's abdomen.

"Eurgh!" Brink tried to swat him away. "I hate it when people do that!"

"Trust me, he wasn't invited," Michael muttered through gritted teeth.

"Oh, that's nice. You know, last time I checked, I'd been your friend a lot longer than these two. Then again, I guess I'm not as pretty as she is..." Brink remarked, snuggling up to Kate, who suddenly went rigid, like an electric shock had just shot up and down her spine.

"Will you knock it off?" Michael growled.

"What's he doing?" Kate asked, looking apprehensive.

"What? I'm not going to sit on *his* lap," Brink pointed his thumb over his shoulder at Gavin.

"He's not doing anything," Michael lied, grateful that for once, his voice didn't crack. "In fact, he just assured me that he's about to go haunt the bathrooms in the back of the plane until we land."

"Yeah, right. I might be dead, but I'm still human. I still get grossed out. Heck, for all we know, I might still have a gag reflex."

"Why would you have a gag reflex? You can't choke!" Michael argued, a little louder than he intended.

"*What* are you talking about?" Kate asked.

"Hey! Is there a ghost over there?" Luke asked, acknowledging them for the first time since he'd been allowed to turn his music back on. Michael wasn't sure what he'd been rocking out to the whole flight, but he had a feeling it was something that would eventually cost him his hearing.

"Yeah, Michael's friend Brad," Gavin replied.

46

"It's Brink," Kate and Brink corrected him at the same time. Of course, Gavin could only hear his sister.

"Brink? That's kind of a weird name, isn't it?"

"You're one to talk, Gavin *Wentworth*," Kate remarked.

"Seriously, bro?" Luke asked.

"It's a family name." Gavin brushed off his sister's attempt at humiliating him.

"Is Brink still there? If so, tell him to stay right where he is. I want to see if I can get a picture!" Luke began digging through his carry-on for his camera. "You know, I don't get the opportunity to really get to know the spirits we work with. But if Brink wouldn't mind, I'd love to have him sit down with me, maybe see if we can get some really solid EVPs. I bet it would be a lot easier to collect evidence if the ghost was actually willing to cooperate and didn't need to be persuaded or taunted."

Once he had found his camera, Luke leaned over the armrest of the chair so far that his head, arms, and upper torso were obscuring the entire aisle.

"That doesn't look very comfortable," Kate remarked.

Luke ignored her.

"Okay, Brink, hold still!" he instructed. Then he started snapping away.

"What are you doing?" a lady sitting behind him asked.

"Hey, turn that flash off!" another man griped.

"You know Luke, maybe now isn't the best time..." Michael offered tentatively.

Luke didn't hear him, or if he did, he ignored him.

"Hey! I think I almost see something in this. Look at this, Gavin. Does this look like a mist to you?" Luke shoved the camera in Gavin's face. "Brink, is that your head?"

"Sir." A flight attendant with auburn hair and a stern look on her face approached him. Luke didn't respond to her either.

"Okay, Brink, I'm going to try some without the flash. This time, I'm really going for the full bodied apparition, so feel free to use a little of Mikey's energy if you - "

"Sir!" This time, the flight attendant's voice made Luke jump. "I don't know what you think you're doing, but you need to remain seated and put the camera away. You're being disruptive and it's making the other passengers uncomfortable."

"Sorry, but real quickly, can I just take one more picture?"

"No!"

"Okay, okay." Luke held his hands up in mock surrender and packed his camera back into his bag.

Kate exchanged a nervous glance with Michael. Then, she leaned in close to him and muttered, "I hope he's not famous enough for this to make People.com."

"Even if he's not, I'm sure the world will hear about it somehow," Michael muttered. Even though he didn't have a Twitter himself, he knew (mostly thanks to Kate) that Luke was notorious for Tweeting every aspect of his life.

Kate nodded in acknowledgement.

"You're probably right."

Then, she laced her fingers through his, rested her head on his shoulder, and closed her eyes for the rest of the flight.

CHAPTER SEVEN

The three remaining members of the *Cemetery Tours* crew were waiting for Luke and his guests at baggage claim. Michael had met Gail Marsh, JT Sawyer, and Peter Jamison once before, but he had been in the hospital under extreme sedation, so he didn't remember a whole lot of the encounter. Kate had assured him that he hadn't said or done anything embarrassing, but she'd been so excited to meet all of them that Michael was pretty sure she hadn't been paying the slightest bit of attention to what he was doing.

Gail, the only female member of the group, greeted Kate with a familiar embrace. Seeing them together, Michael wasn't sure if Kate was actually taller than he'd thought, or if Gail was just really short. She probably stood at around five feet, if that, and was very petite, but she was also very athletic. She had shoulder length brown hair, brown eyes, and she wore cargo shorts and a black tank top.

Meanwhile, JT and Luke were already flipping through both of their iPads, discussing the itinerary for the next couple of days. From what Michael had seen on television, JT and Luke were practically polar opposites. According to Kate, some fan sites even referred to him as the "anti-Luke." While Luke was short, sturdy, and blond, JT was tall and thin, with dark hair and about a week's worth of stubble. Luke's loud, energetic, and outgoing personality sharply contrasted with JT's reserved and rather dry demeanor. But somehow, amidst all their differences, Luke and JT remained the best of friends. They played off each other well and never seemed to have any sort of major disagreements.

After he and JT had all the plans squared away, Luke introduced Gavin to Peter, the team's primary tech guy. Michael had always thought that of the four of them, Peter looked and acted the least like a celebrity ghost hunter. While his fellow crew members dressed in expensive, designer brands, Peter still ran around in jean shorts and extra-large Nintendo 64 T-shirts. He rarely cut his flyaway brown hair, and although he was trying to grow facial hair, it appeared wispy and soft.

Peter greeted Gavin enthusiastically and immediately began giving him the rundown on their equipment. But someone else had turned their attention on Gavin as well. Gail, who moments before had been preoccupied catching up with Kate, was suddenly watching Gavin with keen interest. It was only then that Michael remembered Kate mentioning something about Gail's reputation. When it came to men, she wasn't really into relationships. She was more into two-week flings. And judging by the way she was eyeing Gavin, she was considering making him her next conquest.

Kate didn't seem to notice, however. She'd abandoned the group and had rejoined Michael on the outskirts.

"Kind of crazy, huh?" she asked him as a couple of girls stopped Luke and asked for a photograph with him.

"Hey, Sis!" Gavin called.

Both Michael and Kate turned to see Gavin and Peter, who was carrying one of the team's large cameras on his shoulder. As Peter pointed the lens on them, Michael took an automatic step to the side. Kate, Gavin, and Peter all laughed.

"You know, you're going to have to get used to it," Peter told him.

"I will," Michael said. "You just caught me off guard."

"Since when do you have a camera phobia?" Brink asked, appearing suddenly by Michael's side.

"You're not shooting for the show, are you?" Kate asked.

"Nah, this is for my YouTube channel," Peter replied.

"Oh, great. I'm still in my airplane clothes," Kate grumbled, staring down at her ensemble of torn jeans, T-shirt, and jacket. Her hair was tied up in a messy bun and she wasn't wearing any make-up at all. Michael thought she looked great. But then, he was a little biased.

"Tell her it's okay. She's still hot," Brink quipped.

Michael ignored him.

Once they'd collected their luggage, they piled into the vans that Gail and JT had rented. Peter and JT drove the one with all the equipment and luggage, while Gail opted to ride along in the second van with Luke and the rest of the group.

"So, handsome, why don't you tell me a little about yourself." Gail grinned flirtatiously, twisting around in the front seat so she could talk to Gavin.

At first, Gavin didn't seem to know that she was talking to him. Kate clearly didn't either, because she cast an alarmed and rather possessive glance at Michael. He'd always heard that girls could get territorial when a potential rival was around, but he'd never experienced it firsthand.

It was kind of neat.

It didn't last long, however. One glance at Gail and Kate realized that she hadn't been hitting on her boyfriend at all, but on her brother. Michael had to bite his tongue to keep from laughing as Kate's vengeful expression shifted to one of shock and disgust.

Gavin, on the other hand, was clearly caught off guard.

"Leave him alone, Gail. He's here to learn, not to be harassed," Luke said.

"I'm not *harassing* him. I'm just talking. We are going to be spending the next three days together, after all." Gail batted her eyelashes.

"No. He is going to be spending the next three days with Peter. *You* are going to be doing your job like a professional. I don't need another incident like the Del Coronado," Luke remarked.

For about half a second, Michael wondered what exactly had happened at the Del Coronado, but then he remembered that this was celebrity drama and, as a guy, he wasn't supposed to care.

51

Besides, he could always ask Kate about it later. She was so up-to-date with the latest gossip, he was certain she'd know everything there was to know about the Del Coronado incident.

"Okay, please don't give me that look," Luke was saying to Gail.

"Then stop lecturing me," Gail countered.

"I'm not lecturing you. I'm just saying that you are a professional and I need you to act like it. This investigation is a big deal, for us and for the paranormal community. No one has ever been allowed to film inside Stanton Hall. If there was ever a time I needed you focused, it's now."

Gail huffed and crossed her arms, but she didn't argue.

Michael had to admit, he was taken aback. He'd never seen this side of Luke before. The Luke Rainer he knew was loud and arrogant and an absolute pain in the ass. This Luke was serious, mature, responsible, and every bit as professional as any businessman or CEO Michael had ever met. It was weird.

"They sound like an old married couple," Brink remarked from the trunk of the van.

Michael had to agree with him. It was sort of uncomfortable. As uneasy as he felt, however, it was nothing compared to how Gavin appeared to be feeling. With a sheepish grin, his eyes shifted back and forth from Luke to Gail, then finally over to Michael and Kate. Michael didn't really know what to do, so he just shrugged. Kate, on the other hand, raised her eyebrows and mouthed, *Awkward*.

Unsure of what to say to break the tension inside the car (it was actually probably better that he didn't say anything), Michael turned his attention to the scenic view outside his window. It was a great day. The trees were fiery and vibrant against the sky, which was the kind of deep blue you only saw near the coast. Back in Texas, the leaves had just barely begun to change. In Maine, however, the trees were alive and dancing with a brilliant blend of reds, oranges, and yellows.

"It's gorgeous, isn't it?" Kate asked. "I've always wanted to visit the Northeast."

52

"You and me both, Beautiful," Luke called back to Kate. "You don't mind that, do you Mikey? That I call your girlfriend Beautiful?"

"No, no, I agree with you." Michael grinned bashfully at Kate.

"Get a room," Brink groaned.

"You two are so cute," Gail said, twisting back around to see Michael, Kate, and Gavin. "You're pretty lucky, Sinclair. Luke never lets me bring my boyfriends on investigations."

"That's because your boyfriends aren't boyfriends," Luke said. "I think I could take every single one of your so-called relationships, add them together, and they still wouldn't equal the amount of time I spent with my first girlfriend. And by the way, that was in eighth grade and we dated for about two weeks."

"Whatever," Gail scoffed.

"Besides, Kate's not just here as Mikey's date. She's a sensitive. And she knows what it's like to die."

"So, what you're saying is if I go out and find a boyfriend who's had an NDE, then you'll let me bring him on the show?"

"Sure. Knock yourself out," Luke said.

"What's an NDE?" Michael asked.

To his surprise, it wasn't Luke, but Gavin who answered him. "It's a Near Death Experience." Michael and Kate both glanced at him, curiously. "I've been doing a lot of research after all the stuff that went down a few months ago," he explained.

"Hmm. Sexy *and* smart." Gail grinned.

Luke heaved a frustrated sigh. He seemed to realize he wasn't going to win.

"So, are we actually going to be staying at Stanton Hall?" Kate asked.

"Yes, ma'am," Luke replied. "We'll be there for three nights. There are a few areas that are still under renovation, but from what I understand, there are enough rooms available for each of us to have our own suite."

"Sweet," Kate and Gavin declared at the same time.

"Jinx! You owe me a Coke," Kate exclaimed.

"Okay, middle schooler," Gavin retorted. "Hey, Luke. Are we going to have dinner there or are we on our own?"

"Mrs. Drake is cooking for us tonight. She wanted to do something special to welcome us. I told her that wasn't necessary, but she insisted. It's good though, because it'll give us a chance to settle in and get familiar with the building. But tomorrow, when we take our tour and explore the area, we'll mostly be dining out."

"Will we be filming any of that?"

"Gavin, starting the second we set foot inside that house, we will be filming around the clock," Luke replied.

"We'll be filming you while you eat, while you sleep," Gail rambled. "Heck, we'll even be filming you while you're in the bathroom."

"Are you serious?" Kate's eyebrows furrowed in blatant alarm.

"No," Luke assured her. "Though Mikey, if you see a ghost in the bathroom, feel free to take a camera."

"You know Luke, I know you saved my life and everything, but I think it's best to keep some mystery between us," Michael replied dryly.

Ten minutes later, Luke pulled off the main highway. The scenery around them changed from mostly forest to a small New England town. Coastal waters began appearing on either side of the road. Michael noticed several small fishing docks and marinas, probably privately owned, that had been built on the water. There were a few boats out sailing around, but most were secured to the docks.

Kennebunkport itself was a charming town. Old-fashioned shops, bars, and boutiques lined the streets, and there were several people dressed in fall attire out strolling the sidewalks and enjoying the crisp, cool weather. It was like a scene straight out of an American fairy tale. Michael even spotted a white horse pulling a carriage and for a moment, he forgot that they were about to spend three days at one of the most haunted locations in the country.

What was that supposed to mean, anyway? The "most haunted" location? Did that mean that it had a lot of ghosts or was there just one ghost who liked to stir up trouble? Or maybe the one ghost was just a lot more active than most. Maybe it meant that every living person who went there had some sort of experience.

Or maybe it was just a really spooky old house that got the better of people's vivid and willing imaginations, Michael thought as the van rounded a corner and a building that he presumed to be Stanton Hall Manor came into view.

It was a magnificent building; grand, gothic, and protected by a black iron gate, capped with medieval looking spears. Michael couldn't tell at first glance, but Stanton Hall appeared to be at least three or four stories tall, complete with arches, balconies, towers, and five chimneys. Perhaps the most impressive feature, however, was the clock tower that stood at the center of the building.

"Wow," Gavin breathed.

"It's incredible," Kate said.

Michael remained silent as Luke turned around to face them.

"Well, we're here."

CHAPTER EIGHT

Kate had been fully prepared to leap out of the car and explore the house as soon as Luke parked and turned off the ignition. Ten minutes later, however, she and Michael were still stuck in the van while Gavin helped Luke and the rest of the crew unpack all the equipment. She wasn't quite sure how it had happened, but one of the guys had stacked about three or four heavy (and really expensive-looking) cases of equipment on Gavin's vacated seat next to her, blocking the only way out of the van for her and Michael.

"I kind of feel like we should try to get out and help," Michael said.

"I sort of do too, but at the same time, I really don't want to," Kate confessed. "Besides, it's not like we don't have valid excuses for not helping. I'm a recent head trauma patient and you're still recovering from a broken collarbone and a gunshot wound. Really, it would be wrong of them to expect us to help."

After what seemed like an eternity, partly because of how anxious she was to see the inside of the house and partly because she really needed to stretch her legs, JT and Peter arrived to move the cases out of the way, freeing the way for Kate and Michael to finally slip out of the van.

"All right guys, let's get the cameras rolling," Luke called over to Peter and Gavin.

"Already?" Michael asked.

"Come on, Mikey. You've seen the show. We always film a little introduction before we ring the doorbell," Luke told him as Peter helped hook him up to a clip-on wireless microphone.

"We're going to be standing out here all afternoon, aren't we?" Michael muttered to Kate.

She laughed lightly, but secretly, she was thinking the same thing. It wasn't that she didn't want to watch Luke and the gang in action. She'd always wanted to go behind the scenes. It was just that they'd been traveling all day and she was hungry, thirsty, sort of tired, and absolutely freezing. It turned out, not surprisingly, that Kennebunkport in the fall was a lot chillier than Dallas in the fall.

"Okay, are we rolling?" Luke asked JT and Peter, who were both filming him from different angles. Gail, meanwhile, zipped around the property, getting scenic shots that Kate knew they would use as transition between scenes. Peter, who Gavin was shadowing for the time being, gave Luke a thumbs up.

Luke positioned himself directly in front of the manor's massive windows and began walking forward. "We're here at the infamous Stanton Hall Manor in Kennebunkport, Maine, just less than thirty miles south of Portland." He paused. "How was that? Do we need to go again?"

"Yeah, you sort of sped up there at the end," JT told him.

"What did we tell you about eating sugar straight out of the packets?" Peter teased.

Kate giggled. Of the four of them, Peter was definitely the goofiest.

"Is that all he's going to say?" Michael asked Kate as Luke started the take over again.

"A lot of the show's narrative is voice-over," she replied. Luke would surely go on to explain the history of the building to his viewers later, but Kate suspected he would do all that recording back at their studio in L. A.

Michael nodded before turning his attention to the house. He stuffed his hands into his pockets and took a few steps toward the building, dry leaves crunching and crackling beneath his feet. Kate glanced around and watched him take in the manor with dark, focused eyes. She wondered for a moment what he was thinking about, but before she could dwell for too long, she realized just how handsome he looked in his jacket and scarf. His dark hair was messy and windswept, his eyebrows slightly

57

furrowed in concentration, his eyes set and focused. In that moment, Kate was acutely aware of how intelligent, how compassionate, and how rare a find he was.

"See anything?" she asked, strolling over to him.

"Not yet," he replied.

"Okay, I want to be sure to get a few shots with Mikey before we go inside, sort of introduce him, you know," Luke was saying to his crew. "Let's get Kate in there, too. We could use another girl on this show."

"Really?!" Kate squealed. She couldn't help it. She thought she'd been lucky enough just to be invited along. She never dreamed that she'd actually get to be on the show.

"Absolutely. You didn't think you were just here to look pretty, did you? Now, let's get you hooked up to a mic."

"Do I have to say anything?" Michael asked.

Luke peered at Michael over the rims of his sunglasses.

"Really, Mikey?"

Michael shrugged.

"Where do you want to set up?" JT asked Luke.

"Let's move to the very front. I want a good head-on shot of the house."

Kate and Michael followed Luke to the front staircase and stood next to him as the cameras began rolling once again. Staring into the lens, Kate suddenly felt awkward and very aware of every flaw in her hair, complexion, and outfit. She also felt like she needed to sneeze. She tried to push all of that out of her mind by concentrating on what Luke was saying.

"This week we're joined by my good friends, Michael and Kate - hold up. Cut. Mikey, could you maybe take a few steps back? Maybe stand on the other side of Kate? I don't want you making me look short."

Michael obliged and Luke began his dialogue again.

"This week, we're joined by my good friends, Michael and Kate. Michael is a psychic medium, who actually speaks to the - "

"Wait," Michael interrupted.

"What is it, Mikey?"

"Don't tell people I'm a psychic medium. I'm not psychic."

"Then what do you want me to call you?"

"I don't know. The term 'psychic medium' just gives people all these ideas that I can do things that I - I just can't."

"Okay, well, I'll think of something. Let's go back!"

Filming a television show, Kate realized, was much more work than she'd ever considered. She guessed she hadn't really put all that much thought into it in the past. Of course, she'd known that filming took time and energy, but she'd never thought about just how long it could take to film one short scene.

By the time Luke was finally satisfied with their takes, Kate was so hungry, she thought she might keel over. Fortunately, she was fairly certain that these early scripted scenes were the only ones they'd have to shoot multiple times.

Armed with their video cameras and a boom microphone, the crew made their way up the stairs. Kate, Michael, and Gavin trailed behind as Luke knocked on the front door. A few moments later, a short woman dressed in nice slacks and a button-down blouse answered the door.

"Hi. Are you Carolyn?" Luke greeted her.

"I am," she replied. Her demeanor was gracious and respectful, though Kate could tell that she still had reservations about allowing them to come in and film.

After introductions, Carolyn led them inside. All the while, the cameras kept rolling. But Kate forgot about everything, the cameras, the show, even Michael's hand in hers, once she set foot in the magnificent foyer of Stanton Hall Manor. With glittering, antique chandeliers designed to emulate the sun, stars, and planets, stained-glass windows depicting exotic flowers and beams of light, and intricate tiled designs of every color on every wall, even the glitz and glamour of Karen's beautiful house paled in comparison to this splendid storybook mansion.

"Whoa," Kate breathed.

"You know, I think that every place we investigate is pretty cool, but *this* is awesome," Luke told Carolyn.

"We've been working hard to restore it," Carolyn informed him.

"And I understand that you're hoping to turn it into a bed and breakfast."

"That's right."

"Well, best of luck with that. Hopefully, we can generate some good publicity for you," Luke grinned, turning on his overly friendly, television persona. Though Kate really couldn't see a whole lot of difference between that and his regular personality.

"Yes, well, that would be nice," Carolyn replied stiffly, clasping her hands together. "Now then, I suppose you'll want to know the history of the house."

"Yes, ma'am. Anything you can tell us," Luke replied. "But you know, usually when we do these interviews, we like to sort of change the scenery. Is there a room with a couch? Maybe a fireplace?"

Carolyn gave a curt nod.

"Come with me."

They followed Mrs. Drake into the sitting room, an open space with velvet couches, luxurious drapes, and the largest fireplace that Kate had ever seen. It reminded her of a room straight out of a castle in a fairy tale.

After the guys had their equipment set up, Luke and Carolyn took a seat on the couch.

"This house was constructed in the late 1830s by Sterling Hall. Mr. Hall was the son of one of the wealthiest men in town, a Jeremiah Hall, who died very suddenly in 1832. Shortly after his father's death, Sterling fell in love with Joanna Stanton, the daughter of a local fisherman. Now the story goes that Mr. Stanton didn't trust Sterling. He didn't believe that a man who could have any girl in town would want anything to do with a girl of such humble means."

"He sounds very protective," Luke noted.

"He was. Joanna was his treasure. But Sterling was a very determined man, and endlessly wealthy. He built this house to prove to her father that he was worthy of her. They married three months later."

"So, this house was a symbol of Sterling's dedication and love for Joanna," Luke said.

"Exactly."

"Wow, that's beautiful," Gail said.

"Why do I get the feeling that this story doesn't have a happy ending?" JT asked.

Because stories that result in a haunting rarely do, Kate thought to herself. *Someone always dies. Someone is always left behind. Someone is always caught between worlds.*

"You're right, it doesn't," Carolyn replied. "A few years after they were married, Joanna fell ill. Sterling brought doctors in from as far away as Switzerland hoping to save her. But despite his best efforts, Joanna passed away in this house, the very building Sterling had built for her. Devastated and on the edge of sanity, Sterling lived out the rest of his days alone."

"Did he also die in this house?" Luke asked.

"Yes," Carolyn answered.

"And is he the one who's been haunting the building?" Gail asked.

"Well, that's what everyone else seems to think," Carolyn answered with a wry grin. It was the first time since their arrival that Kate had seen the older woman smile.

"You don't believe this place is haunted?" Peter asked.

"No, I do not."

"That's interesting," Luke commented lightly. "And why don't you think so?"

"I know that investigating these buildings and chasing these so-called 'spirits' are what you've built your careers on, and I do respect you for that. But these ghosts, these hauntings... I believe they are nothing but figments of some people's overactive imaginations."

Kate couldn't help it. She glanced over at Gavin, who stared right back at her. She knew they were both thinking about all the times he'd tried to convince her that she was just imagining the feelings she'd felt and the footsteps she'd heard in the middle of the night. But he'd been wrong and he fully acknowledged it.

"So, let me get this straight. You don't believe in ghosts," Luke said.

"No," Carolyn answered.

"That's fine, that's fine. We're accepting of all sorts here on *Cemetery Tours*," Luke assured her. "I am curious about something, though. If you don't believe in ghosts, then I'm guessing you think my friend Mikey here is a fraud, which brings me to my next question. If you believe all hauntings are made up, then why did you insist that he come with us on this investigation?"

Kate glanced over at Michael, who was listening intently. She had been wondering the answer to that question too.

"To be honest, I didn't insist that he come along with you. My daughter did," Carolyn said.

"You have a daughter?" Gail asked.

"Emily. She just turned fifteen."

"Okay. So why did she insist on having Mikey come with us?" Luke asked.

Carolyn remained silent for a moment while she considered her answer.

"Emily is a wonderful, very bright girl, but I'm afraid that all the stories about this place that people have told her over the years have had a very negative impact on her. From the moment she set foot in this house, she's wanted nothing to do with it. Most of the time, she keeps herself locked in her room. I told her if it would make her feel better, I'd call someone to come and inspect the house. She read about your story on some website, and she asked for you."

Kate looked at Michael to see how he was reacting to all of this. She wasn't surprised to see him looking nervous and unsure of the woman's confidence that he would be able to provide her with the answer she so obviously sought. If there *was* a ghost there in the mansion, he would see it.

"So, you've brought us here, not to prove that Stanton Hall is haunted, but actually to prove that it's not," Luke translated.

"That's exactly right," Carolyn replied.

"That's very honorable of you," Gail told her. "To go to such great lengths for your daughter."

Honorable, Kate thought, *but all too familiar*.

"Thank you. And thank you all for taking the time to do this," Carolyn said.

"Oh, it's our pleasure," Luke assured her. "But I do have to warn you, Carolyn, we might not be able to give you the answer you're hoping for. If there is a haunting here, we're going to find it."

"Understood."

"I also can't guarantee that we can do anything about it if there is a haunting. We try to help these spirits move on as much as we can, but ultimately, it's up to them. They have to make the decision to leave on their own," Luke explained. "I can't promise you either that the activity won't get worse when we leave. You know, we always try to help wherever we investigate, but sometimes, if a spirit doesn't like us or if it feels like we're intruding, we make it angry..."

Kate could see by the assured look in Carolyn's eyes that she wasn't the least bit concerned or frightened. She wasn't sure if that was a good or a bad thing.

"Thank you for the warning, Mr. Rainer, but I think I'll take the chance."

CHAPTER NINE

After the first interview, Carolyn Drake led the entire group on a tour of the mansion. While the others marveled at the stained glass, the gold and silver adorning every doorway, and the swirling patterns of reds and purples and yellows and greens on the walls, Michael found himself distracted. Stanton Hall was everything Luke had described and more, but it was noticeably lacking one thing:

Ghosts.

For a building that was supposed to be so notoriously haunted, Michael was beginning to suspect that perhaps Mrs. Drake was right. Maybe everyone who had heard the story had just expected the house to be haunted and had mistaken the inevitable creaks and moans of an old building for something paranormal.

Well, there was one ghost, but he'd come with the crew.

"This place is kind of creepy, isn't it? You know, for a house that was supposed to be built for the woman he loved, this guy could have made it a little more romantic and a little less mystical-funhouse-where-all-the-demons-play," Brink remarked.

Michael thought he was exaggerating just a little. Stanton Hall was fantastic. A little spooky, sure, but it wasn't something out of an Alfred Hitchcock movie. It was a true work of art, crafted from the mind of a lovelorn genius.

"So Mikey, you think you'd ever build Kate a house like this?" Luke asked him.

"Um..." The question would have been awkward enough without the added bonus of being captured on camera. It wasn't that he was embarrassed by his relationship with Kate, or that there was anything he wouldn't do for her. It was just that the idea of talking about his personal life in front of an international audience didn't exactly thrill him.

He finally responded with, "I'm not sure I could afford it."

Kate and Luke both laughed. Michael took that as a good sign. He'd always liked the idea of being funny, but somehow, he'd never been able to master the art.

"That's okay," Kate assured him as Mrs. Drake led them into one of the many, many bedrooms. "Oh my..."

"Every bedroom in the manor has a theme. This is the Starlight Room," Mrs. Drake explained.

Fitting name, Michael thought, glancing around the magnificent room. Dark blue velvet drapes adorned with silver thread and glittering gemstones surrounded the four-poster bed. The silver chandelier hanging in the center of the room glistened with star-shaped crystals. Paintings of stars and constellations danced across the ceiling. Even the cerulean carpet seemed to shimmer.

Next to him, Kate was about to hyperventilate.

"Oh my God, this is the most beautiful room I've ever seen in my entire life! How much did it cost for you to do this? Would you mind if I took pictures to show my boss? I'm an interior decorator and this is just *amazing!*"

"Well, thank you. And yes, feel free to take as many pictures as you like. However, if you post them online, be sure to mention Stanton Hall," Mrs. Drake told her. "As for the design, I didn't come up with it. Every room in this house was designed by Sterling Hall. In our renovations, of course, we've modernized a little, but for the most part, this is how the house was originally decorated."

"That's incredible," Kate marveled.

"So Carolyn, of all of these rooms, which of them would you say gets the most activity? Ghost activity, I mean? I know you say you don't believe the building is haunted, but you must have a lot of people reporting some crazy stuff, given this house's reputation and everything," Luke said.

"That would have to be the master bedroom. It's the room where Sterling and Joanna slept. It's the room where they probably consummated their marriage. It's also the room where she is believed to have died."

"And are you going to have guests stay in that room?" JT asked.

"Yes, eventually. It's in the part of the house that's still undergoing a few renovations, but eventually it will be the Honeymoon Suite."

"You know, this is just a hunch here, but I'm willing to bet that a guy who loved his wife as much as Sterling did is probably not going to like a bunch of workers coming in and tearing up the room he shared with her. Especially if he's still waiting for her," Luke said.

"How do you know it's him?" Kate asked. "What if she's the one who's still waiting?"

"I guess I don't know. That's an excellent point," Luke acknowledged.

"I'm not sure," Gail chimed in. "After doing this for as long as we have and having seen this kind of haunting before, it would make more sense for him to be the one who stayed behind. After all, he was the one who experienced heartbreak. He was the one who was driven mad. I think in the end, he suffered a lot more than she did."

"But don't you think it pains the ones who've died just as much to be separated from their loved ones as it pains those who are still living?" Kate asked.

At that moment, Michael knew she was thinking not only about Trevor and how much he'd suffered being cut off from her, but about her own time spent in the afterlife.

Gail was silent for a moment.

"I guess I've never really thought about it," she confessed.

Luke, meanwhile, stared at Kate with the kind of admiration a teacher might show for his favorite student.

"Carolyn, you should spend some time talking with Kate. She might be able to change your mind about ghosts," he said.

"And if her experience isn't enough, then I guess we'll just have to capture some damn good EVPs."

EVP, Michael had learned from his first ghost-hunting excursion, stood for Electronic Voice Phenomena. Basically, it was a spirit's voice captured on a digital recorder.

"Well, you can try," Mrs. Drake told him.

"Wow. You know, you might just be the most stubborn skeptic I've ever met." Luke actually sounded impressed.

"Tell her about me," Brink said loudly. Of course, Michael was the only one who could hear him, so he wasn't quite sure why he was almost shouting. "I'm real. We could do one of those tests to prove I'm here. You know, maybe you could have her tell me a secret and make sure no one else is around to hear, and then I could tell you and it would prove that I was there."

"You do know that once the investigation starts, you can't talk at all," Michael hissed to Brink once Carolyn had led the rest of the group down the hall. Only Kate lingered, waiting for him to catch up.

"How come? They want to catch a ghost on tape, right?" Brink asked.

"They want to catch Sterling Hall or Joanna Stanton on tape. Not you."

"Ouch."

"I'm guessing Brink is still here," Kate grinned, making her way back to them.

"You know, if she had stayed dead, then she could be my girlfriend instead of yours," Brink quipped.

Michael glared at him.

"What's he saying?" Kate asked.

"Oh, just that he has a lot of respect for us. You know, the usual," Michael answered.

Kate laughed.

"Have you seen any other ghosts yet?" she asked.

Michael shook his head. "No, I haven't."

"I guess we just haven't found them yet."

"That, or Mrs. Drake is right, and there are no ghosts here."

"What do you think?"

"I don't really know," Michael confessed. "I think a building with a history like this definitely has the potential for a haunting. And with so many people reporting activity, I'd think we'd at least find *something*. Then again, if someone is here, he's apparently not very bent on making his presence known."

"That's weird, isn't it?" Kate asked. "I remember when I had my experience, all I wanted was for someone to acknowledge me. I probably would have been screaming at the top of my lungs if you hadn't asked me if I was okay. Then again, whoever's here has had a lot longer to get used to not being seen or heard."

Michael was about to reply when the faint sound of footsteps trudging down the hall distracted him. Kate must have heard them too, because her head turned immediately to the door and she took an automatic step towards Michael.

Just then, Gavin poked his head inside the room and said, "Luke sent me back to make sure you two hadn't gotten lost."

"Gavin," Kate groaned. "Oh my God, you just about scared me to death."

"What? Did you think I was a ghost? Wooooo..." Gavin waggled his fingers in her face.

"Careful who you taunt, Gav. The last time you pissed off a spirit, you wound up in the emergency room," Kate reminded him.

"Don't worry, I learned my lesson. From now on, there will be no pissing off the spirits. But Luke did want to know what was taking so long."

"We were just talking," Kate assured him. Gavin raised an eyebrow. "We *were*," Kate insisted. "If I was going to try something, I'd at least have the decency to close the door."

"Whatever you say, Sis," Gavin smirked and headed back down the hall.

"He is such a pain," Kate griped.

"Is it just me, or is he starting to act like Luke?" Michael asked.

"What? No way. Luke is way cooler than Gavin."

Michael wasn't sure he agreed with her on that one. In fact, he could have listed all the reasons why Gavin was considerably cooler than Luke, beginning with his wardrobe and leading all the way up to the fact that Gavin had never tried to manipulate him, blackmail him, or screw with any aspect of his life in order to get something he wanted. Unfortunately, he was pretty sure none of that would change her mind.

Together, Michael and Kate (and Brink) followed Gavin down the hall and into the majestic dining hall where Mrs. Drake was introducing the rest of the crew to a young girl sitting at the head of the grand dining room table.

"I am going to ask that for her sake, you do not film her, but she did want to meet all of you," Mrs. Drake said.

"Of course, we understand," Luke told her before turning his attention to the girl. "Hi there, Emily. I'm Luke. It's nice to meet you." He held out his hand, but she didn't take it.

"Nice to meet you, too," she mumbled quietly and averted her eyes. Being at the center of everyone's attention must have embarrassed her. Or maybe she had a crush on Luke. Michael wouldn't have been surprised.

There was a momentary silence amidst the group as Emily's timid brown eyes flitted across the faces of everyone in the room before they finally met Michael's. It was only then that he remembered that he was the reason they'd been allowed to come in the first place. Emily had asked for him.

He wondered if maybe he should say something, formally introduce himself when, without warning, Emily leapt up and bolted out of the room. Suddenly, everyone's eyes were fixated on *him*.

"Were you making faces at her, Mikey?" Luke asked.

"No! I was just looking! I didn't know if maybe I should say something or... I don't know..." Michael said, feeling confused and a little guilty.

"Don't worry about it, dear," Mrs. Drake assured him, sounding weary. "Emily has always been skittish, especially when it comes to meeting new people."

"Carolyn, did Emily ever tell you *why* she wanted Mikey to come with us? She must have had a reason," Luke said.

"She didn't have to tell me. Emily truly believes this building is haunted and she thought that if she could get the young man who supposedly sees spirits up here, then he could get rid of them."

Oh, great. I've gone from psychic medium to exorcist, Michael thought. Seriously, was it really *too* much to ask for a nice normal life? Why couldn't he have a pleasant calling like a gardener? He could totally see himself as a gardener.

"Well, um, I can try but... Um..."

"Oh, dear, don't worry, you don't have to try. You don't have to do anything except assure her that there are no ghosts in this house," Carolyn told him.

Michael thought about telling her that he was really bad at lying, but decided against it. Maybe he wouldn't have to lie. Granted, there was a ghost in the house, and he was standing right behind him, but he wasn't going to stick around. He'd be heading back to Dallas with the rest of them once the investigation was over.

"I'll see what I can do," he promised.

"Good. Now, I'll get you your room assignments. You'll all be on the east side of either the first or second floor. The west is still undergoing a few renovations," Mrs. Drake explained.

"Will we be allowed to investigate there?" Gail asked.

"You'll all have to sign a liability form stating that you understand the risks involved and that you won't hold the workers of Stanton Hall accountable for any injury sustained."

"It won't be the first time," Luke said.

Michael wasn't so eager to agree, but he had a feeling he didn't have much of a choice. Kate, however, was another matter entirely.

70

"Luke." Michael pulled him aside as the others ventured back out to the vans to unpack their luggage. "You're not going to make Kate and Gavin sign those forms, are you?"

"If they want to go on the west side, I think they'll probably have to," Luke replied.

"I mean, they didn't sign on for anything dangerous."

"Mikey, you need to understand something about the society we live in. Everyone is afraid of getting sued. That means if there is the slightest little chance that someone might trip and sprain their toe on a screwdriver, they have to make you sign a release form, because guess what? There are lawyers out there who will take that toe sprain and turn it into a million-dollar lawsuit."

"So, you don't think there's any real danger?" Michael asked.

"Of course not. But if there was, do you really think that would stop Kate?"

Unfortunately, no. And he knew how she felt about people trying to protect her. It didn't matter what he said or thought. There was no way he'd be able to keep her away from experiencing a paranormal investigation to its fullest, especially in the creepiest part of the house.

Luke took a step toward Michael and clapped a brotherly hand on his shoulder. "Don't worry about her. We're all here. We look out for each other. I would promise you that I won't let anything happen to her, but I don't think I need to."

"Why?" Michael asked.

Luke's eyes flitted for a half a second down to Michael's chest, to the spot where Chastity Cannon's bullet had almost torn through his heart.

"Because she's got you."

CHAPTER TEN

Kate was assigned to the Emerald Room. After spending time in the Starlight Room, she had been afraid that any other bed chamber might pale in comparison, but the Emerald Room was yet another interior masterpiece.

As the name suggested, everything in the entire room was some shade of the color of an emerald, with hints of the color of the sun and the color of grapes. A circular mirror hung above the queen-sized bed, also adorned in emerald. The room didn't have a chandelier, but there was a light fixture, framed by swirling shades of sunlight. The construction of the room was also unique. Instead of a rectangle or a square, the Emerald Room had eight walls, forming the shape of an octagon, just like a gem.

After photographing every detail of the room on her phone and texting the pictures to Val, Kate dragged her suitcase to the side of the bed and, without bothering to unpack, scampered out into the hall, eager to see the other rooms.

Gavin had been assigned the Storybook Room, Luke the Mariner's Room, and Michael the Fireside Room. Each room seemed more spectacular than the last, and by the time she'd visited all of them, Kate had taken so many pictures that her phone battery was almost drained. She'd have to dig out her charger after dinner.

"This place is *awesome*," Kate gushed as she and Michael made their way back to the dining hall.

Gavin had gone ahead with the rest of the crew to set up some more film equipment. Kate was happy to pass on that. She realized now that what went on behind the scenes didn't really interest her as much as she thought it would. She liked the stories they learned, the people they met, and the places they visited much better than watching them try to figure out which cord went where and if they had enough battery power and if the camera was set up at just the right angle. It was sort of cool to see how much hard work went into creating that one perfect shot, but after a while, it got a little tedious.

"It's a lot cooler than I was expecting," Michael admitted.

"And still no ghosts, huh?"

"Just Brink," Michael replied, casually slipping his hand into hers.

"Well, maybe they'll show up later."

"You say that as though you *want* them to show up."

"I do! Wouldn't it just suck if the one episode of *Cemetery Tours* that we get to be in turns out to be the one with no ghosts? Seriously, it'd be the worst episode ever."

"It couldn't be any worse than the one where Luke fell into that patch of poison ivy and decided to change his pants right there in the middle of the forest," Michael remarked.

"To be fair, he didn't know that they were still filming him. I'm pretty sure that was all Peter and Gail's idea."

"Yeah, but as executive producer, he could have made the decision *not* to include it in the episode."

Kate threw her head back and laughed. "You're hilarious. You know that, right?" She kissed him swiftly on the cheek. "At least he was wearing boxers that day."

"Yeah. Thank God," Michael quipped dryly, as though that was in no way enough to make up for the fact that he'd had to endure the sight of Luke Rainer in his underwear.

Kate snickered again.

By the time they reached the dining room, where Mrs. Drake had set out a magnificent feast of rosemary roasted chicken, mashed potatoes, and seasoned vegetables, the cameras were already rolling again.

"Hey, there are the two crazy lovebirds," Luke grinned and turned his handheld camera on them. "So Mikey, what do you think of the house so far?"

"Um, it's great. Why are you filming this?"

"In a place like this, you never know what's going to happen. There was one time back when the show had just started, we decided to turn the cameras off for just a second and what happens? A mannequin gets knocked right off its feet in the middle of a department store. No explanation at all. That could have been one of our most compelling pieces of evidence up until that point and we totally missed it. I'm still not over it." Luke sounded genuinely distressed for a brief moment, but he quickly recovered. "And just for future reference, you never question the camera. You just go with it."

"Right."

But it soon became pretty clear that Michael had no intention of "going with it." Apparently, acting natural in front of the camera was not Michael's forte, so instead of even attempting to be normal, he completely clammed up. He didn't say a word throughout the entire meal. Not that he would have had much of an opportunity. Luke, Gail, and Carolyn talked throughout most of the evening. Every once in a while, JT or Peter managed to chime in with a sentence or two, but for the most part, Luke carried the conversation.

"So after dinner, I was thinking we might do a séance. Well, not a séance per se, but you know, some sort of ritual to introduce ourselves to Sterling and Joanna. Maybe have the digital recorder going, see if we can get any responses? What do you guys think?" Luke asked.

"I brought my old Ouija Board. We could see if - "

"No." Kate interrupted Gail without even thinking about it. Suddenly, all eyes were on her.

"Why? What's the problem?" Luke asked.

Kate had her own reasons for not liking Ouija Boards. For one thing, they were creepy. For another, she fully believed that if you invited any sort of entity in, light or dark, good or evil, it would come. But neither of those reasons would have caused her to voice her objection if Luke and his crew had decided to use a Ouija Board.

No, she'd only spoken up because she'd seen the look on Emily Drake's face.

The young girl, who'd remained as silent as Michael throughout all of dinner (truthfully, Kate hadn't even noticed she was there until her mother asked her to pass the mashed potatoes), had gone absolutely rigid with alarm the moment Gail mentioned the Ouija Board. Kate had no idea what had happened to her to elicit such a reaction, but whatever it was had left a deep impact.

However, if Emily Drake was like other shy teenage girls, she wasn't going to want Kate to direct the spotlight over to her. So she simply replied, "I just don't think it's a good idea. If I've learned anything from horror movies, it's stay away from the attic, stay away from the woods, and stay away from Ouija Boards."

"Wait a minute. You used to play with Ouija Boards all the time with your friends. You'd sit around for hours giggling and asking it things like, 'Ooh, will Eric ask me on a date? He's so dreamy. Hee hee hee!'" Gavin imitated his sister's high-pitched voice.

Gail giggled loudly.

Kate, meanwhile, scowled.

"Okay, first of all, we were twelve. Second of all, Eric Jensen was the hottest guy in the eighth grade and he was really tall. Finally, that was before I grew up and had a personal experience with the paranormal that left me a little more cautious around this stuff than I was in my youth." After a brief moment of consideration, she turned to Luke. "This won't make it to the final cut, will it?"

"Probably not," Luke said. "The vast majority of what we film actually doesn't. It's hard to cram three days of footage into forty-five minutes of show time."

Kate was relieved. Unless something spooky happened during dinner, that meant she didn't have to worry about her brother calling her out on television. It also hopefully meant that maybe Michael could relax a little.

Unfortunately, it turned out her little speech about Ouija Boards wasn't very effective. Once they'd finished eating, Gail sprinted back to her room to retrieve the Ouija Board while Luke, Peter, and Gavin transferred all the equipment into the sitting room. Kate, Michael, and to her surprise, JT, lingered behind to help Mrs. Drake clear the table and wash the dishes. Emily had disappeared shortly after dinner.

Of Luke's entire crew, JT was the one who'd always seemed the most like a stereotypical ghost hunter; dark, mysterious, a little broody. Kate realized, watching him carry a pile of plates into the kitchen, that she really didn't know a whole lot about him. Unlike Luke, who'd written a book and who told anyone who would listen about the time he saw the ghost of his grandfather, JT was incredibly reserved about his personal life and experiences. Somewhat odd for a celebrity.

"You know, JT, if you need to go help them set up, I think Michael and I can handle the rest of the dishes," Kate told him as she filled the sink with hot water.

"They're fine. Besides, I don't want anyone thinking that the guys on *Cemetery Tours* are a bunch of divas." He offered a wry grin.

"I think that ship sailed with Luke," Michael remarked, drying off the crystal glasses that Kate handed to him.

To her surprise, JT chuckled.

"Luke is an enormous douche, but he's a good guy. He's my best friend."

"How did you two become friends?" Kate asked. "I mean, I know you met at that bar he used to work at, but how did you go from two guys in a bar to two of the most famous paranormal investigators in the world?"

"Three. Gail worked at the bar, too," he reminded her.

"That's right." Kate felt silly for forgetting.

"It was a while ago. I'd just turned twenty-one, and it was around Halloween. One of the other patrons came in with this wild story about a ghost in his apartment. That was all it took. That night, Luke told us the whole story about his ghost

76

experience and how he'd always wanted to investigate it further. Gail was totally into it. I didn't want to be the only skeptic, which I was at the time, so I agreed to go along with it. I never expected to actually find anything."

"So, you went along even though you didn't believe in ghosts?" Michael asked.

JT just shrugged in response as Luke appeared, clapping his hands loudly.

"Okay, clean-up brigade, are you about done in here? Because we are ready to get our Ouija on!"

Kate hesitated. The neurotic, over-protective, rational part of her wanted nothing to do with the séance or Ouija Board whatsoever. The eager, curious, slightly reckless part of her, however, didn't want to miss a moment of any ghostly interaction. There was no debating which part would win out in the end.

"We're almost done! Don't start without us," Kate told him.

"Are you sure?" Michael asked, looking surprised. "I mean, after everything you said at dinner..."

"That was more for Emily's benefit than mine," Kate confessed.

"Still, you sounded pretty adamant," JT spoke up.

"Okay, yeah, I admit it. Ouija Boards kind of freak me out."

"Any particular reason?" Luke asked.

"So, you heard Gavin giving me a hard time about playing with Ouija Boards as a kid?" Kate began. "It's true, my friends and I used to ask it all these dumb questions about boys and if we were going to grow up to become movie stars. But then one day, my friend Simone and I got curious and we started asking if there were any ghosts or demons around. It said 'yes.' We got chilled. Our cat started freaking out. We asked it to leave, and suddenly, everything was calm again."

"So, you were a sensitive before all that business with Trevor last spring?" Luke asked.

"I don't think so. That was the only time anything like that happened, which makes me think that whatever we contacted was pretty powerful," Kate said. "Anyway, that's why I think Ouija Boards are creepy. But I still want to be a part of whatever you guys are going to do."

"You know, we might not even need the Ouija Board, with Michael here," JT observed.

"Mikey can't call spirits. He can just see them. Since these ghosts seem to be a little camera shy, the Ouija Board might be the best way to actually get them to show up. Mikey, however, will be able to tell us *when* they show up," Luke said. "I for one still think the Ouija Board is a good idea. We don't have to start with it, but if it comes down to it, Gail and I will do all of the communicating. The rest of you don't even have to touch it if you don't want to. Just sit there, look pretty, and Mikey, keep your eyes open for ghosts. Not that you have any control over it, but you know what I mean." Luke grinned like a kid on Christmas and clapped his hands together again. "So... everyone ready?"

CHAPTER ELEVEN

The cameras kept rolling as Kate, Michael, and JT followed Luke into the sitting room, the same room where the crew had filmed their first interview with Mrs. Drake. To no one's surprise, both mother and daughter had elected to pass on the séance. Truthfully, Kate found it a wonder that Mrs. Drake had even agreed to let them perform it in the manor. Her daughter was scared to death of the ghosts that supposedly haunted Stanton Hall. If there were ghosts in the building, then a séance all but guaranteed a surge in supernatural activity.

Then again, since Mrs. Drake didn't believe in the ghosts, then she didn't really have a reason to believe that a séance would be anything more than a group of people holding hands around a ring of candles and an old Ouija Board.

Both Kate and Michael had opted out of the whole Ouija experience, but they were still going to watch from the couch. Luke was surprisingly okay with that. What he wasn't okay with was Kate snuggling up next to Michael while he was supposed to be on ghost patrol.

"I don't want you to have any distractions. Kate is a distraction," Luke explained. Kate threw him a look. "Don't worry, it's a compliment."

"Sure it is," Kate murmured.

"No, really. You wouldn't want to be with a guy who found dead people more interesting than you, would you?" Luke asked.

"Well that explains why *you're* still single," Gail remarked.

Luke ignored her, but Kate could tell that Michael was trying not to snicker.

"For another thing, this is all going to be recorded. I want people to take Mikey seriously, and how serious can he look cuddling up with the cute blonde while the rest of us are here baring our souls to the Ouija Board?" Luke asked.

This time, Peter was the one who chuckled. Everyone turned to look at him. "I'm sorry, man. It's just, do you have any idea how ridiculous you sound every time you say 'Ouija Board?'" He'd almost dissolved into a full-blown giggle fit. "Come on, it's a funny name. 'Wee-Jee' Board."

"How many glasses of wine did you have, Peter?" Luke asked, not sounding very amused at all.

"None, man! I swear!"

"He's just drunk on life," JT remarked. "Come on, let's hit the lights."

As the room descended into darkness, the soft glow of the candlelight dancing around the walls and casting eerie shadows across their faces became their only source of illumination. Careful to avoid being burnt, Gail set the Ouija Board, dirty and faded with age, in the center of the candles.

"Wait a minute, aren't you supposed to touch the Ouija Board to make it work?" Gavin asked.

"We're pretty much just using it as a conduit for now. Besides, if all the stories and myths about Ouija Boards are true, then theoretically, we shouldn't have to touch it to make it work," Gail replied. "But if we do use it later, I'll be sure to ask it if you think I'm cute."

"Gail..." Luke warned her.

JT cleared his throat.

"Shall we commence?" he asked, obviously trying to spare Kate, Michael, and Gavin from his coworkers' bickering.

"Yes," Luke affirmed as he stood to face one of the cameras they had set up. Peter filmed him from a different angle. "It's our first night here at Stanton Hall Manor in Kennebunkport, Maine. This mansion is notorious for being one of the most haunted buildings in North America. Since we haven't had a whole lot of luck making contact with the spirits that dwell here, we've decided to take matters into our own hands by conducting a séance. We have candles burning, we have a Ouija Board, and we will have our digital recorders rolling the entire time just in case we catch a disembodied voice our cameras don't pick up. I've also set up motion detectors in every corner of the room and in the very center. And I think that pretty much covers it. JT, are we good to go?"

"We are ready," JT confirmed.

Kate felt an unnatural chill as Luke took a seat and joined hands with Gail and JT. Subconsciously, she scooted over toward Michael, who wrapped a protective arm around her. If Luke noticed, he didn't say anything.

"Anything yet?" she whispered to Michael.

"No," he answered.

"We're ready to begin," Luke murmured in a hushed, even tone.

Kate took that as a subtle request for them to stop talking.

In the candles' soft glow, Kate could see that Luke, Gail, and JT had all closed their eyes. Their breathing had steadied and slowed, and for an instant, it almost seemed to Kate as though they'd all fallen asleep.

Then Gail began to speak.

"If there are any spirits in this house, we invite you to come and speak with us now." The candles flickered. Kate waited for a response from Michael. Nothing. Gail continued. "You're lonely. You've been lonely for a long time. We know, because you've been reaching out to people. Well, we're here now. Talk to us."

"Do you think this will work?" Kate whispered to Michael.

"I don't know. I've never been to a séance before," he replied.

"I guess you've never really needed to, huh?"

"No."

"What if it doesn't work?"

"Then we'll go to Plan B," Luke muttered.

"What's Plan B?" Kate hissed.

"Working on it. Shh."

Kate had never been a particularly patient person, nor had she ever been all that skilled at sitting in silence. Even in kindergarten, she was the kid who would get sent to time-out for talking during quiet time. It wasn't that she didn't understand the concept of silence, it was that the absence of any and all noise made her antsy. It always had.

"Sterling? Joanna?" Gail continued. "If you're there, we're asking you to give us a sign. We know you're trapped here. We want to help you, but you have to let us. We are opening ourselves up to you. Use our energy. Speak through us. We're here for you."

Suddenly, one of Luke's devices, a motion sensor that he'd placed in the center of the room, began to wail and light up. Kate flinched, unnerved by the sudden disturbance.

"See anything, Mikey?" Luke asked.

"Not yet..." Michael replied, sounding sleepy. Considering how dark it was, Kate wondered if he'd even be able to see a ghost if one decided to show up.

"The candlelight probably triggered it," Luke murmured.

Kate wasn't so sure. Perhaps it was the eerie shriek of the motion detector, but the hairs on the back of her neck were suddenly standing on end. Something in the atmosphere had shifted. The air was a little too tense, too cold, and too still. So very still. A chilling and invisible presence filled the room, and at that moment, there was no doubt in Kate's mind.

The séance had worked.

Michael was struggling to stay awake as Gail continued to beckon whatever spirits may have been listening. The séance was turning out to be so boring, however, that he really wouldn't have been surprised if they had just tuned her out. His own thoughts were just beginning to drift up to the very comfortable-looking bed back in the Fireside Room when suddenly, he felt Kate go rigid beside him. He turned to look at her. She was sitting up straight, alert and focused.

"What is it?" he asked her.

"Are you sure you don't see anything?" she whispered.

"I don't know," he replied honestly. Glancing around the room, no, he didn't see anything. Then again, the light of the candles being used for the séance only reached so far. The furthest corners of the room were still pitch black.

He strained his eyes, trying to make out items on the shelves: large, old books, an antique globe, framed photographs. As his eyes adjusted, he was able to see an old armchair, probably a reading chair, next to a small round table with a lamp that looked like it belonged in the fifties and then –

There!

The dark, shadowed silhouette of a man stood near the far west end of the room. The figure was so still and so silent that Michael's eyes could have easily passed him over had he not been looking for him.

Unsure of whether or not to speak up, Michael leaned into Kate and whispered, "He's here."

She drew in a quick, shaky breath, too soft to be called a gasp, but sharp enough to get Luke's attention.

"What's going on?" he asked, glancing up at them. "Mikey? We got something?"

Michael simply nodded in reply, hoping that Luke could see his motion in the dim candlelight.

"Sterling?"

Michael nodded again.

"Excellent," Luke whispered. Then he turned to JT. "Do you think we should try the SB7 or should we stick with the digital recorder?"

The SB7, or Spirit Box as it was also called, was an irritating nuisance of a device that scanned radio frequencies and allowed spirits to communicate through the static. Michael had seen it in action back when he'd gone with Luke and Kate on their

83

first investigation. As loud and annoying as the Spirit Box was, however, Michael had to admit... it worked.

"Digital recorder for now," JT said. "This spirit seems reluctant, and the noise from the Spirit Box might discourage him, or even scare him off. We don't know what kind of communication devices he's been exposed to in the past, so it might be safe to say he's never encountered an SB7 before."

"Good call," Luke told his friend. "Gail, proceed."

"Sterling," Gail spoke in her calm, soothing voice. "Are you here with us?" She paused. "My name is Gail. This is Luke and JT. We've come to speak with you." Another pause. "If you're here, give us a sign. Say something."

After a few moments of silence, Luke asked, "Okay. Want to see if we got anything?"

Michael could have told them that they hadn't. Sterling hadn't spoken since he'd appeared. Still, he'd seen enough episodes of *Cemetery Tours* to know this was part of their routine.

They rewound and replayed the digital recorder. Nothing out of the ordinary. Luke glanced over at Michael as if to ask, *Is he still here?*

Michael gave yet another swift nod. Their ghostly visitor hadn't moved much. Michael wished he could get a little closer so he could see the expression on Sterling's face, but he wasn't sure how to do that without seeming... well... really awkward. He was also pretty sure if he got too close to the ghost, he'd vanish. JT was right. This was one of the most reluctant spirits that Michael had ever encountered.

But why? He'd been dead for over a century. Surely he was at least sort of used to it by now. He'd spent more than twice as long wandering the halls of the manor as a spirit than he had in his living, breathing body.

So why was he so hesitant to make contact with them now? If the stories were to be believed, he'd been making his presence known for quite some time. He obviously had something holding him there, to Stanton Hall. And if not Stanton Hall specifically, there had to be a reason he hadn't moved on yet. Did it have something to do with Joanna and her untimely passing? Considering Sterling had built the entire mansion out of adoration for her, Michael was willing to bet that it did.

Could that mean that Joanna was still trapped there too? It would make sense. After all, if Sterling loved Joanna as much as the stories all claimed he did, then the only reason for him not to move on to be with her would be if he was already with her. Ghosts didn't often see or interact with one another, but it wasn't impossible, especially for two people who had loved each other as much as Sterling Hall and Joanna Stanton.

"Hey, Sterling." Luke's voice interrupted Michael's train of thought. He'd apparently taken it upon himself to make contact the Confrontational-and-Obnoxious Luke Rainer way since Gail's gentle and understanding approach hadn't done the trick.

"My name's Luke. How are you doing?" Michael still couldn't see the look on Sterling's face, but he had a feeling he was either very confused or very irritated. Luke just kept on talking. "Okay, so here's the deal, Sterling. See this little device in my hand? This is a digital recorder. If you talk into it, we'll be able to play it back and hear what you have to say. I know others have probably tried to come in and talk to you before, but - "

Eeeeeeeeeeeeeeeeeeeeeeeeeeeee!

Michael, along with everyone else in the room, clamped his hands over his ears, but it wasn't enough to block out the awful high-pitched screech of the digital recorder, now ten feet across the room where Luke had thrown it after the noise started.

"What is going on?" Gavin yelled over the racket.

"He's messing with the - "

CRACK!

The digital recorder gave one final fizzle before the room descended into a stunned silence.

"Well, I guess that's the end of the séance," Luke stated matter-of-factly.

"What the hell was that?" Gavin asked, sounding shaken. "Did he do that?"

"Yep," Peter answered, abandoning his camera to turn the lights back on.

"How?"

"Spirits can interfere with electronics and drain them of their power. That's why our batteries sometimes die for no reason at all, or a television or radio signal gets disrupted. It's especially easy for them to manipulate devices on their own if they have enough energy to go on, and considering how many of us there are in this room, he had more than enough," Gail explained.

"So, what you're saying is he used all of our energy and killed the recorder?"

"Pretty much," Luke replied as he trudged across the room to retrieve the device.

"Is he still here?" Kate asked Michael.

"No." Michael wasn't surprised. Sterling clearly didn't want anything to do with them.

"What did he look like? Is he angry? Scared?" Kate asked.

"I didn't get a good look at him," Michael answered honestly.

"That's okay, Mikey. You did good."

Michael shook his head. "I wouldn't have even noticed him if Kate hadn't said something."

"You could sense him?" Luke asked her. Kate nodded. "What did you feel? I wasn't really paying attention to the energy in the room. I was just trying to get him to talk."

"I'm not sure," Kate replied, crossing her arms. "I just knew that something was here. I don't know what he was feeling or anything."

"That's okay. You'll get more in tune as you work at it. It just takes practice. Practice and exposure," Luke said, glancing around the room. "Well, I don't know about the rest of you, but I'm about ready to call it a night. Tomorrow is another big day and we still need to get this room picked up."

"What are we doing tomorrow?" Michael asked as Gavin, Peter, and JT made their way around the room, unplugging cameras and collecting the motion detectors.

"Going into town. We've scheduled a few interviews here and there, but mostly we're going to try to learn a little more about the history of the manor, see if there's anything that Carolyn neglected to mention," Luke said.

"Like what?" Kate asked, stifling a huge yawn.

"I don't know. That's what we're going to find out," Luke answered. "But for now, you get your gorgeous self into bed. That goes for you too, Mikey. I need you refreshed and rested for tomorrow."

Even though Michael knew that his mother would have scolded him for not offering to stay behind and help, he was so tired that he didn't even try to argue. After bidding everyone in the room goodnight, Michael took Kate's hand and, with her head resting against his shoulder, walked out of the room and into the dim, haunting hallway.

CHAPTER TWELVE

Kate closed her eyes and savored the sudsy feel and freesia scent of the rich, soapy lather on her skin. No doubt about it, there was no better way to end a long, tiring, albeit exciting day than a hot, soothing shower; especially a shower in what was quite possibly the most luxurious bathroom in the world. It had everything: antique mirrors decorated with colorful gemstones, statues of dolphins and ships and seahorses, and towels so soft and fluffy that Kate was almost certain they were made of clouds.

After she climbed out of the shower, she changed into her warmest pair of flannel pajamas and brushed her teeth. She grabbed one of the towels and began to dry her hair when she suddenly realized that her hairbrush wasn't in with her other toiletries. Hopefully, it had just gotten mixed up in Gavin's stuff. If not, she'd just have to borrow Gavin's. She simply couldn't go to bed without brushing the knots out of her hair.

Shivering slightly despite her warm, cozy pajamas, she tiptoed barefoot out of her room and down the hall toward the Storybook Room where Gavin was staying for the next three nights. She considered just letting herself in, but since they weren't at home, she decided against it and knocked on the door.

"Come in!" Gavin called.

Kate opened the door and stepped inside. The Storybook Room was designed like a book store, with antique novels lining each and every corner of each and every wall. It reminded Kate of the castle library in *Beauty and the Beast*. She couldn't help but think how unfair it was that her brother got all those books to himself, especially considering how little he actually read.

Gavin, who had been kneeling beside his bed, apparently searching for something in his suitcase, stood to greet her as soon as he heard her open the door.

"Hey there, I - oh, it's just you." His face fell as soon as he saw his sister. Kate wrinkled her nose, not only out of confusion, but because Gavin was wearing nothing but socks and a pair of boxer shorts.

"Were you expecting somebody else?" she asked, not entirely certain she wanted to know the answer.

"No," he lied.

Kate crossed her arms.

"You were hoping I was Gail, weren't you?"

"No! Well, I mean... Maybe I was thinking she might... She did seem interested in me, after all - "

"Gavin!" Kate interrupted her brother's ridiculous rambling. "No! Just please, stop right there."

"Why? She's cute. She's obviously into me. What's the problem?"

"The problem, Romeo, is we are both incredibly lucky to be here and to be a part of this and it is not the time or the place to be hooking up with someone, especially one of the stars of the show!"

"See, last time I checked, her being the star of a television show is all the more reason to hook up with her. Besides, you're one to talk, Little Miss I-Went-On-A-Date-With-Luke-Rainer."

"Okay, A. That was not a real date. B. There is a big difference between having dinner with someone and hooking up when you're supposed to be learning and working. And C. Luke has made it pretty clear that he expects nothing less than absolute professionalism from the entire team, and for the moment, that includes you!"

"Okay, okay, fine. I get the picture. No fun for Gavin. Why are you in here again?"

"I'm looking for my hairbrush. And you're allowed to have fun, just not that kind of fun."

"All right, Sis," he sighed, not sounding very compliant at all as he dug through his suitcase to retrieve her brush.

"Gavin, I'm serious. Please, please, please do not do anything to encourage Gail. Don't wink at her. Don't flirt with her. Please, just don't reciprocate anything at all."

"You know, this is really rich coming from the girl who was all over her boyfriend during the séance," he remarked, holding out her hairbrush for her to take.

"Oh, right. I sat next to him and held his hand when it got spooky. How scandalous."

"So you're telling me that you're not going to sneak off to his room after you're done scolding me?"

Kate blushed, shocked that her brother would even suggest such a thing. Not that the thought hadn't crossed her mind...

But there was no way she was admitting that to Gavin.

"No, I'm not. I'm going to brush my hair and go to bed."

"But why would you bother brushing your hair if you're not planning on sneaking off to see him? Hmm?" Gavin asked, holding the brush high above Kate's head and acting as though he'd just discovered the key to cracking the ancient mystery of Girl Code.

"Because I've been brushing my hair before bed since I was ten years old," Kate snapped, snatching her brush out of his evil clutches.

"You're welcome," Gavin taunted.

"Thanks," she muttered. *For nothing.* "Goodnight, Gav."

"Goodnight, Sis. Tell Michael I say hello."

"Not going to see him," Kate reiterated. Then, before Gavin could make one more witless comment, she was out the door and once again shivering in the hallway.

She wondered if Sterling or Joanna or maybe even Brink might be the reason the hallway was so cold, but then she realized that unlike southern autumns, October nights in the Northeast were actually cold. If only she didn't have to wake up early. It was the perfect temperature for curling up with a blanket, hot chocolate, and a cute guy for a late-night movie by the fireplace. Alas, Luke had instructed everyone to be awake and ready for breakfast by 8 AM sharp, and it was already close to midnight. Perfect, cozy, cold weather date night would have to wait.

Kate had almost made it back to her room when a tall figure appeared in the hallway, making her jump.

"Don't be afraid. It's just me," Michael assured her, his handsome features becoming clearer as he approached.

"Hey," Kate breathed, trying not to let him see just how startled she'd been. "I thought you'd be asleep by now."

"I'm about to be. I was just getting a drink of water. My nerves are pretty much shot after today."

"How come? Are you feeling all right?" Kate asked. She hoped he wasn't coming down with something.

"I'm fine. It's just been a long day. And after what happened at the séance..."

"I understand," Kate told him. And she did. The last time they'd encountered a spirit that didn't want them around, they'd ended up tangled in a mess of secrets, sins, and murderers. Hopefully this experience would be a little less traumatic. "So uh, is Brink around?"

"No. He gets bored at night so he usually goes exploring."

"Good to know," Kate remarked lightly. Then, hoping to make his day a little better, she wrapped her arms around his slender torso and kissed him lightly on the mouth.

Sure enough, he grinned.

"What have you been up to?" he asked.

"Retrieving my hairbrush from Gavin. Clearly, I haven't had time to use it yet..." she remarked, realizing just how wiry and matted her hair must look.

"You're beautiful," Michael assured her.

"I think you might be sweet-talking me." Kate allowed her arms to linger around his lean body. "Keep going." They both shared a laugh and Michael leaned down to kiss her again. Kate felt her pulse flutter even though the kiss ended far too quickly. "I actually just had a talk with Gavin about this."

Michael's eyes widened with the slightest bit of alarm.

"About... us?" he asked.

"No!" Kate exclaimed, a little too loudly. "No, not about *this*." *Way to be vague, Kate,* she scolded herself. "He has it in his head that he's going to hook up with Gail sometime during our stay and I had to give him the list of reasons why that is a terrible idea and how he shouldn't do it and then he gave me a really hard time about having my boyfriend here and I had to swear up and down that I wasn't going to sneak off to your room in the middle of the night."

Kate blushed, not only because she was rambling, but because she and Michael had never once discussed spending the night together. It wasn't a subject she usually approached lightly, and yet, it had somehow managed to slip out like it was nothing!

Fortunately (or unfortunately, depending on your perspective), Michael didn't even seem fazed by it. Instead, he asked, "I was actually meaning to ask you about Gail."

Wait, what? Kate didn't say the words aloud, but she was definitely thinking them.

"What about her?" she asked.

"What's between her and Luke?" Michael asked.

That actually hadn't been what Kate was expecting either.

"I don't think there's anything between them. I think they're just friends. Why? Do you think there's something going on?"

"I don't know. Brink's the one who brought it up. When we were in the van earlier, he said they sounded like an old married couple. I was just wondering if maybe Luke liked her as more than a friend."

"That would explain why he didn't like her flirting with Gavin," Kate said. "Wow, I don't know. I mean, there have always been speculations. But then again, rumors and tabloids are hard to avoid when you're in the public eye. If you're famous and you're spotted with someone of the opposite sex, it doesn't matter who either of you are. Someone is going to report that you're dating."

It was true. Kate had visited *Cemetery Tours* fan sites and read all the gossip. Possessive fans had always been jealous of the friendship between Luke and Gail, but both had always come back and insisted that friendship was all that existed between them. Both had been incredibly open about other relationships, so there was no reason to expect them to lie about their feelings for each other, unless one of them had some strange reservation about dating a co-worker.

Or if the feelings were unrequited.

Michael definitely wasn't convinced. "It just seemed kind of weird for him. Not that I know him all that well, but in all the times I have seen him, I've never known him to actually be so serious about anything."

"Well, we've also never seen him behind the scenes of an investigation. His job is probably one of the few things that he does take seriously. But on the other hand, maybe that's why neither of them has had very good luck with relationships."

"I can't really fault them on that," Michael murmured. "I've never been good at relationships."

"You're good at this one." Kate smiled up at him. "The best, I'd say."

"I think that's mostly your doing." This time, Michael was the one who blushed.

"Well, I think you're selling yourself short," Kate told him. "You were never the problem. You just had... complicated circumstances."

"That's very diplomatic of you."

"Thanks," Kate grinned. "And if I may say, I'm glad that none of those relationships worked out."

"I am too," Michael told her as she rose up on her tip toes to accept another kiss from his lips.

So very, very tempted to invite him into her room, Kate had to fight against her desire and her impulsiveness as the kiss deepened and his arms tightened around her waist.

Bad idea, bad idea, she chanted inside her head, frustrated with herself for not being able to simply enjoy his embrace. *Don't do it.*

Oh, but this place is so romantic, the lovelorn, whimsical dreamer inside her head argued. *It's so old and beautiful! Wouldn't it just be wonderful in a place like this to just spend the night in his arms?*

Well... yeah, it would...

After the kiss finally ended, Kate looked up into Michael's dark eyes as she brushed a stray lock of hair away from her face and tucked it behind her ear.

"Michael, I..." she whispered. He leaned in and kissed her again, this time lightly, sweetly. She sighed. "I don't want to, but we probably need to say goodnight."

"Probably," he echoed.

Kate wrapped her arms around his shoulders for one more kiss, then she set her feet firmly back on the ground and murmured softly, "Goodnight."

"Goodnight, Kate," he smiled.

Then, he watched her as she made the short walk back to her room. She gave one final wave once she reached the door before locking herself in for the night.

CHAPTER THIRTEEN

Morning came far too early for Michael. Even though the previous day had left him absolutely exhausted, he'd barely slept a wink. He'd only just managed to drift off when the abhorrent alarm on his cell phone began to chime.

Damn you, Luke Rainer. Because of course, it was his fault for insisting that everyone wake up so early.

Michael didn't even know why Luke needed him to go on this little morning excursion. They weren't looking for ghosts. They were interviewing people who might know something about the ghosts. In other words, Michael would be absolutely useless.

He wasn't sure why he hadn't been able to sleep. Maybe it was because he'd been expecting Sterling Hall to show up some time during the night. Ghosts always seemed to have a knack for showing up right as he was about to fall asleep. Being startled awake by dead people was something he'd always especially hated about his "gift." Maybe expecting Sterling to barge in at some point in the night had made him edgy.

Or maybe it had just been the natural unease that came from trying to sleep in new surroundings. Despite the perfect comfort of the Fireside Room's canopied bed, he'd found it nearly impossible to relax beneath the thick, red velvet comforter. The creaks and shudders of the building were different than those of his apartment bedroom and the air was so still and heavy that every sound seemed magnified.

Then again, it could have been Kate. It was the first time they'd ever spent the night under the same roof, and although he tried to convince himself that it should be the last thing on his mind, he couldn't stop fixating on it. How easy would it have been, as she had mentioned, to sneak off to her room after everyone else had fallen asleep? He'd pretended not to catch that only because acknowledging that the temptation existed would have made it that much more difficult to resist.

He'd always known his feelings for her were real, but for the first time, he allowed himself to consider what it truly meant to love someone, and to be with that someone in ways he'd never before dared to fathom. Love, he realized, was more than just a fleeting desire, or a brief glimpse into a fairy tale, or a flash of playful flirtation in her beautiful hazel eyes. It was more than infatuation with a person's best qualities, or reluctant acceptance of their less appealing traits. Real love meant loving the whole person, in every form, in every state, in every way. It was what transformed the ordinary monotony of everyday life into extraordinary moments of warmth and compassion and joy.

He knew, as surely as he'd ever known anything, that saying goodnight to the girl he loved had been the hardest thing he'd ever done.

The second hardest, he thought miserably, *will be getting out of bed this morning.*

Eager as he was to see Kate, he wouldn't have said no to at least a few more hours of sleep.

Unfortunately, that wasn't going to happen. Michael had a terrible feeling that if he didn't show up for breakfast, Luke would send him a personal wake-up call, and Michael could not think of a worse way to be hustled out of bed than by the insufferably cheerful and reprehensibly loud morning person that was Luke Rainer.

With the promise of a hot shower to motivate him, Michael dragged himself out of the warmth and comfort of the scarlet sheets and headed for his personal bathroom.

A quick fifteen minutes later, he marched out of his room and into the hallway, not bothering to lock the door behind him. Although his hair was still dripping wet from his shower, he'd at least managed to shave and brush his teeth before he threw on a pair of jeans, a long-sleeved button-down shirt, and a sweater vest.

Brink appeared as soon as Michael set foot in the hallway.

"You know what really makes me sad? The fact that I have an incredible sense of style, but no one appreciates it because I'm dead. You, however, dress like a stiff even though you're living, breathing, and from what I can tell, incredibly visible."

"What are you talking about?" Michael asked, not nearly awake enough for his friend's senseless rambling.

"*You take no advantage of your visibleness.* If I were alive, I'd go crazy! I might dye my hair, get a few tattoos, and wear the coolest clothes imaginable." When Michael didn't bother to validate that with a response, Brink heaved an exaggerated sigh. "God, everything is wasted on the living."

"So, what I'm getting from this is that you don't approve of my clothes," Michael stated.

"Yes!" Brink cried, pleased that his friend finally got it.

"What's wrong with them?"

That was apparently the wrong question to ask, because Brink didn't look like he knew quite where to begin, thus effectively putting an end to any hope he may have held of cultivating a better sense of what not to wear in Michael. His friend was clearly a helpless case.

"Nothing. Nothing at all," Brink told him. "You are so lucky that Kate's into nerds."

As it turned out, Kate wasn't waiting for him at breakfast. Much to his dismay, Michael was one of the first guests to arrive at the table, second only to...

"Morning, Mikey!" Luke greeted him with a broad, sunny grin. "Did you have any visitors last night?"

Michael was so shocked that for a moment, he couldn't figure out how to make his body function. Luke was seriously asking him about *that*? How close did he think they were?

Fortunately, it took only one curious glance from Luke to make Michael realize that he hadn't meant the girlfriend kind of visitor. He'd of course meant the ghostly kind.

"Oh. No," Michael answered honestly.

"Hmm. Sterling Hall is not being nearly as social as I'd hoped he'd be." Luke looked contemplative as he took a sip of coffee out of a steaming mug. "By the way, Mikey, have some coffee. Mrs. Drake told us to help ourselves to anything in the kitchen, but I thought I'd wait until more of the crew was up before I opened anything."

"Good idea," Michael said, pouring himself a cup of coffee. He was still slightly embarrassed for misinterpreting Luke's earlier inquiry. Thankfully, neither Luke nor Brink, who was staring wistfully at the expensive coffee-maker, had picked up on it.

"I miss coffee," Brink remarked sadly, watching Michael take a sip.

After over ten years of friendship, Michael was used to Brink watching him eat and drink. Brink often said that he missed everything about life, but something he missed most was the simple joy of taste.

As if right on cue, Kate and Gavin trudged into the dining room. Gavin looked moderately awake, but Kate could barely keep her eyes open. She was still dressed in her pajama bottoms and an overly large hooded sweatshirt, and her hair was tied up in a messy bun on top of her head.

"Coffee," Kate murmured, sounding a little like a zombie demanding brains. She perked up, however, as soon as she saw Michael. "Hey," she greeted him with a brief, sleepy hug around the waist. "You look cute."

"She likes nerds," Brink reiterated.

"So do you," Michael told her.

"Oh, no I don't. But I will. After coffee." She maneuvered past him and reached for the coffee pot without even acknowledging Luke.

"Wow. I am seeing a whole new side of you, Kate," he said.

"This is only a glimpse of Kate in her natural morning state," Gavin explained with a yawn. "It usually takes at least two cups of coffee before she's able to make any sort of polite conversation."

Kate muttered something unintelligible, probably not at all polite, into her coffee mug.

The rest of the crew appeared a few minutes later.

"I think he came into my room last night," Gail announced excitedly.

"Sterling?" Luke asked.

"Yeah. I was just about to fall asleep when all of a sudden, the hairs on my arms began to stand on end, even though I was buried beneath my blankets. I noticed it had gotten really cold inside the room, so I went to see if all the windows were closed, when I turned around and saw a tall figure standing in the corner of my bedroom. Well, naturally, I ran to get my digital recorder and EMF detector, but by the time I'd gotten everything together, he was gone."

"Are you sure it was him?" Luke asked.

"Well, I guess it could have been Joanna. But since he was the one who showed up last night during the séance, I figured it was him. Like I said, I didn't get a chance to communicate with him."

"At least we know that he's open to us," JT commented.

"Did you see anything last night, Michael?" Peter asked. Michael simply shook his head. "Wonder why he'd appear to Gail and not to you. You're the one who can see them, right?"

"But Sterling doesn't know that. Besides, Gail was the one doing most of the talking last night. If he was going to make a connection with someone, it would most likely be her," Luke answered. "Besides, if you were dead, wouldn't you rather talk to a pretty girl than a dude? No offense, Mikey."

Michael shrugged it off. He was too busy watching Brink fidget nervously in the corner of the room to pay attention to what was being said. In the several years they had been friends, Michael had never once seen Brink lose his cool. Something was up.

"What?" He cornered his friend once everyone else had disappeared into the kitchen to decide on breakfast.

"What?" Brink echoed, trying and failing to sound like he had no idea what Michael was talking about.

"You look really uncomfortable, which I've come to believe is impossible given that the only thing you've ever been uncomfortable about in your existence is the fact that your mother named you Eugene."

"Dude, don't spread that around," Brink muttered in a low voice that no one else could hear.

Michael looked his friend square in the eye. "What did you do?"

"Okay. If I tell you, will you promise not to get mad and yell at me?"

"I'm not sure that's a promise I'll be able to keep," Michael said. "Talk."

Brink twiddled his fingers for a few moments while he figured out how best to begin.

"Let's just say..." His blue eyes scanned the ceiling while he tapped his chin. "I can pretty much guarantee that the ghost in Gail's bedroom last night... wasn't Sterling."

It took a moment for Michael to register what his best friend was trying to say.

"Wait a minute," Michael stared at him. "It was *you*?"

"Maybe..."

"What the heck were you doing in her bedroom?"

"I've told you before! I spy on people. It's what I do. I'm a perpetual people watcher!"

"So that's what you do at night? You wander around in girls' rooms and watch them sleep?"

"Give me a little credit. I'm not creepy. I watch all kinds of people all the time. Want to know why? *Because being dead is boring.*"

"But here? With the crew? Brink, what are you *thinking*?" Michael asked.

100

"Okay, for the record, Gail is the first person to *ever* notice, and that was just poor judgment on my part. I should have figured that a professional ghost hunter would be able to tell when a ghost was in the room," Brink remarked off-handedly. "You're missing the point of this confession. The only reason I am feeling even remotely guilty about this is because now the *Cemetery Tours* people think that Sterling Silver or whatever his name is is reaching out to them and... he's not. At least not as far as I know."

Before Michael could respond, Kate poked her head back into the dining room.

"Are you okay?" she asked.

"Yeah, fine," he answered automatically.

"Tell her I say hi," Brink said.

"Shut up," Michael hissed.

"Oh. Good morning, Brink," Kate grinned and waved before she retreated back into the kitchen.

"She's so great," Brink said. "You know, I'm a little surprised that the two of you spent the night alone."

The fact that Brink knew that triggered all sorts of alarm bells in Michael's mind.

"Brink, please, please, *please* tell me you did not spy on Kate too."

"I did not spy on Kate," Brink promised. "I used to. But then after I found out about all that sensitivity crap, I figured it was best for me to keep my distance. Besides, it didn't feel right, knowing how you feel about her and everything. I've got to warn you though, she likes to sing when she thinks she's alone, and I can tell you right now, it is not - "

"*Brink!*" Michael exploded. "Okay, starting today, no more spying. No more nightly rendezvous. You either stay with me or you watch a movie. That's it."

"So... you'd rather have me lurking around your room... all the time," Brink translated.

Well, no. Michael really wouldn't prefer that. But in the end, it really didn't matter what he thought or said. It was futile trying to give a ghost an ultimatum because they literally had nothing to lose.

"You know what? Forget it. Do what you want. Just... try to be respectful."

"Bro, you know me. I'm always respectful."

Yeah right, Michael thought grimly as Brink flashed him a cheeky grin before disappearing on the spot.

Resolving to keep their conversation to himself, Michael ran a hand through his damp, messy hair and went to help his friends prepare breakfast in the kitchen.

CHAPTER FOURTEEN

"Our first stop this morning is Dock Square," Luke announced once everyone had piled back into the vans.

Kate and Michael were once again riding with Luke and Gail, but Gavin had been transferred over to the tech van. Luke claimed that since all the luggage had been unpacked, there would be more room over in the other van, but Kate wondered if his actions were truly motivated by space or if they stemmed from a desire to keep Gavin as far away from Gail as possible.

Before Kate could speculate more on the matter, Luke continued, "We'll be interviewing Marian Davis. She owns a gift shop, Waterside Treasures, and yes, you can shop around once we're done filming."

"How do you find people to interview?" Kate asked.

"Most of the time, they come to us. There are a lot of people out there with stories and experiences, but unfortunately there are only so many minutes that we can dedicate to individual interviews. Marian Davis, however, is a direct descendent of Joanna's cousin. She's like, her great-great-great granddaughter or something and she offered to tell us as much as she knows about her family history."

The drive into town was a short one, and in no time at all, the *Cemetery Tours* crew was hard at work once again unloading and assembling various pieces of video and recording equipment. Kate and Michael offered to help in any way that they could, so Luke put them on battery duty for any device that started running low on juice.

After they were finally set up and ready to go, they set out on foot on their way to Route 9, the street at the heart of Dock Square. Kate realized, looking around at the quaint, old-fashioned shops, boutiques, and restaurants, that she could easily fall in love with a small seaside town like Kennebunkport. Everything, from the colorful wooden buildings to the faint scent of saltwater on the cool autumn breeze, appealed to her.

Since neither of them had to carry a camera or a backpack, Kate took the opportunity to link her arm through Michael's. He had looked cute that morning at breakfast, but thanks to the addition of a scarf and jacket, he was absolutely dashing. Kate wasn't sure what it was, but there really was something about a guy in autumn clothes.

Knowing that she'd be spending the day in front of a camera, Kate had tried her best to look nice, especially after her less-than-glamorous appearance at the breakfast table. She didn't think she'd done a bad job. Her hair flowed freely down the shoulders of her stylish pea coat and her form-fitting jeans tucked easily inside her chocolate-colored boots.

"Okay, according to my GPS, it should be right up here on the left," Luke announced.

Sure enough, a sign hanging over the door to the shop read, *Waterside Treasures: Antiques, Sea Shells, and Maritime Collectibles.*

Kate knew the second she set foot inside the nautical-themed gift shop that she'd made a mistake bringing along her credit card. From the collection of lighthouse statues to the picture frames decorated with shells and sea glass, all the way to the model ships and driftwood sculptures, there was no way she'd be able to walk out of the store empty-handed.

"This is pretty neat, huh?" Michael asked.

"I want to own everything in this shop," Kate replied as a door opened in the back and a middle-aged woman with fading sand-colored hair emerged.

"Hello there!" she greeted them with a friendly smile.

"Are you Marian Davis?" Luke asked, stepping forward.

"I am. Welcome to Kennebunkport." She held out a hand for him to shake.

"Thank you for agreeing to meet with us," Luke said.

"Oh, it's my pleasure. I'm a big fan of the show, and something of a history buff, so this is all very exciting for me."

After quick introductions, the crew set the scene for the interview. Peter, JT, and Gavin filmed while Luke and Gail talked with Marian.

"Now, you are actually related to Joanna Stanton, is that right?" Luke asked her.

"Yes. Her cousin, Sarah Baker, was my great-great-great grandmother."

"That's pretty awesome. Can you tell us a little bit about Sarah?"

"Like Joanna, she was an only child. They were only two years apart in age, so they were extremely close, like sisters."

"And did they remain close after Joanna married Sterling Hall?" Gail asked.

"Yes. In fact, Sarah was a bridesmaid in their wedding. They were constant companions up until Joanna's death."

"How about Sterling? Was Sarah close to him?" Luke asked.

"The entire family was close to him. They all knew how much he adored Joanna. He would have done anything for her. He gave her everything he had and more and they loved him for it. He stayed in close contact with them after she passed, and since he had no family of his own, he left everything to the Stantons in his will."

"Including the manor?"

"Yes, but it's no longer in our family. It went to my great-grandfather's brother, but he was something of a gambler, and he had to sell it to pay off his debts. I do, however, have this..."

Marian stepped behind the sales counter and knelt down beneath the cash register. Kate could hear her rummaging around for something. Moments later, she reappeared, clutching a velvet jewelry box the color of raspberries.

The entire crew watched with curious eyes as Marian opened the box to reveal a spectacular antique garnet necklace. Clasp to clasp, garnets glittered, forming a chain of flowers, or perhaps they were snowflakes, or maybe even stars. Larger stars of the blood-colored gems hung at the base of the necklace, reminding Kate of jeweled fireworks. Again, she found herself in awe of an elegant and vastly beautiful piece of Sterling and Joanna's love story.

Luke whistled. "Now *that* is a necklace."

"It was gift from Sterling. He was always showering her with presents, but this necklace was her favorite. He made sure that it went to Sarah after Joanna died, and it's stayed in the family ever since. One day, it will go to my daughter."

"That's incredible," Gail replied.

"You know a lot of times, spirits can become attached to items that they loved or valued when they were still alive. Have you ever noticed anything supernatural about the necklace?" Luke asked.

"Not that I can recall. Of course, if there was any sort of paranormal activity, my house is so hectic that I probably wouldn't even notice. I'd just think it was one of my kids."

"You know, there is a lot of activity that goes unnoticed just because people aren't open to it," Luke told her. "But if I had to guess, I'd say you were pretty open."

Marian grimaced.

"I'm undecided," she confessed.

"I thought you were a fan of the show!" Luke exclaimed, feigning offense.

"I am! But I've never had a reason to believe a ghost would be haunting me."

Kate glanced up at Michael. He'd already tuned out of the interview and his eyes were locked on a wall full of seascape paintings. She took that to mean there wasn't a ghost in sight.

"Well, it's probably best to keep it that way," Luke acknowledged with a wink.

Gail, on the other hand, stared at the necklace with a contemplative crinkle in between her eyebrows.

"What are you thinking about, Gail?" JT asked.

"I'm just wondering..." she replied without tearing her eyes away from the gemstones. "Joanna may not be interested in the necklace anymore, but maybe Sterling would be."

Luke's eyes lit up. "Gail, you're a genius!"

"What do you mean?" Marian asked.

"You know that we're in town investigating the haunting at Stanton Hall Manor," Luke said. "Well, we've made contact with Sterling, but only very briefly. He either doesn't want to talk to us or doesn't understand that he can. Either way, if you'd like to stop by later this evening and bring the necklace, we might be able to use it as a trigger object."

"What's a trigger object?"

"If he sees the necklace, we might be able to get more of a response from him," Gail explained.

"Do you think that would really work?" Marian asked.

"It has in the past. And if Sterling loved Joanna the way that everyone says he did, then he is going to be seeking anything that might be able to connect him to her. I say we give it a shot. That is, if you don't mind," Luke said.

"I don't mind at all. I'm interested to see if it will work," Marian told him. "How will we know if it does? Will you have your little knick-knacks and gadgets that you're always using?"

"We'll have those on hand, but I'm counting on my friend Michael over there to let us know when a spirit shows up. He's sort of our secret psychic weapon."

"I'm not psychic," Michael insisted, but Luke ignored him.

"Can you actually see spirits?" Marian asked him.

"Yes."

Even though his secret had been out for months now, Kate knew that Michael was still hesitant to affirm it. She hoped that this experience would be good for him, maybe help him to be a little more confident.

"And yet, you claim that you're not psychic?" Marian asked.

"He's just being modest," Luke told her.

"It's not that. I've just never thought of myself as a psychic," Michael said. "You know, when you think about psychics, you picture people who can read minds or see into the future. I can't do anything like that. I'm just haunted. To be honest, I've always thought of it as kind of a curse."

"Oh, but it's so wonderful what you can do," Marian told him. "To not have to lose loved ones to death, and to give those who are grieving peace and comfort in the assurance that their loved ones are still with them. It's such an extraordinary gift. I think you are very fortunate."

"You see, Mikey? Everyone gets it but you," Luke remarked.

Michael shrugged. "My grandmother has always told me that it's a gift, and I'm working on seeing it as one. I'm just not there yet."

Kate took his hand and laced her fingers through his. She knew it was difficult for him to acknowledge that there was anything even remotely positive about his ability, and she was proud of him for making the effort. Marian was right. His sixth sense was extraordinary and wonderful and miraculous. But there was something else that Kate had never taken into consideration until that moment.

Ever since she'd found out about Michael's gift, she'd tried, like Luke and Marian, to convince him just how amazing it was. She'd been adamant, almost pushy about it. She hadn't stopped to think that while Michael knew his talent was exceptional, maybe there was a reason he couldn't accept it as a positive thing. Others went out of their way to tell him how wonderful it was, but they never asked or even wondered why he'd worked so hard to keep it a secret all those years, or why he didn't see it as the gift that the rest of the world obviously considered it to be. He was the only one who truly knew what it was like to be in constant communication with the dead, yet rarely did anyone bother to ask his perspective.

Perhaps she too had been a little too quick to try to convince him that his curse was actually a blessing in disguise.

Luke didn't seem quite as burdened. "You'll get there someday, Mikey," he assured his friend before turning his attention back to Mrs. Davis. "So, what do you say, Marian? Care to join us tonight for a little ghost hunting?"

"I'd be honored," she said.

After the interview wrapped, Luke announced that everyone could go off and do their own thing as long as they all met back up at the van at two o'clock.

"Another interview?" Gavin asked.

"Nope. It's a surprise," Luke replied with a grin.

"'A surprise.' In Luke Language, that could mean anything," Michael muttered to Kate once everyone had dispersed. "He probably booked us for a tour of a haunted lighthouse, or maybe he made reservations at a haunted restaurant." When Kate only responded with a feeble nod of her head, he asked, "Are you okay?"

"Yeah," she answered a little too quickly. "How come?"

"You look so serious. Is something bothering you?"

"No, it's just..." she began. Then she stopped and looked around. A gift shop was not at all the proper place to have any sort of meaningful discussion. "Do you want to take a walk?"

"Sure," he replied.

So they made their way back out to the not-at-all-crowded street and began to stroll down past the colorful shops and restaurants and boutiques until they reached the bridge overlooking the Kennebunk River. It was far from the most beautiful river that Kate had ever seen, but the sky was clear, and the water reflected its deep, dazzling color. There were a few small boats out and Kate even noticed a few kids fishing off the dock across the water. A restaurant called The Clam Shack stood at the far end of the bridge, and next to it, a Seafood Market. Both buildings were supported by wooden stilts that extended down into the water, reminding Kate of her very first trip to Galveston, when, at the age of six, she'd asked her father what they were for.

"They protect the houses and buildings from being washed away by the water," he explained.

Kate hadn't been all that impressed by his answer. "Why don't they just not build by the water?" she'd asked.

Her father had just laughed and patted her on the shoulder. "One day, Pumpkin, you'll understand."

Kate did understand now. Everyone wanted waterfront property. Rivers, lakes, oceans, it didn't matter. Waterfront homes sold, and because they in high demand, they were unfortunately way out of her price range. Regardless, Kate had always wanted some sort of small cabin or lake house of her very own to decorate from front door to back porch, and as it turned out, the maritime atmosphere of Kennebunkport only fueled her ambition.

"So, what did you want to talk about?" Michael asked her as they walked hand in hand along the bridge.

"It's nothing really," she answered. "It was just something you said back there... everything kind of resonated with me for the first time."

"What was it?"

"When you were talking about how you have to try to see your ability as a blessing. I don't know, it really made me stop and think that maybe everyone has pushed you too hard to make you accept it as something wonderful. Maybe *I've* pushed you too hard."

"Kate, no. Why would you think that?"

"Because I'm always telling you how cool it is or how lucky you are, but the truth is, I have no idea what it's like to be you. I've never stopped to think about how confusing or lonely or out of place you must have felt because of it. I was too consumed with how interesting it was for me. And I'm sorry for that." Kate hadn't expected to cry, but as she spoke the words, she could feel a knot forming at the back of her throat.

"Kate, look at me," Michael instructed. She did. "You have *nothing* to be sorry for. The only reason I've made as much progress in accepting this gift, or sixth sense, or whatever you want to call it, is because you've made me see it from a different perspective. Until you came along, I only ever thought about how awful my situation was for me. This negativity I've carried around with me my entire life... it's so selfish, and it's something that I'm trying to overcome. Old habits, unfortunately, die hard. And even if I did finally manage to kill them, they'd probably just come back to haunt me like everything else," he offered with a wry grin.

Kate laughed, relieved and happy to hear him joking.

"You know, we still have a while until two," she said. "Do you want to go and try The Clam Shack?"

"Do you like clams?" Michael asked.

"I've never had them, but I'm feeling adventurous."

"Then by all means, let's go."

CHAPTER FIFTEEN

It took a little longer than Luke had instructed for the group to reconvene back at the vans. Michael and Kate were the first to arrive back, followed shortly by Luke, JT, and Peter. Gail and Gavin, however, were noticeably absent.

"I'm going to kill him," Kate muttered to Michael.

Judging by the look on Luke's face, she wasn't the only one who felt that way. As much as Michael enjoyed mocking Luke for his over-enthusiasm and stupid hairstyle, he had to admit, he was sort of scary when he was angry.

"Are you freaking kidding me, Gail?" Luke snarled as he whipped out his phone and began punching in what Michael could only assume was a very aggressive text message.

"Forget texting," Kate told him as she held her phone up to her ear and waited impatiently while the line rang. Michael watched her heave a frustrated sigh when the call went to voicemail. Instead of leaving a message, however, Kate hung up the phone and dialed again. And again. And again.

"What are you doing?" JT asked her.

"Calling him until he answers. Trust me, it annoys him a whole lot more than leaving a catty voicemail," Kate replied, hitting the **Call** button for the fifth time.

"Man, you don't want to miss a call from her, do you?" Peter asked Michael.

"Oh, I'd never do this to Michael," Kate assured him. "My brother, on the other hand..."

"If they don't get back here soon, we're going to miss our boat," Luke said, still visibly aggravated.

"What boat?" Kate asked.

"We're supposed to be going on a whale watching tour. It's the very end of their season, and I thought it would be sort of a fun thing for us to do, especially since we have y'all here. But if they're not back..."

He didn't finish his sentence, but he didn't need to. Kate's expression had gone absolutely blank. It didn't take a psychic to know that if Gavin's tardiness prevented her from going on that whale watch, the afternoon would end in some manner of violence, or at least a tremendous amount of sibling warfare.

It became even more apparent when Kate forsook her attempt to irritate Gavin by flooding his phone with missed calls and actually left him a message, "Gavin, you need to call me back *right now*," she hissed. After she hung up, she turned to Luke. "I am so sorry about all of this. I told him last night that she was off limits."

"Trust me, I don't blame *him*," Luke sneered.

"Okay, good," Kate said. At least somewhat mollified by his response, she moved on to the more pressing matter. "We can't, you know, leave without them, can we?"

"I wish we could. But Gail has the credit card that we need," Luke responded.

"Dang it," Kate muttered through clenched teeth. "I am seriously going to kill him. I am going to kill him, and then I'm going bring him back to life again so he can buy me a plane ticket so that I can come back here at the peak of whale watching season. And then I'm going to make him pay for my tour."

Gavin and Gail finally showed up about thirty minutes later, long after their boat had been scheduled to leave. By that point, Kate and Luke's nerves had both been shot, JT looked like he was fighting a huge headache, and Michael was feeling exceptionally uncomfortable. Peter alone seemed unaffected by the high tensions amongst the group as he wandered around aimlessly, snapping pictures on his phone. Michael wondered briefly what the captions would read.

"Everyone's angry. Great show so far."

No, Peter probably wouldn't post anything like that. He was, by far, the happiest member of the *Cemetery Tours* crew. He never seemed to be in a bad mood, which was pretty incredible, considering how much time he spent chasing down dead people.

As soon as they appeared, both Gavin and Gail tried to explain why they were late, but neither Luke nor Kate cared to listen to excuses.

"Where have you been?" Kate demanded.

"I'm sorry. We went to grab a bite to eat, the restaurant was crowded, and then we started talking..." Gavin trailed off with a sheepish grin.

"And you didn't think to check the time? What about your phone? You really couldn't have taken *ten* seconds to call me back when you saw you had twenty missed calls?"

"Yeah... about that... my phone died and I kind of left my charger back in Dallas."

"Are you kidding me?" Kate asked him. "Why didn't you ask to borrow mine?"

"I didn't think I needed to."

Meanwhile, Luke was giving Gail the lecture of the century.

"... and after I specifically tell you not to let this guy distract you from your job, or *his* job! I don't understand what's wrong with you, Gail! What part of 'Act like a damn professional' don't you get?"

"And *I* don't understand why you're being such an enormous pain in the ass about this! I already apologized for being late. As for me and Gavin, we weren't off robbing a store or desecrating private property. We had lunch. *You* told us that we had some down time and that we could do whatever we wanted, so we went to a restaurant and we ate. Period."

"Oh, yeah right," Luke snapped. "Don't even try to act like I don't know you, Gail. You know I don't have a problem with what you do with your personal life, but this isn't play time. We are on an investigation, and that means even when we have down time, we are *still working*. You need to get your act together."

Gail didn't respond. She just glared at Luke like she would have given anything to be able to defy him, but Michael had a feeling she knew that he was right. Gavin and Kate, on the other hand, were flat out ignoring each other.

Finally, after a painfully awkward silence, Luke suggested they all get in the vans and head back to Stanton Hall for some much-needed rest and relaxation before the big night they had ahead of them.

Once they were on their way, Gail glanced around to Michael and Kate and said, "Sorry we made you all miss the whales."

"It's all right," Michael told her.

"Yeah. Besides, I'm not mad at *you*," Kate replied.

"I am," Luke muttered from behind the wheel.

"Well, you know, Luke, if you were a real *professional*, you'd build a bridge and get over it," Gail retorted. "I said I was sorry. Now are you really going to let your petty little personal issues get in the way of what will hopefully be a very eventful investigation tonight?"

"I won't if you won't," Luke replied.

"Good."

"Good."

Michael and Kate exchanged uneasy glances as the van descended into a strained silence. It let up a little once Luke turned on the radio, but not enough for anyone to speak until they'd once again pulled up to Stanton Hall Manor.

Outside, Kate shuffled her feet through the leaves that had gathered around the front steps. Then, she looked up at Michael and said, "I don't feel like being inside right now."

"What do you want to do?" Michael asked.

"Want to go exploring?"

"Sure."

For the next hour, they wandered the property. The mansion itself sat on nearly two acres of land, and Mrs. Drake had mentioned that the territory extended at least another three or four. Most of that space was occupied by a vast, autumn forest, far more vibrant and colorful than the trees back home. Michael was surprised to discover that, except for the mansion, the land had ultimately remained untouched. No statues, no fountains, not even a patio. Just a wide-open space before the forest began.

"You know, growing up, I always wanted to be part of something like this," Kate said, gazing around at the trees.

"A television show?" Michael asked.

"Well, yeah, that. But I meant a story, an adventure. It's like we're sort of on a mission and there are still questions to be answered and mysteries to be solved. This forest we're walking through right now could be enchanted, or there could be a secret passageway behind one of the paintings in the manor."

"I feel like you're describing an episode of *Scooby-Doo*."

"Well, I did watch a lot of Scooby as a kid. Especially around Halloween," Kate acknowledged with a quick grin.

The sound of approaching footsteps through the dry, fallen leaves distracted them from their conversation and they turned to see Gavin trudging his way toward them.

"Hey," he greeted them a little apprehensively.

"You have got to stop sneaking up on us like that," Kate snapped.

"Sorry," Gavin said, shoving his hands into his pockets. "Can I walk with you guys? There's really not a whole lot to do inside."

Kate didn't look like she was in any mood to have her brother join them, but she shrugged and said, "Do what you want."

Once Gavin fell into stride with them, he asked, "So, are you going to be pissed at me for the rest of the trip?"

"That depends. Are you planning on being a blockhead for the rest of the trip?"

"Come on, Kate. Look, I know you said to stay away from Gail, but I swear, nothing happened. She asked me if I wanted to have lunch, I was hungry, and so we ate. That's it. And I'm sorry that you had to miss your whale watching cruise, but you know what? You're almost twenty-five years old. Holding grudges over something like that is pretty immature."

"So, that's what you think this is about?" Kate rounded on her brother. "You think I'm throwing a temper tantrum because I didn't get to go on a whale watch? Gavin, I'm not some spoiled little kid who runs around stamping her feet every time she doesn't get her way. I'm mad at you because you did exactly what I asked you *not* to do, which was go behind Luke's back after he agreed to let us come along on this investigation. This is about respect. That's it."

"Okay, in my defense, when you were giving me that whole spiel last night, I did not think that having a casual lunch date counted as betraying Luke's trust or whatever. If I had known, then I would not have gone," he said. "But if I, you know, wanted to call her after all this is over..."

"Fine. Go for it. Marry her, for all I care. Just please, for now, stay focused on the task at hand."

"Right. Ghost hunting. Serious business," Gavin remarked. "So Michael, she seriously never nags you like this?"

"Not yet," Michael quipped, hoping for dear life that Kate knew he was being playful.

She seemed to understand.

"He hasn't given me a reason to," she replied, linking her arm through his. "Unlike you, he's actually - "

Michael never got to hear what Kate had to say about him. One moment, he was walking next to her through the forest, the next, he'd tripped over something solid buried underneath a pile of leaves. He tumbled forward onto the forest floor, his left ankle and knee taking the brunt of the fall.

Kate shrieked.

"Oh my God! Michael, are you all right?" she asked.

"Fine. Just tripped," he replied, wincing as he lifted himself off the ground and into an upright position. It was only then that he noticed the enormous rip in his jeans and the bloodied scrapes running all the way down his leg.

117

"We need to get you to a first-aid kit," Kate said, examining his injured knee. "Can you walk?"

"Yeah, I think so," he replied, accepting both her and Gavin's assistance to his feet.

"What the heck did you trip on?" Gavin asked.

"I'm not sure," Michael replied, glancing back at the spot where he'd fallen. The disrupted leaves revealed what appeared to be the corner of something old, weathered, and made of stone.

"I think I may know," Kate said.

She knelt down and brushed the leaves away from the surrounding area. Michael wasn't sure what she thought she was on to. It looked like a piece of scrap concrete, probably left over from all the reconstruction and renovations. But then, Kate began to dig and tear away at the grass and earth that had been rendered dead and brown by the covering of leaves.

"Wait a minute, what are you doing?" Michael asked.

"Believe it or not, she's always enjoyed getting dirty. She used to build castles in the mud when we were kids," Gavin said.

Kate ignored them and kept digging. As she did, bits of earth began to crumble around her, and more concrete broke through the surface of the dirt and grass. As Michael watched, he thought he noticed a design, sort of like a cross, carved into the concrete. Suddenly, something clicked and Michael realized exactly what Kate was expecting to unearth.

"Kate, is that...?"

Kate wiped her sweaty brow with one of her dirt-covered hands and took a deep breath.

"Yeah," she replied. "It's a grave."

CHAPTER SIXTEEN

To no one's surprise, as soon as Kate, Michael, and Gavin announced that they'd found an old headstone behind the manor, Luke rallied up his crew and scampered out to take a look, filming all the way, of course.

"Oh wow, look at that," he marveled over the tiny portion of gravestone that Kate had managed to dig up. "We need shovels. Gail, go see if Carolyn has any shovels or picks that we can borrow."

"I thought running errands was Peter's job," Gail griped.

"Yeah. I don't mind going," Peter said.

"*Peter* is still in my good graces. *You* are not. Go," Luke ordered. As Gail trudged her way back up the hill, muttering the entire way, Luke turned his attention to Kate. "So, how did you even see it down here?"

"Michael's actually the one who found it," she said.

"Correction. It found *me*," Michael remarked. His untreated wound was still exposed by the huge rip in his jeans, and it was beginning to sting. He thought about running inside for a band-aid, but decided to wait it out. He was too curious about the grave and who was buried beneath it.

Once Gail returned with the tools, Luke assigned Peter and Gavin to the cameras while he and JT each took a shovel. Gail, apparently, was still being punished.

After they'd managed to dig up most of the tombstone, Luke turned to the camera.

"We're here again at Stanton Hall Manor, where our crew has just discovered a private cemetery right here in the back acres of the property. Now, we're not sure who this grave belongs to just yet, but I'd say it's a safe bet that it's that of either Sterling or Joanna Hall."

"This is kind of exciting," Peter said.

"Yeah, we've never uncovered a tombstone before," JT joked.

Finally, after several minutes of digging, scraping, and cursing (which would certainly be censored to ensure the show remained suitable for families and young paranormal enthusiasts), Luke finally knelt down to inspect the engraving on the stone.

"It's Sterling," he announced.

Michael leaned to read over his shoulder.

Here Lies the Body of Sterling Samuel Hall
Dearly Departed
Husband of Joanna
March 13, 1817 - October 23, 1865

"He died young," Kate observed.

"It's sad that that's all they wrote on his tombstone," Gail remarked. "Loving Joanna was all that mattered to him in his life. She was obviously his world. And she was taken from him so soon... It's sort of romantic."

"It's not romantic, it's tragic," Luke said, standing up and brushing his hands off on his jeans. "Gavin, make sure you get a close-up of the inscription. I want viewers to be able to see this for themselves."

"If you ask me, this guy was a little creepy," Peter suddenly remarked. All eyes shifted toward him.

"Why do you say that?" Kate asked.

"Think about it. This guy, all alone in the world, falls so deeply in love with this girl that he builds her this mansion that looks like Gomez and Morticia's summer home. Then she dies, so he becomes this lonely hermit who never loved again, even though he was still young and rich. And then the only thing he wants to be remembered for is being her husband?" Peter raised a skeptical eyebrow. "I don't know. It all just seems a little sketchy to me."

"No one ever said love was rational," Gail commented.

"But this guy went beyond love. From what I can tell, he was obsessed to the point where, I don't know, it was a little unhealthy. Maybe even dangerous."

"Yeah, but remember what Marian said? Joanna's family all loved Sterling," Kate reminded him.

"Yeah, I'd love my son-in-law too if he had all that money," Peter remarked.

"It wasn't just for the money," Gail told him.

"Oh yeah? Did you know them? Were you there?" Peter asked. Neither Gail nor Kate responded. "Look, I don't want to be a downer here, I'm just saying that money talks. And I think there's a lot more to this supposedly beautiful love story than we're getting. For example, where's Joanna's grave? Huh?"

"She died at least two decades before Sterling. She could be buried anywhere," JT said.

"I don't think so. I think that if Sterling's love for her was as pure and true as he claimed it was, then he would have insisted they be buried side by side. I don't know, man. Something's just not right."

For a brief moment, no one spoke. Michael figured they were all in shock that Peter - jovial, fun-loving, easy-going Peter - was the one casting shadows of doubt over Sterling and Joanna's love story. But he made valid arguments. Sterling didn't just love Joanna. He'd worshipped her, and Stanton Hall Manor was her shrine. Michael had never thought to question that maybe his incentives weren't entirely pure. Maybe there was a darker side to their historic romance.

In an apparent attempt to break the tension, Luke cleared his throat and said, "We should probably head back up to the manor and get cleaned up for tonight."

Everyone agreed and began to make their way back to the house. Michael took a few steps before he noticed that Kate wasn't next to him. She still lingered behind, staring at the grave. The breeze toyed with strands of her long blonde hair as Michael walked back to her.

"It's strange," she said.

"What is?"

"When we're up there in the house, talking about spirits, trying to communicate with them, I still kind of think of these people as alive. You know, they're there with us, we just can't see them. Seeing this though... It's a little spooky." She shivered. "Even when I go visit Trevor at the cemetery back home, it doesn't feel like this."

"Maybe because you know Trevor's at peace," Michael told her.

Kate turned to look at him. "What do you think about everything Peter was saying?"

"I'm not sure," Michael replied honestly. "I never thought there was anything wrong. It's a beautiful love story. It's tragic, but if you think about it, all love stories eventually end with one of the lovers dying."

Kate offered him a grim smile. "If I go first, I'll be sure to hang around. That way, neither one of us will be alone."

"I don't even want to think about that," Michael said, pulling her into his embrace. They stood in silence for a long time, just holding each other. Then Michael pressed his lips to her forehead and whispered, "I love you, Kate."

Her arms tightened around his slender torso. "I love you, too."

She turned lovely hazel eyes up at him as she rose up on her toes to kiss him. Michael savored the soft and gentle touch of her lips, all the while trying not to think about the silent and haunting figure that had appeared mere meters away, less than a fleeting second before he closed his eyes to accept her kiss.

***

At dinner, Luke announced that Marian planned to stop by with the necklace around eight or so. That gave them two and a half hours to prepare. As Michael saw it, that gave him two and a half hours to take a nap.

After scarfing down three giant pieces of Domino's pizza (not exactly the kind of dining experience he'd expected to have at a haunted manor), he retreated into his room for some much-needed shut-eye.

"So, what's the buzz, Cuz?" Brink asked, appearing as soon as Michael had locked the door.

"Get out. I want to sleep," Michael muttered.

"What? You abandon me all day and now you want me to leave you alone so you can sleep? Some friend you are." Michael didn't have the energy for Brink's ridiculous baiting. Instead of defending himself or whatever Brink wanted him to do, he kicked off his shoes and fell into bed. "So that's it? You're not even going to tell me about your day?"

"Nope," Michael replied, his voice muffled by his pillow.

"Well, can you at least tell me why you and Kate picked the least romantic place in the known universe to host a make-out session?"

Michael's eyes flew open. He sat straight up and pointed an accusatory finger at Brink.

"You were the one spying on us in the woods!"

"Okay, okay, hold on." Brink held up his hands in defense. "First of all, no, I was not spying on you down in the woods. I overheard Gavin make a snarky remark about it while you and Kate were still down there. Second of all, if I wanted to spy on you, I am not stupid enough to do so in plain sight."

"Good," Michael murmured and settled back down onto the pillow. Unfortunately, his mind was suddenly swimming with questions, all thanks to Brink and his big mouth.

If Brink hadn't been the one spying on them, then it must have been either Sterling or Joanna. But why? Had the ghost just been passing through and just happened upon them? Or had they been there all along and Michael just hadn't noticed? Maybe it had been Joanna, visiting the grave of her love. Or maybe Sterling wanted to keep an eye on the investigation. Either way, Michael prayed that the ghost had been checking up on the headstone and not on them.

He must have fallen asleep then, because the next thing he knew, someone was pounding loudly on his door.

"Mikey! Come on, rise and shine!" Luke's irritating voice rang loud and clear from the other side.

Still sleepy, but feeling a little more refreshed, Michael dragged himself out of bed for the second time that day. Brink had disappeared, which meant that he was more than likely loose somewhere in the manor. Probably preparing to eavesdrop on the entire investigation.

Luke had vanished by the time Michael emerged from his bedroom, so he followed the sound of laughter back into the kitchen.

"There you are." Kate grinned when she saw him. "Look, Carolyn made us cupcakes."

Sure enough, a platter of fresh cupcakes, vanilla, chocolate, and strawberry, sat waiting on one of the counters.

"That was nice of her," Michael said, helping himself to a strawberry one.

"She's a nice lady. Even if she is a skeptic," Luke said.

"Did she say how many we're allowed to have?" Kate asked.

"I think they're all for us," Gail answered her.

"Good. Then I'm having another," Kate announced and reached for a chocolate cupcake. "I need to make sure I have plenty of energy, you know, for the investigation tonight."

"Well, that covers tonight. What's your excuse for the past twenty-four and a half years?" Gavin smirked.

"Hey, I eat... sort of healthy," Kate said. "I mean, yeah, I had fried clams and onion rings and pizza today, but this is sort of like a vacation, so it doesn't really count."

"I wish I could find a woman who liked to eat like that," Peter remarked.

"Um... I guess that warrants a thank you?" Kate laughed.

"It does," Peter assured her. "Michael's a lucky man."

"Yeah," Kate teased, nudging Michael with her shoulder. "So you'd better be good to me or I'll start eating salad."

"I will be good to you, no matter what you eat," Michael promised her.

"Oh, you two better cut that lovey-dovey stuff out. Remember, that's not allowed here," Gail threw a dirty look in Luke's direction.

"I know you're trying to piss me off, but it's not going to work because I am too excited about tonight," Luke said. "Okay, so here's what's going to happen. As soon as Marian gets here with the necklace, we're going to do a short segment in the hall, then we're going to take the party into the master bedroom. I already checked with Carolyn, and she said that was fine."

"Will she and Emily be joining us?" Gavin asked.

"No. She's turning in early and Emily has homework," Gail said.

"Probably for the best. Emily is already scared of the ghosts. If this investigation is as eventful as I'm hoping it will be, it will be traumatizing for all of us," Luke added.

"Oh, please don't hope that," Michael deadpanned.

Luke just laughed at him.

When the doorbell rang a few minutes later, all four members of the *Cemetery Tours* crew were out of the room in the blink of an eye. Gavin followed close behind, still licking chocolate frosting off his fingers.

"Do you think this is a good idea?" Michael asked Kate once they were alone. He didn't want to say anything to her, but his thoughts kept drifting back to the ghost that had been watching them down by the grave.

"Oh sure, they'll be fine. They use trigger objects all the time on the show."

"Yeah, but do you think it's still a good idea for us to be involved?"

"I think so. Why? Are you having second thoughts?"

"No, not really. I just..." he trailed off.

"What?" Kate asked, taking both his hands.

"I just hope Luke knows what he's doing."

"I think he does. After all, this is his job," Kate said. "You know, he's kind of like a pilot."

"How so?" Michael asked.

"A pilot doesn't take off if he believes there's a chance the plane could crash. I figure that if Luke thought there was even the slightest chance of something bad or dangerous happening, then he wouldn't go through with whatever he was planning, because he'd be endangering himself just as much as his crew," Kate explained.

Michael wanted to ask if she remembered a little incident involving a Bridal Barn and a preacher's deadly daughter, but he decided against it. None of them could have seen that coming. It was highly unlikely they'd run into any sort of similar situation at Stanton Hall.

At least, that was what Michael was going to tell himself.

CHAPTER SEVENTEEN

Kate had been wondering how Luke expected to fit eight people into one room for the EVP session with Sterling and the necklace. She should have known, given the size of the rest of the manor, that she needn't have worried. The master bedroom was enormous. Although, as Carolyn had told them earlier, it was still in the process of being renovated. While it was by no means as aesthetically pleasing as the rest of the house, its deteriorating condition did lend the tiniest bit of charm. With the peeling wallpaper, boarded up windows, old dusty books and papers scattered on the floor, and bricks and floorboards piled in the corner, it was the perfect setting for a ghostly interview.

"Okay, we're going to set up the main camera here," Luke instructed, pointing to a spot at the foot of the worn and faded four-poster king-sized bed. "Peter, JT, Gavin, I want one of you to have a camera on the necklace at all times. The other two, be on the lookout for any movements, mists, light anomalies, basically anything unusual. We're going to be turning off all the lights and shooting in night vision, so you'll have to keep an eye on your camera screens to know what you're looking at. Mikey, Kate, I think you know your assignments. I want all your senses on high alert."

"We're going to be in the dark?" Michael asked.

"Yeah. That's how we do all of our investigations."

"Will there be any candles this time? Because if it's going to be pitch black in here, I won't be able to see the ghosts any easier than you."

"Look at one of the screens on the camera. Someone will let you watch over their shoulder."

127

"That won't make a difference," Michael said. "I see the same thing as everybody else on camera."

"Really?" Kate asked. "But cameras have captured images of ghosts before. They have a whole show on the Biography Channel that features people who've caught ghosts on film."

"It does happen occasionally, and I can't explain why it does. It probably has something to do with energy, angles, and lighting, but this is the one instance where it works the same for me as it does for everyone else. But," he added. "I'll still be able to hear him if he decides to talk to us this time."

"Good. Then keep your ears open. Kate, this means I'll need you to be extra vigilant," Luke said.

"Okay," she agreed. She still wasn't one hundred percent certain that she was as 'sensitive' as Luke would have the rest of the world believe, but it was nice to feel like she had a purpose in the group.

"Can you see them too?" Marian Davis asked her.

"No, but sometimes I just... know when they're here," she replied. "It's not a reliable skill by any means."

"You've been pretty spot-on for as long as I've known you," Luke assured her.

"Thanks," she grinned.

Neither she nor Michael really had anything to do while the *Cemetery Tours* crew set the scene for the EVP session, so they stood back in the corner of the room and observed. Fortunately, it didn't take Luke and his team very long. Less than ten minutes later, Peter, JT, and Gavin each had a camera in hand and Luke, Gail, and Marian had all seated themselves on the edge of the bed in the center of the room. They placed the box containing the necklace in the middle of the old mattress. Finally, Peter flipped the light switch and the entire room fell dark.

At first, Kate was a little unnerved by the consuming and impenetrable darkness, but then, Gavin opened the small screen on his camera, illuminating his face and his shoulders.

She felt around for Michael's hand, and when she finally found it, she leaned in and whispered, "Let's go stand next to Gavin."

Michael agreed, and very carefully, they made their way blindly across the room to where Gavin stood. Watching the scene through the camera, Kate realized, was a whole lot like watching an episode on a miniature movie screen.

"All right. Everyone ready?" Luke asked.

"Go," JT said. Peter and Gavin echoed his affirmation.

"We're here in the master bedroom of Stanton Hall Manor. This was Joanna and Sterling's bedroom. This is where they actually slept. More significantly, this is also where they both died. This room has had more reports of paranormal activity than any other room in this entire building. Now, we've brought Marian and her necklace in here, hoping that their presence might help stir up some of that activity, since we haven't had a lot of interaction with either Sterling or Joanna. Are you ready for this, Marian?" Luke asked, sounding a lot like a kid about to ride his favorite roller coaster.

"I'm ready," she answered with the same amount of enthusiasm.

"All right then!" Luke exclaimed, and pressed the record button on his digital recorder. "Hi there, Sterling, Joanna. It's us again, from last night. I hope you're around, because we have something to show you. Whoa. Did it just get colder in here?"

"I felt it," Gail agreed.

"Me too," JT said.

They weren't the only ones. Kate felt the chilling rush also. Could a ghost have arrived already? Instinctively, she turned to look at Michael, but then she remembered that he was as incapacitated by the dark as the rest of them.

"Sterling? Joanna? Are you there?"

Beside her, she felt Michael stiffen.

"It's Sterling. He's here," he confirmed.

"You hear him?" Luke asked.

"He wants to know what we're doing in his bedroom."

"We just came here to talk to you, Sterling. And maybe to help you," Luke answered.

Kate heard Michael draw in a shaky breath. "He says he doesn't need our help."

"Okay, I can respect that. But you know, a lot of times, we don't realize we need help until the right person shows up to provide it."

Just then, the image on Gavin's camera dissolved into fuzzy lines of jagged static, and a loud *THUMP* reverberated through the room. Kate didn't have to be a sensitive to know that Luke had just made Sterling very upset.

"Luke, my entire screen just went gray," Peter said.

"Mine did too," Gavin reported.

Luke just kept pushing.

"Sterling, we're not going to go away. Now, we've heard a lot about how you've been causing trouble for some of the workers here. A lot of people are pretty scared of you."

Another loud noise, this time a *STOMP* and the shuffling of papers. Kate jumped and tightened her grip on Michael's hand.

"He says he's aggravated," Michael translated. "Luke, maybe we shouldn't - "

"You're aggravated. Hate to break it to you, Sterling, but a lot of people are aggravated." Sterling must have said something then, because Kate felt Michael flinch, but Luke never gave him the chance to relay the message. "Believe it or not, we're not here to make you angry. We just want to talk to you."

Beside her, Kate heard Michael take a deep breath. Was he suddenly experiencing the same queasy feeling that had just befallen her? It wasn't awful, but it was enough to make her want to lie down and rest her head on something soft. Was that Sterling making her feel that way? She couldn't be sure. The last time a spirit had affected her, she'd felt dizzy and a little light-headed, but never sick. Was it the ghost? Or were the clams she'd consumed earlier finally catching up to her?

"He says there's nothing to talk about," Michael said. "We're all trespassers here, and he wants us to leave immediately."

"Trespassers? That's a pretty strong word there, Sterling. We're not trespassers. We're guests. Carolyn Drake asked us to come here. You know Carolyn, don't you? The nice lady who owns this place? You're pretty lucky she doesn't believe in you, or she might have called in someone a lot less understanding than we are. You know, like an exorcist."

"Why is he doing this?" Kate whispered to Michael. "Why is Luke being so aggressive?"

"Isn't this just how he is?" Michael asked, sounding ill and exhausted.

"Maybe you'll recognize this, Sterling. Huh? Does this necklace look familiar to you?" As he asked the question, Luke grabbed a flashlight, flipped it on, and cast the beam onto the sparkling blood-colored gems. "Is this the necklace you gave to Joanna?"

Kate felt Michael wince again.

"He wants to know where you got it. Luke... I think maybe we should - "

"You gave it away, remember? To Joanna's cousin Sarah. This is her great, great, great granddaughter, Marian. She owns the necklace no - "

But before he could get the words out, a blood-curdling scream rang out from the darkness, scaring Kate so badly that she shrieked too.

With trembling hands, Luke turned the flashlight on Marian, who was curled up in a ball, quivering and sobbing, on the bed.

"What just happened?" JT asked.

"Marian, are you all right?" Luke asked urgently, resting his hand on her shoulder.

"No... No... He came at me... I could feel him. It was the worst... the worst feeling..." she wept.

"This is my fault," Luke said. "Mikey tried to warn me, but I kept pushing. I'm so sorry, Marian."

"I thought he was going to kill me," she whimpered.

"Well, hopefully, he's gone now. Gee, never thought I'd say that," Luke said. "Kate, would you mind hitting the lights?"

Kate barely heard him. Michael's palm had suddenly gone cold and clammy, and she could feel him swaying, struggling to stay upright.

"Kate, is everything okay?" Gail asked.

She never got the chance to answer. Half a second later, Michael collapsed.

"Michael!" Kate gasped.

Quickly, Gavin ran to turn the lights back on.

Thankfully, Michael hadn't passed out. He was kneeling, however, with his arm and head pressed to the old, rickety footboard of the bed. All the color had drained from his face, and he was taking deep, slow breaths.

"What's the matter?" Luke asked.

"It was Sterling," Kate answered. "He made him sick."

"You gonna be okay, Mikey?" Luke asked, leaning over to look at him. "Do we need to get you a trash can or something?"

Michael just closed his eyes and shook his head. Kate was glad that he didn't seem to think so, but she was beginning to worry that maybe it wasn't the ghost affecting them at all. No one else in the room seemed to feel sick. Maybe it was the clams.

Then she noticed Peter and Marian, both looking just as pale and sickly, and Kate felt oddly relieved. Strange as it may have been, she'd much rather have a ghost make her ill than succumb to something like food poisoning. She truly couldn't imagine anything worse.

"Wait a minute. Where's the necklace?" Gail asked.

Everyone, even Michael, turned their attention to the empty jewelry box on the bed.

"Marian, do you have it?" Luke asked.

She meekly shook her head.

"Maybe you hit it? Or kicked it? You know, during all the commotion?" Gail asked.

"I don't think so," Marian answered.

"Well, everyone look around. It's got to be here," Luke said. "Mikey, you can just stay where you are. Don't want you fainting, or worse, puking."

"Thanks, Luke," Michael muttered.

Kate was relieved. He was already sounding more like himself.

"So, did you get any sort of look at him? At all?" Luke asked.

"No."

"Oh well. Next time."

"There's going to be a next time?" Michael asked, sounding perplexed.

"Of course. What, do you think we came all this way for one EVP session? Mikey, we're just getting started."

"Oh boy."

They searched the room for half an hour, but still, there was no trace of the necklace.

"Do you think he took it?" Gail asked.

"Who? Sterling?" Peter asked.

"No, the mailman. Of course Sterling!"

"Can he do that?" Kate asked.

"Trevor trashed our apartment last year," Gavin reminded her.

"Yeah, but he just kind of threw stuff around. He didn't physically carry one thing out of the room and put it somewhere else," Kate said. Though even as she spoke the words, a memory resurfaced of one of her neighbors back in Dallas who'd once told her about household items turning up in places they were never supposed to be. A curling iron in a china cabinet, for example.

"Well, wherever it is, it's definitely not here," Luke said. "Marian, I'm sorry."

"No, I'm sorry. I feel like this is my fault."

"Of course it's not your fault," Luke said. "We're the ones who brought you here. We should be apologizing to you. And buying you a new necklace."

But Marian shook her head.

"That necklace is irreplaceable. I'm just hoping that it shows up."

Kate was surprised by how well Marian was handling the loss of a precious family heirloom. Then again, she was also exhausted, physically and mentally, from their encounter with Sterling. Maybe she simply didn't have the energy to be upset.

Once they finally decided to call it a night, Kate walked with Michael back to his room.

"Are you feeling better?"

"Yeah. I think I just need to get some rest."

"Then you go do that," Kate said, rising up on her toes to give him a gentle kiss.

After they'd said their goodnights, Kate retreated to the Emerald Room. After such a stressful day, a long, hot, soothing shower was in order. As exciting as it could be, fraternizing with spirits was draining and, as previous experience had taught her, could even be a little dangerous.

She just hoped that Luke hadn't pushed Sterling too far.

Since her very first EVP session with Luke, to the night Michael had told her about his gift, she'd believed that the world of ghosts was a mystical one, full of wondrous possibilities, and she'd persistently plagued Michael, trying to persuade him to embrace her viewpoint. Now, she felt foolish and naïve for her complete and utter disrespect for the harsh realities of life and loss, death and despair, and for the first time that trip, Kate found herself hoping they would have no further encounters with the ghost of Sterling Hall.

CHAPTER EIGHTEEN

For the second night in a row, Michael found himself tossing and turning, not because he was unable to sleep, but because when he did, his dreams were full of frightening and troubling images. Even though he'd spent a good portion of his life in the company of the spirits of the dead, they very rarely haunted him in his dreams. At times, it seemed that sleep was his only refuge, the one place in the world where the dead couldn't find him.

Not anymore.

He knew it wasn't actually the ghost of Sterling Hall inside his mind, but that didn't make the visuals any less disturbing. Because he still hadn't gotten a good look at the man who had built the manor, his brain had taken what little it knew about Hall and used it to construct a woeful and rather sinister character to torment him in what should have been a peaceful rest.

In his first dream, he'd been walking alone in the woods behind the manor, when he again stumbled upon Sterling's grave. Instead of an old weathered headstone, however, a black and gold plaque had been set at the head of an open tomb, containing a single black, gold, and crimson casket. The plaque read, *In Death, In Life, In Love. Do Not Open the Coffin.*

Although Conscious Michael wouldn't even think of touching the casket, much less opening it, Dream Michael possessed no such inhibitions. Without a second thought, he leapt down into the grave and lifted the lid. The coffin was empty, except for a single red rose. Michael reached down to take the flower, but as soon as his fingers grazed the stem, the rose began to melt, dissolving into a puddle of hot, thick blood that began to fill the casket. The form of a body began to rise out of the blood, but the dream ended before Michael could identify it.

In his second dream, Luke and JT had discovered a body in the parking lot of his apartment complex back in Dallas. The body belonged to a young woman, possibly Joanna Stanton, wearing a white dress. Her long dark hair was stringy and matted, and she'd clearly been dead for at least a few days. Luke theorized that she'd been hit in the head with a brick. Insisting that it was Michael's responsibility to take care of her, Luke and JT left her inside his apartment. She didn't bother him at first, but as he was getting ready for bed, she got up and began to wander around his apartment, moaning and crying.

His last dream found him back at Dock Square. He and Kate were enjoying the afternoon on the bridge when someone began to scream. Michael bolted across the bridge and back into the square, where he searched desperately for whoever was in trouble. He finally came across the same young woman lying dead on the river bank, a thin trail of blood dripping from her mouth and onto the damp sand beneath her.

Michael tried calling for help, but no one was around, so he retreated back to the bridge where he'd left Kate. That was when Sterling Hall finally made his debut. He was tall, with light brown hair and piercing black eyes, and he wore a black suit. He stood behind Kate, pulling her hair back, and whispering into her ear.

When he sensed Michael approaching, he looked up and sneered. Then, he reached into his pocket, pulled out Marian's garnet necklace, and fastened it around Kate's neck.

It was only then that Michael finally opened his eyes. Weary of ghosts and gory nightmares, Michael sought solace once again in the kitchen. Moonlight spilled through the large window above the sink, flooding the room with silvery blue shadows. Like the night before, Michael filled a crystal glass up with tap water and sipped at it until his head was a little clearer and his thoughts a little purer.

136

One more night, he told himself. *Just one more night in this place, and then you'll be home.*

He'd just drained the glass when a timid movement on the far side of the room caught his eye. Emily Drake stood in the doorway, looking small and mousey with her messy reddish-brown hair and long white nightgown. Michael wondered how long she'd been standing there.

"Oh. Um..." he mumbled, unsure of how to address her. "Hi."

She pursed her mouth as though she was trying to think of something to say, but she remained silent.

Suddenly feeling like he needed to explain his presence in the kitchen at almost three in the morning, he said, "I uh, I was just getting a drink of water. I'm sorry."

"That's okay," Emily spoke in a hushed yet high-pitched voice. "I heard something."

"That was probably me," Michael told her.

"It wasn't," Emily replied with a certainty that sent a dreadful chill down Michael's spine.

"Oh. Okay then," Michael said, wondering how awkward it would be if he just walked out of the room. Emily's curious stare, however, seemed to prevent him from moving.

"Is it true?" she asked.

"Is what true?"

"That you can see them."

Michael bit the inside of his cheek. He didn't need to ask who she meant by *them.* What he didn't know was whether or not to answer her honestly. Although he could guarantee her that there was at least one restless spirit haunting Stanton Hall, he wasn't sure what her mother would think. Carolyn still adamantly rejected the idea of ghosts, and Michael knew that the last thing she wanted was for her daughter to be scared of something that didn't exist. Then again, she had said that she wanted Michael to assure Emily that there weren't any ghosts inside the manor. While he couldn't do that in any sort of good conscience, he could at least be honest with her about his so-called "gift."

137

"Yeah. It's true," he replied.

He expected her to interrogate him about Sterling, about whether or not he'd seen him, or if they'd been able to make any contact at all.

Instead, she asked, "Do they scare you?"

That was a complicated question. No, they'd never scared him, at least not in the Hollywood horror movie sense. They startled him constantly. A few of them had made him uncomfortable. A few had yelled. Trevor had just about scared him out of his wits the first time he saw him. But it hadn't been a fear like the one he presumed Emily meant.

Of course, after the way Sterling Hall had made all of them feel tonight, he couldn't blame her for being wary of him.

"Not really," he answered. "They just look like people to me. True, some of them are a little more... dramatic than others. But they're no different than they were in life."

Emily looked like she'd never considered that. "But what if they weren't good people in life?"

"Then I'd probably be a little scared of them." *Or a lot*, his subconscious added. But he was supposed to be reassuring her, so he kept that thought to himself. "But you've got to remember that they can't hurt you." *Another white lie.* But truthfully, Trevor throwing Gavin into a wall was a pretty rare exception. Even if a violent spirit did appear, it took a tremendous amount of energy just to move a small object. Tossing a full-grown man across the room was just about unheard of.

Emily seemed to accept that.

"Have you seen *him*?" she asked, surely meaning Sterling Hall.

"I haven't gotten a very good look at him yet," Michael confessed. "But he has... contacted us." He guessed that was the word that Luke would use.

Emily's lower lip trembled. "Why is he still here?"

Now that one, Michael couldn't answer.

"Your guess is as good as mine. We haven't really been able to get a lot out of him. But since he spent so much of his life loving Joanna, I can only - "

Before he could finish, a shadow crossed the room, accompanied by faint footsteps against the hardwood floor. The spirit of Sterling Hall appeared, looking somber and despondent as he slowly made his way across the dark kitchen. At first, Michael thought he might be coming to talk to him, but then he noticed that Sterling's eyes were fixed on something and nothing, like he was staring into space or lost in his own thoughts. Michael wondered if the ghost even noticed them standing there at all.

"Do you see him?" Emily's voice was barely a whisper.

Michael nodded.

Without another word, the young girl fled the kitchen.

The sound of her retreating footsteps snapped Sterling out of his stupor. Silently, he looked around the room, like he was trying to remember where he was or why he'd come to the kitchen in the first place. Michael observed the ghost standing before him in the pale glow of moonlight.

He didn't look like the Sterling Hall from his dream at all. Although not very tall, only five foot eight or so, he was handsome. His dark hair was thick with a slight scattering of gray amidst the black and the only sign of aging on his still-youthful face were the crows' feet around his blue eyes. What surprised Michael the most, however, was how impeccably dressed Sterling appeared to be. He didn't know much about fashion trends in the 1800s, but he was willing to bet that black trousers and a dark tail coat were usually reserved for special occasions.

Michael had half a mind to slip right past Sterling, all the while pretending not to notice him, but the look on the ghost's face, like he'd never been more lost or alone in his existence, forced him to reconsider. As miserable as that last encounter had been, Michael couldn't help but feel a little sorry for Sterling Hall.

"Are you all right?" Michael asked him.

Sterling turned his head and looked Michael right in the eye.

"You're speaking to me." It wasn't a question.

"Uh... yeah. I guess I am."

"That's refreshing. Do you know how long it's been since anyone has bothered to approach me at all?"

"Yeah. That sort of happens when... well, you know."

"I most certainly do not know," Sterling retorted. "These men and women intrude upon my property and privacy without so much as a second thought. Foul, disgusting, downright cowardly. Why, not one of them has the decency to even look me in the eye."

Okay... Michael thought. Not quite the conversation he'd been expecting to have, but he could go with it.

"Well maybe they just don't know you're there."

"How couldn't they know when I'm standing there before their eyes?" Sterling asked, a bewildered look in his eye.

"Because you're - " Michael paused mid-sentence.

He didn't know.

Sterling Hall didn't know that he was dead. But how? How could he not realize? Did he truly believe he'd been alive for the past century and a half?

Michael had met ghosts who hadn't realized they were dead before. It was sad, but he'd never thought it was his place to tell them. Usually, he just let them pass by and hoped that they'd eventually find their way to the next world on their own. But he'd never known a spirit to exist in ignorance for almost one hundred and fifty years. It was simply unfathomable. And yet, the look on Sterling's face was unmistakable. In his mind, he was still very much alive.

Did that mean it was Michael's responsibility to tell him the truth? He wasn't sure, mostly because he had no idea how Sterling would react. He might accept it, thank Michael for his time, and move on. But if he was as moody and cantankerous as he seemed earlier that night, that probably wasn't the most likely scenario.

"Never mind," Michael finally said. "I don't know."

"Well, in that case, I trust that you are a decent young man and will see to it that all of your companions leave my house at once."

"I know that's what you want, but to be honest, it's not really that simple - "

"Of course it's that simple, and I will tell you why. My wife will be home any moment now and she expects and deserves her home to be free of trespassers and burglars."

"Your... wife?" Michael asked.

"Yes. My Joanna. She's coming home from a long trip and I want everything to be perfect, just as it was before you and your kind showed up."

"So Joanna is coming... here?"

"Of course. Where else would she go? I daresay, for such a courteous young man, you're not very quick, are you?"

No, apparently he wasn't, because he wasn't comprehending a word that Sterling Hall was saying to him. When he said that Joanna was coming home, did that mean her spirit had been away and would return to Sterling? Were they together in death? Or did his delusions extend even beyond his inability to accept his passing?

Michael intended to question Sterling further and try to explain to him why neither he nor Luke nor any of the other "trespassers" would be clearing out any time soon, but with one last condescending sneer, Sterling said, "I want all of you, every last one, gone by morning."

Then, in the blink of an eye, he was gone, leaving Michael alone and bewildered in the soft glow of moonlight.

CHAPTER NINETEEN

"So let me get this straight," Luke said as he paced back and forth across his bedroom. "This guy kicked it almost a hundred and fifty years ago and he still hasn't figured out that he's dead?"

"That's the impression I got," Michael answered. He, Kate, Gavin, and the rest of the *Cemetery Tours* crew were all gathered inside Luke's room. Michael had only intended to tell Luke about his conversation with Sterling, but Luke being Luke had insisted on filming. Thirty minutes and several questions later, what was supposed to be a simple conversation between colleagues had turned into a regular pajama party... and all recorded for national television.

All things considered, Michael probably should have waited until morning instead of waking everybody up in the middle of the night, but he hadn't been thinking straight.

Not that any of them seemed to mind. In fact, Michael was willing to bet that Luke enjoyed being woken up to talk about anything weird, be it hauntings, space aliens, or the boogeyman.

Oh God, please don't let those things exist, Michael thought sleepily, as Luke continued to wander anxiously around the room.

"And he said Joanna is still here?" Luke asked.

"Yeah, but I'm not sure how much his word is worth. If he's deluded himself into thinking he's still alive, then it's also possible that he hasn't come to terms with Joanna's death."

"So we're talking about a spirit who's essentially a head case," Luke translated.

"Is that even possible?" Kate asked. "I mean, mental illness always has something to do with the brain. When a person dies, it's because their body can't function anymore for whatever reason-- injury, illness, old age -- but the brain dies with it."

"What's your point, Kate?" Gavin asked. He was the only one of the bunch who looked like he'd rather be back in bed than filming a late night paranormal pow-wow.

"My point is when you think about it logically, any sort of mental illness, or any malady at all, also dies with the body."

"When you think about it logically, none of this stuff should exist, period. But it does," Gavin reminded her. "I think that means just about anything is possible."

"Even mental illness among those who no longer possess a brain. Interesting," JT remarked.

"I don't think it's mental. I think it's emotional," Luke said. "It's true a damaged brain dies with the body, but a damaged soul never perishes. And what's more damaging on a soul than heartbreak? Or the death of the one person you cherish above all others, even yourself?"

"That's uncharacteristically deep of you, Luke," Michael said.

"What can I say? I'm a romantic at heart."

"Bull," Gail muttered. "You just have a flare for dramatics and a secret *Lifetime* addiction."

"That second part is not true," Luke insisted. "But think about it. Aren't most of the ghosts that hang around just as equally damaged?"

"Yeah, but they're not all equally delusional," Peter said. "I still think this guy is hiding something. That's the only rational explanation."

"I don't think so. I think he really loved her. Besides, we've met other spirits who weren't aware that they'd died. Think of all those civil war soldiers who still patrol battle grounds, or haunted bars where ghosts still play poker," JT said.

"There's a big difference between this and an eternal poker game. Those guys aren't taking their deaths or losses out on other people."

"It's still not impossible," Luke told him before addressing Michael again. "Did he say anything about the necklace?"

"No, but he did call us trespassers and burglars."

"Ouch," Luke remarked dryly.

"Do you think he was talking about Marian?" Kate asked.

"He could have been talking about anyone: Marian for taking the necklace, or Carolyn and Emily for taking the house," Luke said.

Emily. The sound of her name reminded Michael of his brief meeting with the teen in the kitchen.

"I saw her," Michael said.

"Who? Joanna?" Luke asked.

"No, Emily. I was talking to her in the kitchen right before Sterling showed up."

"What did she say?"

"Not a lot. She just asked me if it was true, if I could really see them. I think she's like Kate, a sensitive. She could tell when Sterling entered the room."

"What if it's more than that?" Peter asked. "What if that girl reminds him of his wife? That would explain why she's so scared of him that she asked you to come here."

"Pete, that's - " Luke began, but Peter cut him off.

"Look, I know you all think I'm nuts and that this is just the most romantic story ever, but I'm telling you, I *feel* it. Something is not right in this house. This Sterling guy is a whack job and now he's preying on innocent girls - "

BOOM!

A violent burst of energy shook the room. Gail and Gavin both cried out. Kate reached out for Michael, who looked around frantically for any sign of Sterling or Joanna, but there was none.

"Pete, you really need to watch what you're saying, man," Luke told him. "Come on, you know better than to go around accusing spirits of stuff like that. Even if you think you have reason to believe it."

"You seriously think this guy is innocent?" Peter asked.

"Yeah, I do," Luke said. "Until I see hard evidence to the contrary, I'm choosing to believe his story. And I think Mikey is, too."

Oh, please don't drag me into this, Michael wanted to say. Unfortunately, it was a little late for that. He was already about as far in as he could get.

"I think he's telling the truth," he answered, choosing his words carefully. "I think he's lonely, confused... I think he needs help. Whether we're the ones to give it to him is another matter."

"Why?" Luke asked. "Who better to give it to him? We've got four professional ghost hunters, a psychic medium - "

"I'm not psychic," Michael interrupted, but Luke ignored him.

"A sensitive who has actually experienced the afterlife, and, well, Gavin," Luke concluded.

"Hey, I've got experience. Any of the rest of you know what it's like to have a ghost sucking the life out of you every damn day?" Gavin asked.

"Fair point," Luke acknowledged.

"So, how are we going to help him?" Kate asked.

"We make him see reason and help him move on. Since his life seemed to revolve around his love for Joanna, I'm guessing that's what's holding him here in death."

"Obsessed," Peter murmured.

Luke threw him a look, but didn't say anything. Michael, on the other hand, didn't care all that much about Peter's theories. He was more concerned about how Luke intended to make Sterling "see reason." It was hard enough to make the living see reason, and they didn't come with all those fun supernatural tricks like draining energy and making a whole room full of people nauseated. True, it was easier for the living to throw things, but in Michael's experience, angry spirits could be just as dangerous and sometimes twice as quick-tempered as their living counterparts.

"Well, whatever we do, it's going to have to wait until tomorrow. I'm beat," Gail announced.

"That might not give us enough time," Luke said.

"What? You want to do this tonight? Luke, we've already had one bad session with this guy, two if you count Michael's experience in the kitchen, and we're going to be up late again tomorrow night for the last investigation. We need to get some rest," Gail argued.

"Fine. Go get some rest," Luke told her, sliding his feet into his old green Converse shoes. "I'm going to take a camera out and see if I can find him. Mikey, you with me?"

Somehow, Michael figured that no wasn't the right answer, so he pulled himself off the bed and said, "Let's go."

"I'm going too," Kate said, standing up beside him.

JT also volunteered.

"Have fun," Gail told them as she, Peter, and Gavin headed back to their rooms.

Michael couldn't help noticing Kate's eyes following her brother out the door. Although his rendezvous with Gail hadn't come up since that afternoon, Michael could tell that neither Luke nor Kate had forgotten about it.

"Don't you want to turn on the lights?" Michael asked as they ventured out into the dark hallway.

"Night vision," Luke reminded him. "Just follow the glow of the screen."

"Easy for him to say," Michael muttered to Kate, who snickered and took his hand.

"So, where exactly are we heading?" JT asked. "Does anyone know where we're supposed to find this guy?"

"Mikey, any ideas?"

Now why would Luke even ask him that? Did he *ever* have any ideas as far as ghosts were concerned? Sterling hadn't revealed anything deep or personal enough to give him any sort of insight on things like where he liked to hang out when he wasn't tormenting the living.

Although, if there was one thing anyone knew about Sterling, it was how his life had revolved around his devotion to Joanna.

146

"My guess would be anywhere that reminds him of his wife," Michael said.

"The master bedroom?" JT suggested.

Even though deep down, he knew that was where they were headed, Michael was reluctant to return. Kate seemed equally hesitant.

"Are you sure that's a good idea?" she asked.

"Now that we know a little more about him, we should be able to communicate more effectively," Luke explained. "This evening, we thought he was just another asshole spirit throwing a hissy fit. If I had known just how confused he was, I would've tried to be a little more sensitive."

"Sensitivity. Who knew?" Michael quipped as they approached the dark and abandoned master bedroom.

"All right, now I know we didn't have the best experience here a few hours ago, so maybe if we just stand in the doorway, we can still get in touch with him," Luke said.

"That is fine with me," Kate said, snuggling closer to Michael. He wrapped his arm around her shoulders with a very false sense of confidence and bravado.

"Okay Mikey, since you're the last one he talked to, I think you should try summoning him. Who knows? Maybe he trusts you," Luke said.

Michael highly doubted that, but he figured it was worth a shot.

"Okay," he agreed. Then he remembered that he had never actually "summoned" a spirit before and had no idea how to go about doing so. He knew he couldn't dwell on it for too long without seeming incompetent, so he cleared his throat and mumbled, "Um... Sterling?"

No response.

After a few moments of silence and stillness, Michael decided to try again. "It's me, Michael, the uh... decent young man from the kitchen. I'm here with my friends. We'd like to talk to you."

Still nothing.

147

"I told them what you said... about the house and Joanna. We don't want to hurt you or upset you any more than we already have. We just... we need to talk to you. We think maybe we can help you."

"Why do you keep insisting that I need help?"

The voice cut through the darkness so suddenly that Michael gasped. Kate looked up at him, the alarm on her pretty face visible even in the poor lighting.

"Is he here?" JT asked.

"Yeah." Michael squinted, trying desperately to make out a form or a shadow, but his eyes were no match for the pitch blackness of the master bedroom.

"I thought it might go without saying that I don't appreciate you talking about me as though I were not present, but I see that it in fact does not," Sterling said.

"Sorry," Michael apologized. And he really was sorry. He hadn't realized up until then how rude they would seem to a ghost. Sterling must have thought they were a few of the most inconsiderate folks on the planet.

"Sorry for wh - oh, right. Never mind," Luke said after he figured out that Michael wasn't talking to him. "Listen, Sterling, we're not here to offend you or to try to take over your house. We just need to talk to you. We think there are things that you... well, that you don't quite realize about yourself."

"What are you talking about?" Sterling asked.

Michael wasn't sure if he should repeat what Sterling had said or not. He knew there was no way Luke could answer him unless he knew about the question. But he wasn't sure that repeating what Sterling had just said wouldn't upset the spirit even more.

Nervously, he cleared his throat again and muttered, "What are you talking about?" to Luke.

"You know, Sterling, there are some things.... Well, there's no easy way to say them. And I'm not one for beating around the bush."

"Then don't," Sterling snapped.

"Don't," Michael repeated.

"Sterling, I want to ask you a question. Have you noticed anything strange about the way you spend most of your days? People don't talk to you. They don't even look at you. The world is changing all around you and yet, you're still about the same as you were, say, a hundred and fifty years ago."

Michael held his breath as he anticipated Sterling's response, but the ghost remained silent.

"Anything?" Luke hissed back at Michael.

"Nope," Michael murmured. He felt Kate tense next to him. He held her closer.

"Sterling, look, I know this is hard for you to accept," Luke continued. "I know you probably don't want to accept it, but death is just a part of our existence. You know, everything that lives eventually has to die."

Michael longed more than anything to tell Luke to *shut up*, but he couldn't make his mouth form the words. The master bedroom, which only moments prior had been as quiet as a tomb, now radiated a terrible and violent energy, so intense it was almost tangible. A near-crippling wave of nausea washed over Michael as he leaned against the wall, taking deep breaths and willing himself not to be sick.

Kate meanwhile took his clammy hand in hers and gripped it until he thought she might cut off the circulation. Her fingers were cold and trembling.

In that moment, Michael hated Luke for dragging them into this, hated Sterling for what he was doing to them, and most of all, hated himself for going along with all of it, especially because he knew how dangerous it could be.

JT, meanwhile, seemed utterly unaffected. "Luke, the camera's dead," he said, apparently unaware of the spirit's powerful attack.

He must not be a sensitive, Michael thought bitterly.

"Yeah, so is mine," Luke replied, but he sounded a little uncomfortable, which gave Michael an admittedly sick sense of satisfaction. If he and Kate were going to be miserable, at least

Luke was suffering right along with them. "Sterling, I know this isn't what you want to hear, but if you wouldn't mind, could you maybe dial it down a bit on the psychic attack? I'm really not in the mood to lose my lunch."

That was it.

A screeching, ear-piercing howl arose from the center of the room as a gust of cold air engulfed them in a strange cyclone of despair and heartache. In the midst of everything, Michael managed to flip the lights on just in time to witness every boarded-up window in the master bedroom burst open, sending splinters and chunks of wood showering down into the center of the room.

Kate screamed.

Luke was so startled that he stumbled backwards, catching his foot on one of the old pieces of wood sticking up out of the floor. With a panicked yell, he and his camera toppled to the ground.

"Luke! Oh my God, are you all right?" Kate asked.

"Yeah, fine," he grunted. "Ow..."

"Man, *why* are we not getting this on tape?" JT moaned.

Definitely not a sensitive, Michael thought again as he scanned the bedroom for Sterling, but the ghost had managed to slip away in the midst of all the commotion. Finally, the dust in the room started to settle and the sickening heaviness of Sterling's psychic assault slowly but surely began to lift. Michael turned to face his friends, still wide-eyed and weary from the encounter.

"Well," Luke said, pulling himself back up to his feet. "That could've gone a lot better."

150

CHAPTER TWENTY

No one said a word as they all made their way back to their own rooms for a few more hours of sleep. For Kate, the silence came as a substantial relief. She didn't want to talk or think about how she was feeling after that confrontation.

Truth be told, she didn't really know how she was feeling. She just knew that coming to Stanton Hall Manor had been a mistake. She couldn't say how or why she thought that, just that she wanted nothing more than to be back home, safe in her own bed, miles and miles and miles away from that horrible place. Kate wondered if maybe, just maybe, Luke would consider leaving a day early. Surely, they had more than enough footage for their episode.

After Luke and JT bade them listless goodnights and disappeared into their bedrooms, Michael walked Kate back to hers. Of the four of them, she knew that he'd been the most affected by Sterling's attack. He was still shaken and pale as a sheet, with dark circles under his tired eyes.

Naturally, though, Michael was more concerned for her well-being than his own.

"Are you going to be all right?" he asked her as soon as they reached her room.

She wanted to tell him, yes, that she was totally fine, having the time of her life, and so happy that they'd come on this exciting adventure. But she couldn't lie, especially to him.

"I don't know," she replied, her voice small and timid. "I - I feel like this is my fault."

"How could it be your fault?" Michael asked.

"Because I pushed you into this. I knew you didn't want to come, but I made you come anyway." She could feel a knot forming in the back of her throat, but she tried to swallow it. She didn't want to cry. She was too exhausted to cry.

"Kate..." he whispered, sounding heartbroken. "How could you possibly think that?"

"Because it's true. And I'm sorry. I'm so sorry..." Kate whimpered as the tears that had threatened finally began to flow freely down her cheeks.

Michael had her in his arms immediately.

"Kate, listen to me. This is no one's fault; not yours, not even Luke's. Okay well, it's sort of Luke's, but in the end, it was still my decision to come. But even that doesn't matter. None of us could have known what was waiting for us up here. We all thought this was going to be a great experience."

"You didn't," she reminded him.

"Yeah, but it's me. I never think anything is going to be a great experience."

Kate managed to choke out a laugh. It was kind of true. And she loved him for it. She looked up at him through the tears clinging to her eyelashes.

"Will you stay with me tonight?" she whispered. "Please. I don't want to be alone."

"Of course," Michael replied.

In that moment, Kate couldn't imagine being more thankful for one person. She wrapped her arms around his torso and buried her face in his T-shirt. He would be there, and he would protect her. From the very beginning, she'd found comfort in his arms, in his scent, in his warm eyes.

Feeling that she could drift off at any moment, Kate unwillingly pulled herself from Michael's embrace to unlock her bedroom door.

"It's kind of silly, isn't it?"

"What is?" Michael asked.

"Locking a door in a haunted house," Kate replied dryly.

"Oh, yeah. Whoa." He stopped and stared once she finally opened the door. Kate felt her blood freeze in her veins. Had something followed them back to her room? She waited, terrified, for some sort of explanation. Finally, he said, "That is a lot of green."

Kate breathed a heavy sigh of relief. He was just talking about the color of the room. At least, she thought that was what "green" meant. Ever since her car accident, it was pretty safe to assume that any word she didn't understand was the name of a color.

But at least there were no ghosts.

He must have sensed her weariness, because he glanced down at her and asked, "Are you all right?"

"Yeah. You just scared me," she said. "The way you reacted, I thought you'd seen a ghost. Literally."

Michael managed a mild chuckle.

"I'm sorry," he told her, taking her back into his arms.

She savored his embrace for only a moment before she pulled away and looked him in the eye. "What if Peter's right?"

"What?" he asked, her question clearly having caught him off guard.

"What if Sterling did do something to Joanna and he's acting this way because he doesn't want anyone to know? Or maybe he doesn't realize that he did it. I mean, obsession... it can be a scary thing. And he's so aggressive with these attacks. I just... I can't help thinking that there's something we're missing... something that maybe he doesn't want us to know, that maybe he doesn't want to acknowledge himself, and that's why he's acting like he doesn't realize he's dead."

"I don't think that's the case, at least I hope not. He really seemed to believe that he was still alive," Michael replied, but Kate couldn't tell if he really believed that or if he was just trying to make her feel better.

"Did he say that?"

"Not in those words. But he did talk about how no one ever acknowledged him, even when he was standing in front of their eyes. I figure that's kind of the same thing."

"I guess," Kate said, still not entirely convinced. "I wish we were back home. I don't want to be here anymore."

153

"I don't either," Michael said. "At least we only have one more night."

"Thank goodness," Kate murmured as she slipped off her bedroom shoes. Glancing at the clock on her bed-stand, she saw that it was almost four in the morning. Thinking about how little rest they would actually be able to get that night made her even more exhausted than she already felt.

But even after she was nestled safely in Michael's warm arms, she still couldn't relax. Her mind was racing and her nerves were completely shot, and for the life of her, she couldn't figure out why. By all reasoning, these encounters should be nothing compared to storming into an open field to save Michael from a mad woman with a gun, and she'd slept just fine after that -- once she knew that Michael would be all right, that is.

But, a small voice in the back of her mind whispered, *you did have trouble sleeping whenever Trevor was around.*

Was that it, then? Was she really that scared of ghosts? She didn't think she was. She thought she understood that ghosts were simply people, not the monsters or unearthly beings that horror movies portrayed. But if she knew that, really and truly knew that, then why did the presence of a spirit still send unpleasant shivers down her spine? Why was her initial inclination to flee rather than to embrace? Was it because of some innate fear of the unknown? Or perhaps even a fear of death? It sort of made sense. The human body was designed for life, after all, and every instinct and function were geared for self-preservation. Maybe what she called a "fear of ghosts" was actually her body's primal response to the presence of death.

Or maybe you're just scared of ghosts, that rational little voice argued again.

I have no reason to be scared of them, though, she argued back.

You have no reason to be scared of roaches either, and yet you were ready to chop your own foot off after one crawled across your shoe.

Her rational voice made a point (if talking to herself in the middle of the night counted as any sort of rational). She was scared of all kinds of things she knew weren't actually dangerous.

154

So why didn't she lie awake at night trying to justify her fear of them? Or try to convince herself that she wasn't actually afraid?

Beside her, Michael shifted and his arm tightened around her waist. She listened to the sound of his slow, steady breathing and realized that he was already asleep.

Because of him, she realized. Not just him, but because of Trevor and Gavin and Luke... and even because of her own experience.

She, of all people, should understand and want to reach out to these spirits. After all, she knew firsthand how it felt to stand in a room full of people only to have every eye pass through her as though she didn't exist. She'd never wanted to hurt or to alarm any of the people around her. She'd just wanted answers. She was frightened and confused and so alone.

That was probably how most, if not all, spirits felt. If anything, those ghosts should be pitied, not feared. But even as she repeated that to herself in her mind, she still shivered at the thought of an unseen presence wandering silently across the shadows of her room. Although she was fairly certain that she and Michael were alone, she knew that Sterling Hall wasn't far. He would be upset. He would be angry. And he'd more than likely want the truth.

Too bad Brink couldn't see other ghosts. Kate would have had him come and stand guard while she tried to get some sleep.

Hey! You're not scared of Brink, the little rational voice reminded her.

Perhaps it was because she was so exhausted, but she felt an odd sense of triumph. Maybe she *wasn't* scared of ghosts, not all ghosts anyway. Maybe she was only scared of a select few, Sterling Hall being one of them. She had been scared of Trevor also, back before she knew why he was haunting her apartment.

Honestly, though, Trevor had stalked their apartment for months, trashing it, pacing back and forth in the middle of the night, and feeding off of Gavin's energy, draining him of his health. Of course he'd scared her. That kind of supernatural activity would have scared anyone.

But Sterling Hall was worse. Much worse. The way he made her feel during those attacks, it was more than nausea and physical discomfort. There was something emotional about his assault as well, almost like he was trying to inflict onto them the same pain and isolation and loss which he had endured for decades. In her mind, Kate had felt trapped, crushed, and weighed down by something that would never let her escape. She could handle the flu-like symptoms. She'd endured far worse and lived. But that dreadful sense of hopelessness and abandonment, it was pure despair, more miserable than any physical ailment. If that was what Sterling Hall had lived, or perhaps the more appropriate term would be "existed," with for all those years, it was no wonder that he'd allowed himself to believe that he was still alive and well, just waiting for his love to return to him.

Joanna.

For a woman so adored that a man had devoted his heart, his soul, his entire existence to proclaiming his love for her, Kate found it strange how little they actually knew about Joanna Stanton. They knew that she had been the daughter of a fisherman, that she had married Sterling Hall, and that she had died a few years after their wedding. Her story was something of an empty shell. They knew all of the facts, but what had driven Joanna in life? Her love for Sterling? Perhaps painting, or maybe walks down by the river? Had she spent her days inside the manor, relishing the temple that Sterling had constructed for her? Or had she been more of a free spirit, running barefoot through the forest?

Maybe if they knew more about her, they would be able to contact her. Unless, of course, she'd already moved on. But would she have gone on without her husband? It was a possibility. It was a romantic notion, that ghosts might wait around for their spouses or significant others to join them, but Kate knew that wasn't always the case. And part of her didn't think it should be. Although she wished she'd had more time to talk with Trevor, she was glad that he was at peace, and that his love for her hadn't kept him from Heaven or Paradise or whatever was waiting for them on the other side.

Having lost herself in her thoughts, Kate finally felt her body begin to relax. Anxious to embrace sleep, she snuggled closer to Michael, closed her eyes, and breathed him in.

Her movement stirred him slightly, and she heard him whisper, "Kate..."

"Mm-hmm?" she murmured.

"...Love you..."

Kate felt her heart melting.

"I love you, too," she whispered back.

But he was sound asleep. Kate wondered if he'd actually been awake to begin with, or if he'd just spoken her name in his dreams. She smiled, wondering why she'd ever thought she had anything to fear. And finally, just as the sky outside began to glow with the pale shades of early morning, she drifted off to sleep.

CHAPTER TWENTY-ONE

By the next morning, Michael was beginning to suspect that he and Kate were not the only ones ready to return home and leave Stanton Hall Manor once and for all. No one was in a very good mood. Although Kate assured him that no one blamed him, Michael couldn't help but feel like it was all his fault. His fault for seeing ghosts and for being stupid enough to talk to them. His fault for disturbing everyone in the middle of the night. His fault for agreeing to come in the first place.

Only Luke seemed as cheerful and optimistic as ever, and for the first time, it didn't get on Michael's nerves. He was actually grateful for Luke, because as long as someone was happy, there was the slightest chance that the whole awful experience hadn't been for nothing.

"All right troops, here is the plan," Luke announced, not sounding a bit like a person who'd spent half the night provoking a distraught spirit into destroying what remained of the master bedroom. "As you all know, tonight is our last night here - "

"Thank God," Gail muttered.

"- and I would like to make it a special one, especially for our hosts. So, along with one last evening of absolute kick-ass ghost hunting, I'd also like to thank Mrs. Drake and Emily, not only for inviting us into their home, but for granting all of us, well me anyway, the wish of a lifetime by preparing them the best filet mignon they have ever tasted."

"I didn't know you could cook," Kate remarked with a wry grin.

"One of my several not-so hidden talents," Luke gloated. "Then after dinner, we get back to work. I was reviewing some of our footage this morning and we do have some good material, but

Sterling seems to have made a habit of draining our cameras right before the really great stuff happens. So our goal for tonight is to make sure we get some absolutely can-not-believe-it, blow-your-mind, awesome evidence on camera."

"You think we'll be able to do that after last night?" JT asked.

"What happened last night?" Peter asked.

"Well, while all of you lazy loggers were catching up on your much-needed beauty sleep, the rest of us were actually trying to do our jobs, which is to communicate with spirits and find out what makes them tick or go bump in the night or whatever," Luke answered.

"Luke, buddy, I say this with love, but you have had way too much coffee this morning," JT muttered.

"Wrong. Haven't had a drop. Now, we are going to have to take a trip into town for the food, unless someone knows where to get groceries around here, but considering how none of us actually live here, I'm going to guess that's not as likely - oh! Hello, Carolyn."

Michael turned to see their hostess standing in the doorway. She wore a black skirt and blazer, and her graying brown hair was pulled up into a tight bun.

"Good morning. I hope I'm not interrupting," she greeted them.

"Of course you're not. Is there anything we can do for you?" Luke asked.

"No, actually, thank you. I was just hoping I might have a word with Mr. Sinclair." Her tone was conversational enough, but the way she said his name reminded him of how adults addressed children when they wanted to "discuss" something.

Uh-oh, Michael thought as all eyes turned on him.

He didn't think he'd done anything wrong. Maybe she'd seen the damage done to the master bedroom and thought it was his fault. Or what if she'd found out about him spending the night in Kate's room? He could assure her that nothing had happened, but maybe she was really old-fashioned.

He stood up, hoping he didn't look guilty. Not that he really had anything to feel guilty about. Still, he was barely able to meet Kate's eyes as he left the table to join Mrs. Drake in the hallway.

"Have you enjoyed your stay here?" she asked, leading him away from the kitchen and back into the sitting room.

The honest answer to that question was, "No, it's been miserable, I'd rather amputate my own leg than spend one more night in this awful place," but that may have been a little harsh. So instead he answered, "Oh yeah, it's been great. I really love the uh... the decorations." He didn't know if he sounded convincing at all, but he figured it was something Kate might say to be polite. Then again, she was an interior decorator, so it would probably sound a lot more natural coming from her.

Oh well.

"That's good. I thought I heard some commotion last night."

Michael wasn't sure how much Luke wanted him to say, or honestly, how much she really wanted to hear, so he just said, "Nothing out of the ordinary."

It was kind of true.

"Good. Very good," Mrs. Drake said, closing the door to the sitting room. "Now then, so much for small talk. What did you say to my daughter last night?"

She changed the subject so abruptly that Michael wasn't sure he'd heard her correctly.

"I'm sorry?" he asked.

"Emily told me that you spoke to her last night. I want to know exactly what you said."

"Oh. Well, I... Um..." He'd been so caught up in the Sterling Hall fiasco that he had completely forgotten about his encounter with Emily the night before. Now of course, he remembered the meeting, but he had no recollection of what had actually been said. "I don't know. We really didn't talk for that long."

"Well, you must have said something significant. This morning she could barely look me in the eye. It was only after she mentioned your name that I realized you must have said something to her, something about this house or the nightmares that it brings to life in her mind. You need to tell me what you said."

Suddenly, the words exchanged with Emily rang as loud and clear in his memory as though he'd just spoken them.

"Is it true... That you can see them?"

"Yeah, it's true."

"Well, um..." Michael began, certain that Mrs. Drake was about to yell at him. "She asked me a few questions about um... them."

"Your ghosts."

"Yeah."

"And what did you tell her?"

Michael considered a variety of answers before he replied, with a lot more confidence than he felt, "I told her the truth." He was going to get in trouble anyway. He might as well go down swinging. "I told her that yes, I can see them. And that you've got one here in the house. And he's... not happy."

For a moment, Mrs. Drake's face fell completely blank. Michael tried to read her expression, but he couldn't tell if she was angry or relieved or confused, or perhaps somewhere in the middle. When she finally spoke, her voice was hushed and guarded.

"I don't know if you actually believe that, or if you're trying to mock me."

"It's not a matter of belief, Mrs. Drake, and I'm certainly not trying to mock you. But I think your daughter deserves to know the truth. I didn't want to scare her or make things worse, but I've spent my entire life lying to people about what I see and what I hear. It wasn't until this past year, meeting Kate and opening up to her and to Luke, that I've finally found some sense of, well, of freedom. I know what it's like to have people think that I'm crazy and that there's something off about me. But what makes it worse is being told by the people I love that they don't believe me."

Michael had no idea where he'd found the guts to say all that to the woman's face, but he didn't back down. He believed in what he'd said. If Emily was truly as terrified of Sterling Hall as she seemed to be, then she needed to be able to confide in her mother.

To his utter shock (and relief), Mrs. Drake's eyes softened. "You really think that there's something here?"

"I know there is, Ma'am."

"Do you think it's dangerous?"

That was a loaded question. Had Sterling caused them physical discomfort, illness, and injury? Yes. Did Michael think he would intentionally bring harm to Carolyn or her daughter? No.

"Not dangerous in the sense that he would hurt you. But I do think he's unstable, and that he can, and probably will, make life here unpleasant."

Mrs. Drake took a deep breath. Michael realized that she was struggling to fight back tears. "Can you help us?"

Again, Michael didn't know how to answer her.

"I don't know," he replied honestly. "I've tried - we've all tried - to make contact with him, to talk with him, but I'm not sure we've made very much progress." That wasn't altogether true. They had made some progress. He only hoped that they hadn't done more harm than good.

Fortunately, Mrs. Drake seemed to accept that.

"I was only trying to do what was best for her. I was raised not to believe in such nonsense. In our family, ghosts were nothing more than folklore and fairy tales. I thought if I treated my daughter the same way, in a calm and rational manner, then she would never have to be afraid like this. It's the last thing I ever wanted."

"I think she knows that," Michael told her.

Mrs. Drake nodded as she pulled out a handkerchief and dried her eyes. "Well, thank you for saying that. And thank you

162

also for coming. I know I haven't been the warmest of hosts, but I do appreciate your willingness to come up here."

Michael wanted to tell her that he didn't deserve her gratitude, but maybe, if he played his cards right, he could still earn it.

"I'm pretty sure Luke would have never spoken to me again if I'd refused," Michael grinned. On that thought, why *hadn't* he refused?

"He is quite the character, isn't he?" Mrs. Drake asked.

"He's one of a kind," Michael agreed.

Just then, the clock on the wall began to chime.

"Oh dear, already nine," Mrs. Drake sighed. "Time to begin my daily chores. I hope you enjoy your last day here, Mr. Sinclair."

"Thank you," Michael said. Watching her walk away, the image of Marian's lost necklace suddenly flashed across his mind. "Oh, Mrs. Drake?"

"Yes?" She turned back.

"You haven't found an antique garnet necklace around the manor, have you?"

"I haven't. Has your girlfriend lost one?"

"Well, no. It wasn't hers. It was Marian's, the woman who was here last night. She uh, took it into the master bedroom and it just sort of vanished." Even though Carolyn seemed a little more open to the idea of ghosts, Michael wasn't sure she was ready to hear that they suspected one had stolen the necklace right out of their hands.

"Oh. I'm sorry to hear that. I'll be sure to keep an eye out for it. Unfortunately, it wouldn't be the first time something precious has gone missing in this place."

Then, she turned around and marched swiftly out the door.

Michael lingered behind a few moments before he also left the sitting room and made his way back toward the kitchen, following the smell of fresh coffee and scrambled eggs. It was only then that he realized how hungry he felt. Maybe a good breakfast was exactly what he needed.

Hell, it definitely couldn't make things worse –

"*Somebody* didn't make it back to their own bed last night."

- unless of course, he never got to eat it.

Brink appeared, as he often did, completely out of nowhere and fell into step beside his best friend. The young ghost had a broad, cheeky grin plastered across his face. Michael knew he'd come to interrogate him about spending the night with Kate.

"Is there any way I could make you believe that I'd suddenly lost my ability to see you?" Michael asked.

"Dude, I don't think you're hearing me. I saw - "

"Oh no, I'm hearing you perfectly, and I know what you saw, but there is nothing to talk about because it was totally innocent. She was scared and she asked me to stay. That's it."

"Whoa, wait a minute. Back up. What?" Brink asked.

"What?" Michael echoed. Brink was confused? Did that mean...? "Wait, who are you talking about?"

"I'm talking about Gavin and Gail. Who are you talking about?"

"What?!" Michael yelped, much louder than he'd intended. "I mean... Yeah, I'm talking about them too."

"Oh no you weren't. Did you - ?" Brink's face fell. "Oh my GOD."

"No! No, it wasn't like that. We just... ugh," Michael moaned into his hands. "We had a stressful night, okay? I don't know where you were... Well, yeah, I guess I *do* know where you were, but I just... I don't even know how to begin explaining it to you."

"Dude, it's okay. Calm down." Brink stuck his arm out and awkwardly moved it through Michael's collarbone. "If I had real hands, I would be patting you on the shoulder right now."

"Thanks," Michael said.

He may have been offbeat and a little reckless when it came to boundaries, but Brink was a good friend. He always had been.

164

"Are you okay?" Brink asked.

"Yeah, I am," Michael responded honestly. "I'm just ready to go home."

"Me too. Don't get me wrong, this place is great and everything, but I like it when it's just you and me. I'm tired of all these other yahoos thinking that you're *their* best friend."

"I didn't know you got jealous," Michael grinned.

"Well, yeah. I mean, I know that I exude charisma and a devilishly refined sense of fashion, but it's hard to compete with guys who have cool cars and heartbeats..." Brink trailed off.

Michael shrugged. "Heartbeats are overrated."

"You know, I think so, but then again, I haven't had one in like, twenty years."

"And you're totally awesome without one," Michael assured him with a laugh.

"Thank you. Finally, you acknowledge this!" Brink held his hands up in mock victory. "So, you wanna hear more about Gavin and Gail?"

"No." Michael didn't even need to think about it.

"What? Why not?"

"Several reasons. One, I don't want Kate finding out. Two, I don't want Luke finding out. Three, I'm a really terrible liar, and I especially don't want to lie to my girlfriend. And four, we only have one more night in this place and I'd really like this last day here to be as uneventful and peaceful as possible."

"You know everyone is going to find out, don't you?" Brink asked.

Michael didn't answer. His attention had fallen on the stained-glass window near the end of the hall. If he'd glanced up a second later, he'd have missed it: the figure of a man, his outline distorted by the contours and textures of the glass, passing by, unseen and unheard, just outside the window.

CHAPTER TWENTY-TWO

Michael should have just let him go. He knew that. Every rational voice inside his mind scolded him for sprinting out the front door of the manor and following the spirit's footsteps into the forest. But something else, perhaps a flawed and rather egotistical belief that he could still make a difference for the guests and residents of Stanton Hall, kept him moving forward.

He knew that he had no obligation to go after Sterling. In fact, if he was smart, he'd have just pretended he'd never seen the ghost and gone back to the dining hall. He was sure the others were wondering what was taking him so long and he'd probably missed any chance he had of a hot breakfast. Not to mention, they were leaving first thing the next morning. He had no real reason to even attempt to talk to Sterling again.

And yet, he sort of did. He remembered the look in Mrs. Drake's eyes as he confirmed her daughter's fears, and he knew that he had to at least try to help them. The only way to do that, of course, was to help Sterling. Loathe as he was to admit it, perhaps there was a reason he'd been granted his ability, or his gift, or whatever he was supposed to call it. If he had to live with it, at least he could try to do some good.

He followed Sterling down what he realized was a familiar path through the forest and toward the place where he had fallen the day before. He knew where they were headed before they arrived.

Sterling was leading him to his tombstone.

So what did that mean? Had Sterling really known all along? If he knew where he was buried, then surely he knew, at least on some level of consciousness, that he was... well... dead.

166

Unsure of whether or not Sterling knew he was there, Michael kept a fair distance between them as the ghost slowed to a stop in front of his grave. He wasn't close enough to read the expression on Sterling's face, but he could have sworn he detected a sense of relief. Perhaps facing his untimely fate had been what he had needed all along.

Michael could only hope.

He'd just made the decision not to disturb Sterling and head back up to the manor when the ghost called out, "So it's true, then."

His eyes drifted up to where Michael stood half-hidden by a tree. Michael immediately felt ashamed and a little cowardly for hiding, but he really didn't know what he was doing, following Sterling out there.

Almost as if Sterling had read his thoughts, he continued, "It's all right. I knew you were following me. Impossible not to notice with your clumsy footsteps shuffling through the leaves."

Well, so much for stealth.

"Are you all right?" Michael asked, taking a few hesitant steps toward him.

"I'm dead," Sterling answered shortly.

"I know how hard that must be for you -"

"No. I don't think you do. How could you? How could any of you know?" Sterling demanded. "What once was my life, my existence, my love, my memories, all of that lies buried in a filthy, forsaken tomb. I am nothing. I have nothing."

"You have Joanna," Michael reminded him.

At the sound of her name, Sterling's eyes widened, and his forlorn expression evolved into one of hope and redemption.

"You've seen her?" he asked.

The look on his face tore at Michael's conscience. He hadn't considered that by mentioning Joanna, he may have inadvertently been making false promises to a man stricken - no, *crippled* - by grief. He should have known by now that Joanna was Sterling's life, his everything, his one vulnerability. To use her against him, to give him hope for her where there was little, was simply cruel.

"Well, no..." Michael could hear the shame in his own voice. "But she is out there *somewhere*. If not here, then she's waiting for you."

"Where?" Sterling demanded.

Where? That was a good question. Michael only wished he knew the answer.

"Wherever's next," he finally said.

"You believe that? You believe that there's more than this?"

"I've spent my entire life surrounded by ghosts. I think I kind of have to believe it."

"But you believe in a world beyond this one. In a Heaven or Paradise where all souls will be reunited after death?"

For a guy who'd been too distraught to notice a little thing like being dead for a hundred and fifty years, he asked surprisingly deep and complicated questions.

"I can't say for sure what I think is out there." Michael tried to choose his words carefully. "I've never seen it, and I've never met anyone who has. I've read accounts of people who say they have, and it sounds wonderful. But I don't really know."

"How do you get there if you don't even know where or what it is?"

"You'd have to ask someone who's already there. But from what I've seen and experienced, the reason people stay behind even after they've died is because there's still something holding them here. A secret they never shared, an unspoken injustice, a lost love, or maybe they just weren't prepared for death. I can think of a hundred reasons why a spirit might still be bound to this world, but there's no way to know for sure. I've met people who chose to stay behind, and I've met people who didn't know why they were still here. People tend to think that death is absolute, the one thing we can all be certain about, but that's not the case. Death is complex. It's powerful and timeless. The truth is when it comes to death, nothing is impossible."

Sterling stood for a long while, staring down at his grave and absorbing everything Michael had just said. He hoped he hadn't gone too far or given Sterling the impression that he was an expert on the afterlife. After all, what did he really know about death? When all was said and done, he wasn't anything special. Anyone could communicate with another person. The only difference was he talked to people whose bodies were no longer functioning. But all things considered, it was pretty much the same thing.

After a long silence, Sterling finally spoke. "She's not there."

"I'm sorry?" Michael asked.

"Joanna. She hasn't moved on."

"How do you know?"

"Because she wouldn't!" Sterling exclaimed, startling Michael by his outburst. "Because she loves me and she wouldn't leave me behind. She wouldn't do that to me."

"Okay, I believe you." Michael held up both hands, hoping to soothe Sterling and to remind him that he wasn't a threat. "Tell me about her, Sterling."

"Why?" the ghost demanded.

The real reason Michael had asked was because he thought it might distract Sterling from his foul mood. He knew it worked for him. Just the thought of Kate could make him smile, even on the most dreadful of days. He wasn't sure that would be enough for Sterling, however, so he said, in the sincerest tone he could muster, "I want to know what she was like. From what I've heard, she sounds incredible."

Sterling's expression softened, and for a moment, Michael thought he might actually smile.

"She's more than incredible," Sterling said. "Joanna Elizabeth Stanton is the most glorious, the most radiant, the most magnificent creature to ever walk this Earth. Her hair is the color of ebony velvet and her eyes, bluer than the deepest ocean. When she smiles, the light of every star in the sky begins to fade, because they consider it a crime to outshine her."

169

Okay, that was very romantic, and a little sickeningly poetic, but that hadn't been what Michael had been hoping to hear. He'd thought that if he knew a little bit more about Joanna's personality, her interests and hobbies, then maybe he could find her, bring her to Sterling, and have the two of them move on together. Unfortunately, he wasn't very optimistic. Despite Sterling's insistence that Joanna wouldn't have left him behind, Michael couldn't shake the feeling that that was exactly what had happened.

So what then? If it turned out he was right and Joanna had gone on to the next world, where did that leave Sterling? Would he ever be able to move on? Perhaps his love for Joanna and his desire to see her again would be enough to motivate him to cross over.

"When you see her, you'll know," Sterling continued. "You'll know why I love her."

"I'm sure I will," Michael conceded.

"This is our favorite place, you know," Sterling smiled fondly. "Here, beneath these trees. Her father was a fishmonger, and she always feared for his safety out on the open ocean. She often said she couldn't bear to even look at the waves, so she turned to the forest. It made her feel protected. It was in this very spot that we shared our first kiss. It was also the spot where I took her hand and asked her to be my wife."

So that explained why Sterling had also chosen it as his final resting place. It was the one place in the world, perhaps besides the house itself, that he felt closest to his beloved Joanna. It also explained why he had been there the day before. He hadn't been spying on Michael and Kate after all. He'd been there for his love. That was something Michael should have realized long before, that Sterling's complete and utter adoration for Joanna moved and motivated him. It was the driving force behind his every thought and every action. It was honorable and romantic, but in Michael's mind, it was also a little sad.

He loved Kate, and he knew his world would come shattering down on him if anything were to ever happen to her, but he also had an identity outside of his love for her, and he knew that she was the same way. That was the way he preferred it to be. He wouldn't want Kate to be so consumed by her love for him that she no longer found value in anything else. He wanted her to live a rich life, full of love and laughter and memories of all kinds of people and places. He wanted to be the one she loved, but he never, not for one moment, wanted to be her everything. Wherever Joanna was, he couldn't imagine she'd wanted it for Sterling either.

As though he had read Michael's mind, Sterling asked, "The young lady who was here with you yesterday, is she your wife?"

"No," Michael replied.

"But you love her."

"With all my heart," Michael confirmed.

"Then you understand the lengths to which I would go to be reunited with Joanna."

"Of course I do. I completely empathize. But Sterling, I need to ask you a question, and I don't want you to get upset, but what if..." Michael chose his next words very carefully and hoped that what he was about to say wouldn't come back to haunt him. Literally. "What if you don't find her?"

The look on Sterling's face made Michael want to take his words back immediately. He couldn't tell if Sterling was more hurt that Michael would suggest such a thing or outraged that he would even think it.

"You don't know my Joanna. She would never leave me. She loves me."

"I know she loves you. But I don't think you get to decide whether you stay or go. If you're here, it means that something is keeping you here. If she's not... it only means she was ready. It doesn't mean that she didn't care for you or want to be with you." He could tell by the look on Sterling's face that he still wasn't convinced. "Listen, I know this is hard for you, but it might do you good to at least consider -"

"She's waiting for me. I know she is," Sterling insisted.

"You're right. She is waiting for you. But she might not be waiting here." Michael anticipated Sterling's wrath, a rebuttal, anything that might contradict what he was trying to say, but it never came. Instead, Sterling turned his gaze down at his tombstone once again, his eyes lost and vacant. "Sterling, I want you to know that I am trying to help you. So are Luke and the crew, even though I know that we don't always seem like it. I wish that I had more answers for you. If I could, I would find Joanna for you and bring her back. Any of us would."

"Just like your Kate?" Sterling said. Michael wasn't sure he understood what he was asking. "If she was lost, you would do everything within your power to bring her back?"

"I'd do more," Michael assured him.

Sterling looked him in the eye. He seemed... proud. Almost like a guide or a mentor whose pupil had just answered a trick question correctly.

"Good."

And without another word, Sterling Hall vanished, leaving Michael standing alone and confused at the foot of his grave.

CHAPTER TWENTY-THREE

After having been absent for what seemed like hours, but in fact had only been about thirty minutes, Michael finally returned to the dining hall, looking pensive, but thankfully no worse for the wear.

"Hey, there he is," Luke announced loudly as Michael took a seat next to Kate. She'd covered his plate with a paper towel, hoping to keep his food warm, but she wasn't sure how much good it had done. "Glad you're back, buddy. Any longer and we would have sent out a search party."

"Is everything okay?" Kate asked him.

"Yeah," he replied a little too hastily.

No one else seemed to pick up on it, but Kate knew Michael well enough to know when he wasn't telling the whole truth. However, she also knew that if he wasn't telling her, it was because he didn't want to say it in front of the entire group.

In an attempt to help take his mind off of whatever was troubling him, Kate smiled at him and said, "So guess what?"

"What?" Michael asked once he'd swallowed his mouthful of toast.

"Luke says that he doesn't need us for filming this afternoon. I was thinking, you know, if you want to, maybe we could do some sight-seeing or go to the beach. I hear the area around Cape Porpoise is amazing. There are lobster traps everywhere and boats and I think there's a lighthouse somewhere. What do you think?"

Michael didn't have to think about it. "That sounds perfect."

An hour later, Michael and Kate were enjoying the sights and sounds of Goose Rocks Beach. It was a beautiful day: sunny and cool, but not chilly enough to deter a few dedicated beach-goers. The beach itself was lovely, with sand as pure and soft as any Kate had ever seen, bright sparkling waves that reflected the color of the vibrant sky, and small patches of beach grass here and there.

"One day, I'm going to live at the beach," she told Michael. "Or at least have a really nice beach house that I can visit whenever I want."

"I think I could live with that," Michael grinned. "Where would you want it?"

"I think the Gulf Shores."

"Not here?"

Kate shook her head. "Don't get me wrong, this place is beautiful. But I like the south. It's warmer there."

"That's very true," Michael acknowledged and wrapped an arm around her shoulders. "So, you really didn't want to spend the last day with the crew?"

"No. I wanted to spend it with you."

"But you didn't want to see what goes on behind the scenes when they're just out filming?"

"No offense to the guys, but I think I've gotten enough behind the scenes action to last me a lifetime. Parts of it have been fun, but I think after this experience, I'm just going to enjoy *Cemetery Tours* as it's meant to be enjoyed."

"And how's that?"

"From my television screen," she quipped. "No, I would much rather spend my last day here enjoying the beach or exploring the village or watching a bunch of men on boats catch lobsters."

"Boats and lobsters, huh?" Michael grinned.

"I've never told you this, but I am a big, geeky tourist at heart. Even when I was little and my parents would take Gav and me places, I was always the one carrying around the disposable

174

cameras or dragging them in to see the world's biggest toothpick or whatever other bizarre attraction happened to pop up."

"You like to experience things."

"I do," Kate said. "That's part of what makes the whole losing two years of memories thing so frustrating. But I'm excited to make new ones."

Then, she whirled around, threw her arms around his neck, and kissed him swiftly as a salty gust of sea wind toyed mercilessly with her hair, sending it flying in all different directions.

Of all the days to forget a hair-tie.

Fortunately, Michael still smiled at her in a way that made her feel like the most beautiful girl in the world. Just for that smile, she kissed him again.

"Finally, this trip is beginning to seem worth it," Michael remarked with a wry grin.

"Tell me about it," Kate agreed as they took each other's hand and resumed their walk along the shore. "So what happened this morning? I know you went to talk with Mrs. Drake, but I could tell you had something on your mind afterward."

"Well, to be honest, I really didn't spend a whole lot of time talking with Mrs. Drake." He proceeded to tell her about his talk with Sterling down by the gravesite. It sounded like it had been a surprisingly amicable and constructive conversation.

"So, do you think you got through to him?" Kate asked once he'd told her everything.

"I think so," he replied, but there wasn't a lot of confidence in his tone.

"You sound hesitant."

"The thing is, near the end, he almost seemed to take it *too* well. I had to talk in circles trying to convince him that moving on wasn't the same thing as abandonment. He got so upset every time I even hinted that Joanna might not be here anymore. And then, just like that, he seemed to accept it."

"It must have been something you said right at the end."

"The only thing I said then that I didn't say before was that I knew what it was like to love someone." He looked down at her with his big, dark eyes and she felt herself begin to blush.

"Maybe that's what did it," she told him. "You empathized with him. You let him know that he's not alone. Maybe connecting with him on that level finally convinced him that he could trust you."

"I hope so. Except..."

"Except what?"

"Well, if he's accepted it, then there's a good chance he's moved on."

"And what's so bad about that?"

"If he doesn't show up, Luke doesn't get his investigation, and then he'll be complaining about it the entire way home," he griped playfully.

Kate cast him a sidelong glance. He looked back, a cheeky grin on his handsome face. Kate tried to maintain a straight face, but he was too cute.

"You're never going to give poor Luke a break, are you?" she asked.

"You think I'm joking, but I'm telling you, we'll never hear the end of it!"

Kate just laughed.

They spent the remainder of their day exploring the small coastal village of Cape Porpoise. First, they stopped for lunch at a local bar and grill called The Ramp. They ate outside in the small patio, set right on the shoreline. It was decorated with strands of big, colorful light bulbs and surrounded by driftwood piers and oars and paddles of all colors and sizes. Kate decided that it was easily one of her top five favorite restaurants.

After lunch, they took a walking tour of the area, which resulted in a recommendation that they visit Goat Island Lighthouse. The lighthouse, it turned out, wasn't accessible by land, so they decided to rent a couple of kayaks and paddle out to see it.

It was a small lighthouse, no bigger than two stories or so, but it was quaint and beautiful, and it reminded Kate of stories she'd read growing up about mermaids and pirates and ships lost at sea. She wished she could have seen it at night when it was all lit up, but she knew they'd be back at that dreadful mansion by then.

Maybe it won't be so bad, she told herself. *Be positive. You are having one of the best days of your life and you're going to ruin it if you start to dwell on the house and things you can't control.*

Having decided to stay optimistic, Kate called back to Michael, whose feeble kayaking skills had left him trailing a few meters behind her, "Isn't this great?"

"My arms are about to fall off!" he yelled back.

Kate tried not to laugh, but it was difficult. Out there on the water, with the wind in her hair and a breathtakingly beautiful sky above her, she felt happier and more alive than she'd felt... well, since waking up from the accident, if she was being honest. She'd felt joy and love and laughter, especially in the days since she'd met Michael, but something about that moment there on the waves of Cape Porpoise, she felt what she'd always craved above everything else, and that was freedom.

Finally, she felt as though she'd really moved on from what had passed and as a result, she felt confident enough to fully embrace the future. It was a lot to get out of one short kayak expedition, but if there was one thing she'd learned in the last year, it was that life didn't like to teach lessons directly. It preferred to throw you an experience and let you learn for yourself.

By the time they made it back to the mainland, Kate was wiped out and already hungry again, but every moment had been worth it. Michael tried to complain about how much his arms hurt, but Kate could tell by the suppressed smile on his face that he'd had just as much fun as she had.

Eager for food, a shower, and comfortable clothes, Kate suggested heading back to the mansion. She wasn't eager to return to the eerie feelings or the haunted hallways, but Michael's revelation earlier had left her feeling hopeful. Maybe, just maybe, Stanton Hall Manor had finally been fumigated. Or perhaps the more appropriate word was *exorcised*.

"So, what do you think our chances are of Luke having that fancy dinner ready by the time we get back?" she asked Michael.

"I'd say even worse than the chances of Luke even being there when we get back."

"Darn it."

Sure enough, Michael was right. They were the first ones back. Too hungry to wait for the crew, Kate grabbed a snack out of her secret stash for her and Michael before each of them returned to their respective rooms, Michael for a nap, and Kate for a shower.

When Luke and the crew returned about an hour later, Kate emerged from her bedroom, clean and dressed in the nicest outfit she'd brought: slacks, a low-neck sweater, and pearls. As tempted as she'd been to wear sweat pants and a comfortable T-shirt, she wanted to look pretty for their last night and the thank-you dinner for Mrs. Drake and Emily.

However, no one at all (except for Michael) even noticed the extra effort she'd put into her appearance. Everyone, even Luke, seemed agitated and on edge. Gavin came in last, hauling a case of what was probably really expensive equipment, which he promptly dropped.

"Hey, how was the -"

"Not now, Kate," Gavin snapped as he stormed past her. Gail followed shortly behind. Moments later, Kate heard two separate doors slam.

Kate felt her temper flare. She thought about marching after her brother, smacking him upside the head, and demanding to know what the hell his problem was, but Michael's voice brought her back to what remained of her feeble senses.

"What was that all about?" he asked.

"Don't ask," Peter murmured, grabbing the case that Gavin had dropped.

"No, I'm going to ask," Kate told him. "If my brother is acting like a brat, then I want to know about it."

"He's not being a brat, it's just..."

"What?" Kate asked. "It has something to do with Gail, doesn't it?"

Peter sighed. Getting involved in his coworkers' tiff was clearly the last thing he wanted to do, but maybe he figured that it would be better coming from him than someone more emotionally involved because he explained, "Look, Gail's a good person, but whenever she finds a new guy, she likes to flaunt it. And knowing that she's not supposed to be with your brother made it even more fun for her."

"Oh, no..."

"I don't even remember how it all started, but Gail ended up telling everyone about last night, which made Gavin angry and-"

"Whoa, whoa, wait. Back up. What happened last night?" Kate asked.

"Um..." Peter trailed off, but Kate knew exactly what he was trying to tell her.

"Oh *great*. That's just *perfect*," she growled. Of course this would happen. She'd been having what was turning out to be one of the best days of her life and her stupid brother had to go and ruin it. That settled it. She was never bringing him to anything that was supposed to be fun ever again. Turning swiftly to Michael, she said, "You know, maybe you should have just let Trevor drain the life out of him."

"So why is Gail upset?" Michael asked.

"Where do I even begin? First, she was upset that Gavin was upset. I guess she thought he would want to brag about it, but he apparently thought it was something special just between them and he wanted to keep it private. Then Luke lost his temper and yelled at her and she started yelling back, so JT and I just sort

179

of went off and did some filming while they all screamed at each other. Finally, Luke got sick of it and made them go after us while he went to the supermarket and... The rest is history."

Well, at least the home-cooked meal was still on. Not that it would be all that enjoyable if tensions were still running high. Hoping to make amends for her brother, Kate slipped into the kitchen, where Luke was chopping up vegetables.

"Hey," she said.

Her voice startled him, and she realized that, for the first time in their friendship, she'd caught him off guard.

"Hey Beautiful," he smiled. "Boy, you got some sun. Did you and Mikey have fun today?"

"Yeah, we did. But I'm sorry to hear that you didn't."

"Yeah well, that's show biz for you. You never know when someone is going to go completely off their rocker."

"Actually, I think that's any biz," Kate remarked.

Luke grinned. "You're probably right."

Kate was relieved that he didn't sound too angry. At least, not with her. "Listen, I just wanted to apologize. I've been trying to get it through Gavin's head all week that Gail is off limits but he's a stubborn jackass and he does want he wants."

"Kate, you don't have to apologize. I do not blame you in the slightest."

"I know, but he's my brother and I -"

"Nope. I am going to stop you right there. You are not allowed to apologize to me. You are, however, more than allowed to give me a hand chopping up these carrots," he offered with a broad smile, clearly hoping she'd take the bait.

"Just as long as you don't Tweet about it. I don't want the world suddenly thinking I can cook."

"Why not?"

"Because then people would actually expect me to cook."

Luke chuckled. "Fair enough."

180

CHAPTER TWENTY-FOUR

Dinner that night was excruciating.

Well, not dinner itself. The food was great. In fact, Luke hadn't been exaggerating when he'd said he could prepare the best filet mignon any of them had ever tasted. Not that Michael would ever admit that he thought so. After all, how hard could it really be to prepare a filet mignon?

No, the excruciating part was the horrible tension that hovered over the entire table. Gavin, Gail, and Luke were all still clearly ticked at each other. The rest of them, JT and Peter who'd witnessed the whole event and Kate and Michael who hadn't been there but still knew what had happened, were left in the awkward position of being forced to pretend everything was fine despite knowing that that wasn't true at all.

Carolyn and Emily seemed to enjoy themselves though, and that was really all that mattered.

"You really didn't have to do this, Luke," Carolyn said.

"It was my pleasure, Carolyn," he assured her. Even though he was clearly still upset with Gavin and Gail, Luke was trying his best to act his normal loud and cheerful self. "Are you enjoying it, Emily?"

"Yes. Thank you," the teen replied politely. Then, she stole a quick glance up at Michael. He couldn't be sure if she was trying to communicate with him or if she was still wary of his presence. Maybe she knew that her mother had confronted him earlier that morning. It seemed like ages ago.

"It's a shame we didn't get to spend much time with you," Luke continued.

"That's all right. You're busy," Emily told him.

"That's a pretty lousy excuse on our part. Tell you what. We're doing one final investigation tonight to see if we can get in touch with Sterling Hall. You could join us if you want. Be on a TV show. Make all your friends jealous."

Emily's eyes widened, as though she'd never dreamed such an exciting thing could happen to her. But the more Michael observed her face, the more he realized that the look on her face was one of genuine terror.

"Oh, no!" she exclaimed. "I mean, no. No, thank you."

"Are you sure? We'd be happy to have you."

"*Luke,*" Gail hissed.

"What?" he snapped.

"She doesn't want to, okay? Just drop it."

Luke looked like he wanted to strike back with a bitter comment, probably pertaining to what had happened earlier that afternoon, but he kept his mouth shut. Again, the table descended into an uncomfortable silence.

Their agenda after dinner played out very much like their first night at the manor. Kate, Michael, and JT all tended to the dirty dishes in the kitchen while the rest of the crew set up for their final night of filming.

"So do you think we'll actually make it through the night without any of them tearing at each other's throats?" Kate asked as she dried the dishes that Michael and JT scrubbed.

"Hard to say," JT replied.

"You seem pretty unfazed by all the drama," Kate observed.

JT gave a mirthless chuckle. "I've been hanging around with them for years. Trust me, this isn't the first time I've seen something like this."

"So, this isn't Gavin's fault?"

"Oh, no. It's just what happens when people with big personalities are around each other for prolonged periods of time. Occasionally, they clash."

"Does Luke have a thing for her?" Kate asked outright.

Michael wished he could have said that he'd never cared to know anything less in his life, but the sad truth was he was really curious. He hoped his face didn't project any signs of interest whatsoever while he waited for JT's answer.

"No," JT said, but he sounded unsure.

"Really? It sure seems like he does," Kate said.

"Trust me, it's not like that with them. Luke is just a huge perfectionist when it comes to this job and Gail... she can be a bit of a loose cannon."

"You don't say," Kate scoffed.

"I mean that in the most complimentary of ways, of course. She's a great addition to the team. She's passionate, she's a hard worker, but she's also a free spirit who doesn't like being told what to do. And Luke loves telling people what to do."

"You don't say," Michael echoed Kate with the same sarcastic bite. Kate snickered.

Luke must have felt his ears burning or something, because moments later, he appeared and announced that they were ready to begin filming. This time, however, instead of sitting in a room and waiting for the ghost to come to them, they were going to turn out every light in the mansion and search for him.

"Why do we have to turn the lights out?" Michael asked. That was something he'd never understood about those ghost shows. Did they honestly believe they were more likely to find Sterling in the dark? The ghosts that found him never seemed to care what time of day it was or if it was dark or light, rain or shine.

Of course, he expected Luke to go into some longwinded speech about how lighting affects the visibility of the spirit's ectoplasm or that the magical veil between portals is thinnest between the hours of midnight and 3 AM. But to his surprise, all Luke said was, "For effect."

Oh. Well, for a ghost show trying to get ratings, he guessed that made sense too. Unfortunately, if the first few hours of exploring the dark and empty manor were any indication, the ratings for that particular episode weren't exactly going to soar.

183

Michael realized, as Luke led them through the upstairs hallway for what must have been the dozenth time, that while he'd told Kate all about his earlier conversation with Sterling, he'd never mentioned it to Luke or the crew. He'd intended to, but with all the hurt feelings and relationship drama that had gone down, he'd forgotten to bring it up. Now that he thought about it, he really wasn't sure they were actually going to find anything.

"Come on, Sterling. I know you can hear me right now. Please, just do something. Slam a door, talk to us, anything," Luke begged.

Listening to his friend pleading with a ghost that might not even be there anymore tugged at Michael's conscience. He should have told him about his encounter down at the gravesite as soon as it had happened. But he hadn't been thinking, and now he'd let all of them go on this wild goose chase for a ghost that he may have very well encouraged to move on.

But then, if he had moved on, why was he still apprehensive about what they might find in that manor? They hadn't encountered any spirits yet, but Michael still felt off, like something was waiting to happen.

It's the setting, he told himself. It was late at night, dark as all hell, and he was tired and not thinking straight.

"It doesn't make sense. It just doesn't make sense," Luke began muttering. "Mikey, are you sure you haven't seen or heard anything?"

"There's nothing," Michael told him honestly. "And you know, now that I think about it, there might be a reason for that."

"What are you talking about?" Gail asked, sounding listless.

"I saw Sterling this morning, down by his tombstone." Michael briefly recounted their talk for the second time that day.

"Wait a minute, what are you trying to say?" Luke demanded. "Are you saying that you think he might have crossed over?"

"I don't know," Michael admitted. He hadn't actually seen Sterling move on to the other side, but that didn't mean that it hadn't happened in his absence. In fact, he'd only seen a ghost cross over once before, three months earlier in his hospital room. Trevor had come to thank him before disappearing into a flash of golden light.

"Maybe."

"You've known that this entire time and you didn't say anything?" Luke asked. "Geez, Mikey. Look, I know we've had a rough couple of days, but you could have told us that before we wasted hours of our time and film for nothing!"

"Luke, calm down," Gail told him.

"Gail, just stop it. I do not need you telling me what to do."

"Why not? You tell us what to do all the time!"

"Gail," JT spoke softly. "Not now."

"JT's right," Peter said. "There may be a time and a place for this confrontation, but it's not here. Now we've all had a long couple of days. It seems pretty obvious that we're not going to get anything tonight. We have plenty of good footage to work with. I suggest we all take a deep breath, bid each other a goodnight, and go to bed. Besides, our flight leaves tomorrow at eleven and I don't know about all of you, but I still have packing to do."

Almost everyone murmured their agreement.

"So, that's it then? We're done?" Luke asked.

"We do have some good stuff to work with, Luke," JT said.

"But we missed out on all the *great* stuff because our equipment was always going haywire," Luke argued.

"Well, that's a risk we take in this business. We still got plenty of evidence, more than enough to fill forty-two minutes of screen time," JT reminded him.

The long silence that followed told Michael that Luke still wasn't convinced, but he finally relented.

"All right fine," he sighed. "That's it. Goodnight, everyone."

And without waiting for anyone to reciprocate, Luke brushed past them all and disappeared into the darkness. The rest of them followed silently, bidding each other awkward and stiff goodnights as one by one, they broke off and headed to their rooms. By the time they'd reached the Storybook Room, only Michael, Kate, and Gavin remained.

"Well, goodnight," Gavin muttered gruffly without looking either of them in the eye.

"Hey," Kate said, grabbing her brother's arm. "Are you okay?"

"Yeah, I'm fine," he told her. "I'm just ready to get the hell out of here."

"Okay, I just wanted to make sure that -" But before she could finish, Gavin had slammed the door in her face. "... that you weren't hurt... Right. Okay then."

Michael was considering barging into Gavin's room and forcing him to apologize (how, he wasn't sure, considering that Gavin could probably beat him up if he really wanted to), when he felt Kate's cool hand slip into his. Her touch calmed him immediately.

"Come on," she said.

He followed her unquestioningly to her room. Once again, they sought solace in each other's arms. Michael thought he'd be asleep in seconds, but suddenly, his mind was wide awake.

"Are *you* okay?" Kate asked, as though she'd read his thoughts.

"Yeah," he replied half-heartedly.

"You just seem really quiet tonight."

"I feel like an idiot," he confessed.

"How come?" she asked, propping herself up to look down at him. Michael almost didn't answer her. He'd become distracted by the way the pale moonlight illuminated her hair. She was beautiful, ethereal, and in that glow, she should have reminded him of an angel. But to his horror, he realized that she didn't.

She reminded him of a ghost.

"Um..." he mumbled. He'd forgotten the question. "What? I'm sorry. I'm... I'm really tired."

"That's all right," Kate leaned down and kissed him gently. Then, she rested her head back down on his chest and wrapped her arms around him. "God, what is it about this place?"

"What do you mean?"

"Don't you feel it? It gets inside your head. It messes with everything and it's making everybody miserable," she said. "I'm just glad that this time tomorrow, we'll be home."

Thank God. Michael thought.

"Sorry that Luke didn't get his evidence," he heard himself mutter.

What the heck? Where did that come from?

"Don't be. Like Peter said, they've got plenty to work with."

"But I could have told him about Sterling."

"So could I, but I sort of forgot, to be honest," she told him. "Besides, I don't know that it would have made much difference even if we had said something. He was so hell-bent on getting that footage that he probably would have ignored us and gone on filming anyway." Then, he felt Kate kiss his neck. The touch of her lips made him shiver. Did she not know the effect that she had on him? She didn't seem to, because she continued, nonchalantly, "Don't worry about it. Before you know it, Luke will be back to his old self, talking about how this was the greatest investigation ever."

To his utter shock, he found himself hoping that she was right. He must have drifted off then, because the next thing he knew, he was opening his eyes to the soft glow of morning light drifting through the green, purple, and gold curtains of the Emerald Room.

His head still thick and heavy with sleep, he closed his eyes and tried not to wonder what had woken him, when a cool draft compelled him to pull the comforter up to his chin. It was only then that he realized how empty the queen-sized bed felt.

He opened his eyes again and looked around the elegant yet empty room.

Kate was gone.

CHAPTER TWENTY-FIVE

At first, he didn't think anything of it. Kate probably just got up to get a drink of water, or maybe to stretch her legs. Maybe she wasn't feeling well and was down in Gavin's room asking if he had any Advil. Or maybe someone had called her because of an emergency back home and she'd stepped out of the room so that she wouldn't wake him. There were multiple scenarios, each as plausible as the next. But as the minutes ticked by and she still didn't return, he began to worry.

It's this place, he told himself. *It gets inside your head. She said that just last night. You're just being paranoid. She's okay. She has to be okay.*

Still, he figured it was probably best to find her, just to make sure.

There was no sign of her in the hallway, the master bedroom, or the sitting room. He didn't want to panic, because panicking would mean acknowledging that something was very, *very* wrong, and that was something he did not want to do.

He was overreacting. He simply had to be.

Kate could very well have woken up early, decided she couldn't fall back asleep, and gone into the kitchen for coffee. He didn't smell coffee, but it was better than considering certain other alternatives.

His fleeting attempt at optimism proved in vain, however. There was no sign that she'd ever been in the kitchen or the dining hall.

Desperate, and unsure of what else to do, Michael sprinted back into the entry hall, the one spot in the manor that connected all the other halls and rooms and staircases and parlors. Standing beneath the extravagant and sparkling crystal chandelier, Michael called out, "Brink. Brink!"

His friend appeared immediately.

"Wow, you're up early."

"Have you seen Kate?" he asked, ignoring his friend's remark.

"What?"

"I can't find her. I woke up and she was gone. I have no idea where she went."

"Okay, buddy, calm down. Take a deep breath. She probably just had to use the bathroom or something."

"She didn't. The one in our room is empty. I'm telling you, Brink, I've checked everywhere."

"Are you sure? It's a big mansion. To be honest, you guys haven't even seen most of it. Granted, a lot of parts are under renovation, but there's still a lot up there. There's the old piano room and the library, and there's this room at the very top of the stairs with the -"

"Brink!" Michael snapped. His friend looked startled. "I'm sorry, I'm sorry, but this isn't helping."

"You don't know that. Kate's a pretty adventurous girl. Maybe she wanted to get one last look at the house before we leave in a few hours."

"No. No, I really don't think she would do that. This house scares her. She wouldn't have just gone wandering off on her own."

Brink sighed. "I don't know what else to tell you, brother. I mean, it's not like she could have just vanished into thin air."

The problem was Michael was beginning to dread that that was exactly what had happened. How or why, he couldn't say. All he knew was that Kate was gone and he didn't have a clue where she might be or why she might have left.

"But what if she did?" he asked meekly.

"Michael. Come on, you know that didn't happen. I know that you're pretty open-minded about this kind of stuff, as you should be, but people - living, breathing people - do not just

189

disappear," Brink insisted. "Listen. I am going to search the entire house. It won't take me that long; I can walk through walls. In the meantime, you go look and see if she's outside. I'll come get you if I find her."

"Okay," Michael agreed, relieved and grateful that he could rely on his best friend to be calm and cool during a crisis. He hadn't forgotten that it had been Brink who'd gone to alert Kate when he'd been abducted. If not for Brink, then Kate and Luke would never have found him in time. If not for Brink, he might very well be a ghost himself. He owed Brink a great debt that he would never be able to repay.

Of course, at the end of the day, Brink was just happy to have a friend.

As soon as Brink disappeared, Michael darted outside, not bothering with shoes or a jacket. The early morning air was still cool and damp, but Michael barely noticed as he ran around the side of the house to the hill overlooking the forest. Still no sign of her.

There was, he realized, one place he still hadn't checked, and it was the place that he'd been deliberately avoiding. Not because he was afraid he wouldn't find her there, but because he was afraid that he would.

Anxiously, he dashed through the woods, cold, dry leaves crackling beneath his bare feet. His heart pounded in anticipation of what he might find at Sterling's grave, but when he finally arrived, he found... nothing. The headstone stood alone and untouched as last he'd seen it. He was relieved that he hadn't found her there, but at the same time, he was totally lost. If she wasn't there...

Stop it. Just stop it, Michael. She's here somewhere. She has to be.

He could try calling her. He hadn't even thought to check to see if her cell phone was still in the room. If she had gone off exploring, then she may have taken it with her to take more pictures to send to Val.

190

Yes! Yes, that had to be it! She'd been so taken by all the fantastic rooms and windows and decorations. She just wanted to take a few more pictures before their flight left. It was so obvious Michael didn't know why he hadn't realized it sooner!

His hopes were so high that as he practically flew back up the hill, he almost didn't notice the figure waiting for him at the top.

"Michael!" Brink called down to him. "I found her!"

"Oh, thank God. Where is -"

But before the words were out of his mouth, Brink broke into a sprint that Michael wasn't sure he'd be able to match.

Running as fast as he could, he followed his friend around to the side of the manor, until, all of a sudden, Brink stopped. Michael looked frantically around, but Kate was still nowhere to be seen.

"Where is she? I don't see her!"

"Not here. There!" Brink pointed upward.

Michael's heart stammered to a stop. There, in the open window of one of the many towers, a figure stood, dressed in a white, billowy nightdress. Her arms were extended across the length of the window, her hands pressing against the aged and splintered shutters.

"Kate!" Michael shouted. "KATE!"

She didn't respond. Michael didn't even think she looked down. What was wrong with her? What was she doing?

"Come on!" Brink beckoned him.

Without a second thought, Michael followed his friend back into the manor and up the grand staircase.

"What is she doing up there?" Michael panted as Brink led him through the derelict halls of the upper floors. "Is she all right?"

"I don't know, man. As soon as I found her, I came to get you. I mean, it's not like she could have heard me if I'd tried to say anything to her." It was true. "You know, that window does face east. Maybe she wanted to get a picture of the sunrise."

That may have been it, but somehow, Michael doubted it.

191

Racing through the dust and decayed fragments that had piled up over years of neglect, they finally reached what may have at one point been a beautiful mahogany door but now just seemed like rotten red wood on a hinge.

"This is it! Come on!" Brink said before he disappeared right through the door.

Michael yanked the door open so hard that a cloud of dust and splinters rained down on him, irritating his eyes and his throat. He coughed and sputtered, but nevertheless raced up the rickety, enclosed stairwell and into what appeared to be an attic.

At first glance, Michael thought they had the wrong tower. The room was a cluttered wreck of old tables, maps, books, a globe, a spyglass, a full-length mirror, and several bookshelves, all ancient, broken, and dusty. It must have been Sterling's study.

"Michael! Over here!" Brink called from the far side of the room, where a sunlit shimmer of blonde hair caught Michael's eye. He hastily maneuvered his way through the maze of tables, shelves, books, and scattered papers to the window.

"Kate!" he called.

She turned her head slowly to look at him. It was only then that he realized what exactly she was doing. She was standing in the window, her feet perched on the sill, her hands gripping the sides to hold herself steady. But one wrong move, one little slip...

"Kate, what are doing? Get down from there!" he cried.

Still, she said nothing. Michael felt his mouth run dry as he struggled to read the expression on her abnormally solemn face. Her hazel eyes bore into him, but what he saw wasn't love or relief, joy or sorrow. Her eyes were simply... blank.

Was she sleep-walking? He'd never known anyone who sleepwalked before, but he'd always heard that you weren't supposed to wake them. Then again, he wasn't sure that rule applied when the sleepwalker was standing on the ledge of a window over five stories high.

"Kate, please. Listen to me. Get down."

Finally, she acknowledged him.

"And?"

Michael was confused. "And what?"

"What would you do for me in return?" Her voice was softer, lower than usual.

"In return? Kate, what are you talking about?"

"You said you would do anything for her, didn't you?"

At first Michael didn't understand what she meant. But as she stared him down with cold, conniving eyes, eyes that did not belong to the girl that he loved, the true meaning behind the words hit him like a ton of bricks.

"No..." He croaked, almost too breathless to speak.

It couldn't be true. Sterling had moved on. There was no way.

"Michael, what is going on?" Brink asked.

"She's possessed." Michael answered without tearing his eyes away from Kate's. Her beautiful face broke into a strange, sadistic smile. "Sterling... Listen, I know you're mad. You're mad because of Joanna, you're mad because of the intruders, and you're especially mad at me, because I couldn't help you. But please, please hear me when I say that she had nothing to do with this. If you want to punish me, then do it. Just please, let her go."

"I don't want to punish you, young man." Hearing Kate speak in such a slimy, condescending tone made Michael's skin crawl. "If I wanted to punish you, she would have jumped three hours ago."

Three hours. He'd had her up there for three hours. And where had Michael been? Safe and warm and fast asleep in bed. He should have been awake. He should have been protecting her. What was worse, he *could* have protected her, if only he'd seen the ghost coming. But Sterling had made sure that that didn't happen. He'd stayed away all night and given all of them the false hope that maybe, just maybe, he was gone for good.

"Then what are you doing?"

"You mean you haven't figured it out?"

"Well, maybe if you'd let my girlfriend come down from that windowsill, I'd be able to think a little clearer."

"It's simple. You help me find Joanna; I let your Kate go."

Michael was flabbergasted. He thought he'd made it clear to Sterling that it might not be possible to find Joanna.

"Sterling, listen to me. If I could find Joanna, if I even knew where to begin, I would get her for you in a heartbeat. But what you're asking... I'm not sure anyone in the world can do that."

"But you can, and you will. For her."

Michael didn't want to ask the question, because he was fairly certain he already knew the answer, but he asked anyway.

"And if I don't?"

"If you don't," Sterling answered slowly, "she jumps."

CHAPTER TWENTY-SIX

Michael listened intently as Sterling laid down his ultimatum. He wanted Joanna. If Michael couldn't find her, then Sterling wanted to know where she'd gone and why she hadn't waited for him. Furthermore, he didn't want Michael telling anyone, especially Luke, about their deal, a word that Michael would have used very loosely under his current circumstances. A deal required some sort of agreement. What Sterling was doing was coercion.

"But Luke might be able to help us," Michael argued. "This is what he does for a living. He investigates the paranormal."

"I don't trust him." Sterling crossed Kate's arms and narrowed her eye. It would have been funny to see Kate so put off by the idea of Luke if it weren't for the current circumstances.

"Why not?" Michael asked, though it really wasn't that difficult to figure out. Luke was rash and brazen and loud, all the qualities of a confrontational reality television star who spent most of his time screaming at ghosts hoping to get some sort of reaction from them. Not so much the qualities of someone altogether trustworthy, like a therapist.

"He's a brute, a bully. If he were to find out, he would try to force me to let her go," Sterling explained. "You must understand that I don't want to hurt her." *But I will.* The words, though unspoken, were there.

"Look, I know Luke seems a little thick, and yeah, he can be a bully, but he's smart. He's going to know something's off."

"Then you'll assure him otherwise."

Michael wanted to argue, but he had a feeling it wouldn't do him much good. He'd never dealt with a possession before, but he'd had enough exposure to Sterling and his twisted mind to know that reasoning didn't work. If he'd had any sort of logic on his side at all, Sterling would have realized that there was no way Michael could ever hope to know anything more about Joanna than her own husband. If Joanna had already moved on, Sterling already knew about it, at least on some level. He just wasn't willing to accept it.

"And Kate's brother," Michael continued. "Come on, he's definitely going to notice. Sterling, we're supposed to leave today. Please..."

But the callous look in Kate's eyes told him that there was no point in begging. Sterling wasn't going to yield, and he knew that Michael could threaten and bargain all he wanted, he would never do anything that might put Kate in danger. There was only one option.

"Tell the others to leave. I don't want them here."

"You think that Luke and the others are just going to agree to leave Kate and me behind? You think Gavin is going to agree?"

"You are in love with her. Tell them that you've decided to stay. That should require no further explanation."

Oh, it shouldn't, but it would. Luke and Gavin and the rest were all fully aware of how miserable Kate had been. Michael too, for that matter. They'd never believe that they'd willingly extend their stay at Stanton Hall, even for a romantic getaway. But if he had no other choice...

"Okay," he agreed.

"Good." Kate's face broke into a satisfied smiled.

For one fleeting moment, Michael could have sworn he saw a flicker of Kate, the real Kate, peeking out at him. It was all he could do not to grab her by the shoulders and scream her name, imploring her to hear his voice and to fight against the entity that held her captive. But if he failed, and Sterling tore her away from him, he could lose her. He couldn't take that risk.

Brink, who had remained uncharacteristically silent throughout the entire exchange, stood staring at Kate with what Michael could only describe as helplessness. Even though she'd

196

never seen Brink, Kate always acknowledged him whenever she knew he was around, and Michael knew how much Brink cared about her. She was the second-best friend he had, and he didn't want anything happening to her any more than Michael did.

Wordlessly, the three of them, or perhaps the four of them was more accurate, descended back down to the ground floor, with Sterling leading the way. Although he never said as much, Michael got the feeling that Sterling wasn't going to leave anything to chance. He was going to direct Michael every step of the way.

By the time they reached the entry hall, everyone else already had their luggage ready and waiting by the front doors. Michael realized then that he hadn't even begun to pack. He'd been too distracted by, well, everything.

Good thing I'm not leaving yet, he thought bitterly.

"Morning, Mikey," Luke greeted him, lugging one of his equipment bags to the entry hall. "Hi, Gorgeous," he said to Kate.

Michael felt a bony elbow jab him in the side. Sterling cleared Kate's throat. There was no beating around the bush with him.

"Uh, Luke?" Michael began, hoping he sounded at least a little like he was telling the truth.

"Yeah, buddy?" Luke asked, sounding tired and distant. "You two are packed, aren't you? We're getting out of here as soon as we finish breakfast."

"Well, that's actually what I wanted to talk to you about," Michael said. "You see, Kate and I... well, we've decided to stay."

That got Luke's attention.

"You've what?"

"Just for a few days," Michael added hastily.

"I'm sorry, I'm not comprehending," Luke said, rubbing his forehead with his fingertips. "You want to *stay* here? I thought you were both miserable."

"Well yesterday, you know, we spent some time on the beach and... you know, we might not even stay here. We might go get a place a little closer to town." Even to his own ears, the words sounded phony.

Luke heard it too.

"What aren't you telling me?" he asked, crossing his arms and staring Michael down like a policeman interrogating a suspect.

"Nothing," Michael responded a little too quickly. He cleared his throat and then said again, with a little more confidence, "Nothing."

"Kate?" Luke asked. "You're being awfully quiet. Are you sure this is what you want to do?"

"Yes, of course," Sterling replied. Although it was Kate's voice that spoke, anyone listening could've told it wasn't her at all. The response was too distant, too robotic; not at all like Kate's normal chipper and lively timbre.

"Well, if that's what the two of you really want to do," Luke said. His eyebrows furrowed ever so slightly, but it was enough to let Michael know that he still wasn't convinced. "You think Gavin will be okay with it?"

"Um... Probably not," Michael answered.

"What we do is none of his concern." Sterling spoke in a tone much harsher than Kate would ever use.

Michael closed his eyes. There was no way Luke would ever believe that there was nothing wrong with her. Sure enough, when he opened his eyes again, Luke was staring at him, and he knew that his friend could see the truth written all over his face. Parts of the truth, anyway. He knew something was wrong. Michael could deny it all he wanted, but it wouldn't do him a shred of good. He only hoped that Sterling wouldn't take it out on Kate.

Of course, Michael couldn't be sure how much of the truth Luke had figured out. Did he know that Kate wasn't herself? Luke had been a paranormal investigator for a while now. Surely he'd recognize a possession when he saw one. For a moment, Michael wished he was as psychic as everyone believed him to be. Then he

198

could communicate telepathically and tell Luke everything he needed to know.

But maybe, just maybe, Luke was "sensitive" enough to figure it out on his own.

"All right," he finally sighed. "I personally don't understand why you'd want to stay, but I will respect your decision."

"Thank you." Sterling sounded pleased.

"Oh, by the way, Kate? Can you tell me what color my shoes are?" Luke asked.

Sterling looked confused, like he couldn't figure out why Luke would ask him such a question, but he replied without hesitation, "They're green."

Luke flashed sharp and suspicious eyes over to Michael, who nodded grimly.

"I see," Luke said. For a moment, Michael thought he might call Sterling out, but instead, he clapped his hands together and announced, "Well, I'd better get back in there and tell the others to get a move on. Plane leaves soon, don't want to be late."

And just like that, he was gone. Michael suddenly felt more at a loss than ever. He'd thought, or at least hoped, that Luke might be able to help him. But maybe it was all for the best. Kate was already in enough danger. If Luke had indicated in any way that he knew about Sterling...

Michael didn't want to think about it. Not that he could really think of anything else. He was supposed to be trying to find Joanna, but the truth was he didn't know where to start.

Sterling, on the other hand, didn't seem worried at all.

"Well done, young man," he said, resting Kate's hand on Michael's shoulder. "Well done."

Sterling suggested they wait in the Fireside Room until the others had left in order to avoid any further confrontations. Half an hour later, Michael watched from the window of his bedroom as the crew loaded up the vans they had rented and drove them through the gate and off the premises. Kate, or Sterling, sat straight-backed and rigid on the foot of the bed while Brink paced anxiously back and forth through the walls.

"Okay, they're gone," Michael told them as soon as the vans were out of sight.

"Good. Now then -"

But before Sterling could get the words out, the bedroom door slammed open and Luke appeared, camera in tow.

"All right, it is time for someone to explain to me what the hell is going on," he announced loudly.

Sterling was on his feet in an instant.

"What are you doing here?" he hissed.

"I don't know, Sterling. What *am* I doing here?" Luke shot back. Sterling stared at him, mouth agape. "Funny thing about possessions. If you want to pull them off, you'd better know everything about the person you're supposed to be. Otherwise, you might slip up and ruin the whole damn thing."

"How did you know?"

"Well, for one thing, you're mean. Kate is not mean. For another, she has that thing with colors. What is it Mikey?"

"Color Anomia. Are you filming this?" Michael asked.

"You see, Sterling," Luke continued, "the real Kate wouldn't know green from purple from traffic cone orange. But you did. And finally, there's no way Kate would want to stay here after all the crap you've pulled the last few days. I'm a huge advocate for the dead, Sterling. I like to give people hope, but I also like to show them that ghosts aren't evil. They're not out to get the living or make them suffer. But you? Wow. You are a genuine asshole. And I stood up for you! Those first few nights when Peter thought you were some kind of weird stalker, I defended you. Even after the way you've been scaring poor Emily Drake and basically anyone who sets foot in this house, I still tried to cut you some slack. But this? This is over-the-line unacceptable."

"You're filming this, aren't you?" Michael asked.

"Shh," Luke hushed him. "So Sterling, are you going to let Kate go?"

That was it. As grateful as he was that Luke had stayed behind to help, Michael wasn't going to have him risking Kate's life just for a few minutes of film.

"Luke, stop it," he said, placing himself between Kate and the camera. "Please, just don't provoke him."

"Mikey, relax. This isn't my first possession. I know you're not a fan of the show, but trust me. I know what I'm doing. We've all been possessed."

"Not like this," Michael assured him. "Luke, if we don't help him find Joanna, he's going to kill her."

Finally, Luke lowered the camera and looked Michael in the eye, his expression absolutely serious.

"Well," he said. "That changes a few things, doesn't it?"

CHAPTER TWENTY-SEVEN

Things could have been worse. Luke didn't really know how, but he was sure if he put some serious thought into it, he could come up with something.

It was true, they had dealt with possessions before on the show. The first time, it had been Peter, and it was one of the scariest moments of Luke's life. His friend had gone completely lethargic, his eyes blank, his breathing deep and rattling. He hadn't said much. Occasionally, he'd mumble a bit of nonsense. After the spirit had left him, Peter had no recollection of the event. Luke had experienced the same phenomenon.

The problem was all of those possessions had lasted about ten minutes, if that. He'd never seen a spirit hold on to a host for so long, and although he had his theories, he had no way of knowing how Sterling did it, how long it would last, or what kind of effect it might have on Kate. Of course, he wasn't about to bring that up. He knew Michael was doing his best to stay calm, but the distress he felt was written all over his face.

For a kid who'd been trying to live a lie his entire life, he wasn't very good at it.

As for Sterling, Luke wasn't convinced that he would follow through on his threats to end Kate's life if they didn't help him track down his precious Joanna, but he didn't want to take any chances. After all, the guy had existed as a ghost for a hundred and fifty years without realizing he'd bit the dust, so they knew he wasn't exactly sane.

"All right, Sterling. You want us to help you find Joanna? You tell us where to start looking. We're all yours," Luke said.

"No," Kate - or Sterling - snapped.

"No?" Luke wasn't quite sure he'd heard that correctly. "I don't understand, Sterling. I thought you wanted our help."

"I want his help. Not yours."

Luke shook his head. He'd seen a lot of weird stuff in his years of investigating. For the most part, he'd learned to shrug it all off and accept it. But it was hard to see Kate - sweet, happy, beautiful Kate - look at him with such intense revulsion. And if it was hard on him, he couldn't imagine how Michael felt. What was it like to look into the eyes of the girl you loved and see another person? Not only that, but a person who was willing to let you and your love suffer for his own agenda?

"Well, that's too bad, Sterling. Because you see, Kate and Mikey, they're my friends. They're two of the best friends I have, and the only way you're going to get me out of here is to let them go with me."

Out of the corner of his eye, Luke noticed Michael staring at him with a funny expression on his face. Was that actual *gratitude*? From the world's most reluctant medium? Luke might have fainted from the shock if he hadn't had a more pressing issue on his hands.

"So, there you have it. You want these two, you get me. I would ask you if you could live with that, but that might be a little insensitive of me, so I'm just going to go ahead and assume it's okay." Luke recognized the look on Kate's face. It was the look everybody gave him when they wanted to punch his lights out because deep down, they knew they weren't going to win. He got that look a lot. "You know, Sterling, you really should be thanking me. After all, two brains are better than one, and let me tell you, with Mikey, you're not getting much."

Both Sterling and Michael glared at him.

Okay, it was too soon for jokes. Noted.

"One wrong move from you," Sterling warned, "and she's gone."

"Sterling, I have been telling you from the beginning that all I wanted was to help you out. That's what I do. I find troubled spirits, I figure out why they're troubled, and I try to help them

203

out. But what I'm going to need from you is cooperation, and frankly, a better attitude. You know, there are ways of asking for favors that don't involve possessing and endangering a young woman's life." Sterling didn't seem to agree, but at least he kept his mouth shut. Luke took a deep breath. "Well, I think I've said everything that I wanted to say. Now we just need a game plan. Any thoughts?"

"What about Marian?" Michael asked.

"The thief?" Sterling asked.

"Technically, you stole from her," Luke reminded him. "You know, she might be more inclined to help us out if we could get that necklace back to her."

Sterling still didn't acknowledge him. Luke scowled. That was going to get really old really fast. He'd rather have someone flat out yell at him than ignore him completely. Maybe it was the egotistical narcissist coming out in him, but he needed at least some sort of response.

"Do you think she'll be at the store today?" Michael asked.

"She should be. If not, someone there will have her phone number. We'll be able to track her down somehow," Luke replied. "Now, we still have a few things we need to take care of. First, we need to talk to Carolyn and make sure it's okay that we stay here a few extra days, but I don't think she'll mind. Also, I had to let the guys take the vans back to the rental place, so we'll need to call a cab to take us into town. Mikey, why don't you take care of that since I'm assuming our friend Sterling here has never used a cell phone and I'll explain things to Carolyn."

"Wait. You're not going to tell her -" Sterling began, but Luke cut him off.

"Relax, Sterling, I'm not going to tell her anything. Not that she'd believe me if I did."

"Actually, she's more open to it now," Michael remarked.

"Oh. Well, good to know."

Still, Luke figured it was in everyone's best interests (Kate's especially) to keep things on a need-to-know basis. He decided to tell Carolyn the same thing he'd told the crew: that he,

Kate, and Michael had decided to stick around for a few more days of filming. Unlike the others, she didn't question him at all and assured him they were more than welcome.

Later, while they waited for the cab that would take them back to Dock Square, Michael asked, "So, what did the others say when you told them that we were staying?"

"That we were crazy, but to each their own," Luke summarized. There had been a bit more profanity, but they were all so eager to get away from the manor that they really didn't care what their friends wanted to do.

"What about Gavin? Is he worried about Kate?"

"He didn't seem to be. Of course, he doesn't know that he has a reason to worry about her. He thinks she's safe and sound with her boyfriend and the Chuck Norris of ghost-hunting."

"*The Chuck Norris of ghost-hunting?*" Michael sounded incredulous.

"What?" Luke asked. He'd thought it was a perfect metaphor.

"You know what? Never mind," Michael sighed.

"Who is Chuck Norris?" Sterling asked.

Neither Luke nor Michael bothered to explain. Though the question did bring to light another flaw in Sterling's oh-so-brilliant plan to manipulate them into bowing to his selfish and cowardly will.

"You know Sterling, you've been cooped up in that mansion for a long time. A lot has changed since you were alive."

"Yes?" Sterling asked, clearly waiting for him to get to the point.

"If you don't want people thinking there's something wrong with Kate, then you'd better act like a functioning member of the twenty-first century. In other words, don't draw attention to yourself."

"Why would I do that?" Sterling asked.

"Oh, you just never know," Luke replied lightly.

Sure enough, when the cab pulled up ten minutes later, Sterling flew into a full-blown panic attack. It took Luke and

Michael an additional few minutes to convince him that the vehicle was perfectly safe, that people rode in them all the time, and that they weren't trying to send him to yet another death. By that point, Luke was sure that the poor cab driver was more than a little wary of the crazy girl who'd apparently never seen a modern automobile in her life, but fortunately, he didn't say anything. Luke made a mental note to leave an extra generous tip.

By the time they finally made it into town, Sterling had settled down, but he still wasn't doing a very good job of blending. He reacted to the new world outside his window with startled gasps and looks of astonishment. It was like he'd stepped straight out of one of those bad time-travel flicks that Peter loved so much. At least this time, they could just write his odd behavior off as extreme tourist syndrome. If that was even a thing.

It probably wasn't.

Thankfully, the walk to Marian's *Waterside Treasures* shop was a short one. The store was open and already bustling with souvenir shoppers. However, Marian herself was nowhere to be seen.

"She is here, isn't she?" Michael asked.

"I'll go ask the girl at the cash register," Luke said. With that, he marched right up to the counter, stepping in front of several customers who'd lined up to make their purchases.

"Hey!" the chubby woman who'd been next snapped at him.

"Do you not see the line?" another younger woman asked.

The girl behind the counter was equally unimpressed.

"Sir, I'm afraid you'll have to wait -" she began, but Luke quickly cut her off.

"Don't have time for a lecture. I just need to know if Marian Davis is in today."

"No, she isn't, Sir. Now, if you'd please step aside -"

"Do you have her phone number by any chance?"

"If I did, I wouldn't give it to you."

"No, it's all right, she knows me. I'm Luke Rainer, we met a few days ago. She's going to be a guest on my nationally acclaimed television series, *Cemetery Tours*. Perhaps you've heard of it?"

"I'm sorry, but I haven't. Now if you'll please get out of my way and let me see to these customers."

Luke could tell by her tone that she was almost done being polite. Almost.

"Please. I just need to talk to her for a few minutes. It's about Joanna Stanton."

"I don't know who that is and if you do not step away from this counter in the next sixty seconds, I'm going to call the police."

As much as Luke liked to think he could charm his way into or out of any situation, he also knew when it was time to bow out gracefully. Hoping the sad and defeated look on his face would at least make the salesgirl feel a little guilty for refusing to give him Marian's phone number, Luke sighed and turned away.

He found Michael near the front of the store, attempting to explain the workings of a disposable camera to a visibly perplexed Sterling.

"But if you wind it, doesn't that scratch the image? How do you get the photograph out?"

"You take it to the store and - oh, look! There's Luke!" Michael announced, probably a lot louder than he'd intended. "Anything?"

"Nada. Looks like we're on our own on this one, friends."

"Excuse me." A new voice interjected. Luke turned to see a woman, probably in her mid-thirties, with light brown hair tied back into a ponytail. "I couldn't help but overhear... you have a question about Joanna Stanton?"

"Not a question so much as quest to unearth any and every piece of information you could possibly tell us about her," Luke answered. "I'm Luke, by the way."

"Luke Rainer, I know. I recognize you from your show," the woman smiled and shook his hand. "I'm Beth. Are you filming over at Stanton Hall?"

"We were, actually. Now we're just doing a little bit of follow-up research."

"Oh, all right. Well, I can't tell you much, but I do know that Joanna is buried over in Cape Porpoise Cemetery with the rest of her family."

"The cemetery?" Michael asked.

Luke was equally surprised.

"She wasn't buried at the manor with her husband?" he asked.

"No, there was some kind of feud between Hall and her father. Old Man Stanton thought Sterling may have had something to do with her death, so he demanded that she be buried with the family. Hall didn't even try to fight him."

Luke turned back to Sterling.

"Any of this ringing a bell?"

Sterling just stood there, eyebrows furrowed, like he was trying to work it all out for himself.

"How do you know all this?" Michael asked.

"I wrote a report on the history of Stanton Hall Manor in high school," she replied.

"*Did* Sterling have something to do with Joanna's death?" Luke asked.

Sterling immediately snapped out of whatever stupor he'd been in and glared at Luke with such a look of insult and betrayal that Luke was surprised that Beth wasn't whipping out her phone to call the cops. Or the nuthouse.

"Most of the records I found indicate no, he didn't. It was natural causes. But she was Stanton's only daughter, and he wanted to take his anger out on someone. Sterling became his scapegoat."

"That's interesting," Luke said. "You know, we talked to a lady a few days back who is a descendent of the Stanton family, and she told us that Sterling remained on good terms with the family after Joanna's death. He even left his entire estate to them."

"For the most part, I think that's true, especially after her father died, which wasn't too long after she passed."

208

"Let me ask you something else. Do you think that not being buried with her husband would have upset her?"

"It would upset me," Beth said. "I wouldn't care how angry my family was. I'd want to be buried next to my husband."

Luke turned to Michael and Sterling.

"Comrades, I think we have a cemetery to investigate." Then he looked back to Beth. "Thank you so much for your help."

"Oh, it was my pleasure. Here, I'll give you my business card. I can't guarantee that I'll have the answers, but if you have any more questions, feel free to give me a call."

"Thank you. We might just do that," Luke told her. To Michael and Sterling he said, "Let's head out."

CHAPTER TWENTY-EIGHT

Michael had never really liked cemeteries.

It wasn't because they were haunted. He actually rarely encountered spirits who enjoyed hanging around their burial sites, which was partially why he doubted they would find Joanna there. There was always the possibility, but despite ancient folklore and spiritual beliefs, he'd never been convinced that cemeteries were meant for the dead. No, cemeteries, just like everything else, were designed for the living so that they'd have a place to visit their loved ones, or at least their bodies.

Michael had only lost one person to death. His brother Jonathan had taken his own life almost a decade earlier, and he was the only person Michael had known and loved who hadn't found him as a ghost. For the first time, Michael understood just how excruciating it felt to be separated by something that before had never been a barrier. Even still, he'd felt neither comfort nor closure at the gravesite. It wasn't his brother lying beneath the ground. His body was no more than a shell, as cold and empty and hollow as a vacant tomb.

He knew that others might be consoled by the idea of visiting their loved ones at a cemetery, and to be honest, Michael envied them, but for him, Jonathan's death only reaffirmed his belief that a body without a soul was just... nothing. And yet, century after century, headstones and grave markers were crafted, marble shrines to lost life and to bodies that could neither see nor touch nor think nor feel, bodies that were respected and appreciated more after death than some ever could have hoped to be in life.

It was a little sickening, really.

Cape Porpoise Cemetery was small, no more than fifty graves or so, and protected by a border of trees. Most of the graves were from the late 1800s to the early 1900s, and according to a quick Google search Luke had conducted, several of them belonged to sea captains. Michael caught a glimpse of one lonely spirit meandering through the trees, but judging by his modern clothes, he was not there to haunt his final resting place.

"Anything, Mikey?" Luke asked.

"No," Michael confirmed. "She's not here."

"Why would she be? Who wants to hang around a bunch of corpses all day?" Brink commented. Michael knew his friend had never understood the haunted graveyard stereotype.

"Are you sure we've come to the right place?" Sterling asked.

"Cape Porpoise Cemetery, 1812. This is it," Luke said.

"Then she is here," Sterling said.

"Just her body. Her spirit... it could be anywhere," Michael told him honestly.

Sterling either didn't hear him or didn't care to acknowledge what he was trying to tell him.

"I want to see her," he announced. Then, without waiting for Michael or Luke, he set off, moving Kate's body gracefully through the graveyard.

"Mikey, you go after him. Keep an eye on Kate. I'll go search the other half of the cemetery," Luke told Michael before sprinting off in the opposite direction.

Michael didn't hesitate a moment in catching up to Sterling.

"Wait a minute," he said to the ghost. "Are you sure you want to do this? Maybe it's not a good idea."

"And why wouldn't it be?" Sterling demanded.

"You have this idea of Joanna in your head. You see her alive and vibrant and loving, the way she was with you. That's not what you're going to find here."

"You speak as though you think I don't know that," Sterling snapped.

211

"I just want to make sure that you're ready. Seeing her grave... it might make it too real for you," Michael warned him.

Sterling made no reply. He just kept walking, staring at each grave as he passed.

Brink glanced over at Michael. "You tried, brother."

Just then, Luke called out across the yard, "Hey, I found her!"

Sterling stopped in his tracks and turned to look at Luke. Michael recognized the look in his eyes, or rather, Kate's eyes: pure, unadulterated, and heartbreakingly false hope.

"Sterling, wait -" Michael began, but it was no use. Sterling was already marching straight over grass and graves to reach his love's resting place.

The inscription on the tombstone had faded so much that Michael couldn't make out any of the dates. The name Hall, however, was clearly legible across the top of the stone. Below it, he saw the faint tracings of her name, Joanna Elizabeth.

"God, I wish I had my camera," Luke lamented. "If I'd known this was here, I'd have definitely gotten some shots of -"

But before he could finish his sentence, Kate - or Sterling - dropped to her knees and clutched the ground with her fingers. Michael was beside her in an instant.

"Kate!" he cried.

Frantically, she reached out and grabbed his shoulder, digging her fingernails so hard into his shirt that it ripped. Michael barely even noticed. He called her name again.

"Kate! Look at me! Can you hear me?"

She took several deep, labored breaths before slowly turning her hazel gaze upward. His eyes held hers, and in that brief moment, Michael knew she was seeing him. It was Kate. Sterling had let her go.

"Michael?" she whispered. Then, she seized up again as her eyes faded and then closed. She leaned her head forward, hunching over like some strange animal.

"NO!" Michael yelled. "Sterling! Sterling, let her go! Don't *do* this!" he pleaded, but it was no use.

By now, Luke was next to him, trying to pull him away from Kate. "Mikey, give her some air. Don't upset him," he advised.

But Michael was in no mood to listen.

"Kate! Kate, fight him! I know you can! Please!"

It was no use. Kate was already straightening herself back up. But it wasn't Kate anymore. Sterling brushed the grass and dirt off of Kate's jeans and said, "She caught me off guard."

In that moment, Michael felt a vile contempt unlike any he'd ever known he was capable of experiencing. The only thing keeping him from pummeling Sterling to the ground was the fact that he was using Kate as a shield. It was brilliant, really. Sterling knew that neither Luke nor Michael could do him any harm without hurting Kate more.

"I think it's time we seek answers elsewhere," Luke suggested lightly, pulling out his cell phone and Beth's business card.

Michael glared at Sterling.

"Agreed."

Beth offered to meet them at the public library. She explained that in high school, she'd been able to access information on Joanna and Sterling Hall through the town's public records.

"Everything there is to know about Sterling and Joanna, you'll find here in these databases," Beth said, leading them to a computer.

"Probably not everything," Brink muttered.

Luke sat down at the desk and began browsing.

"So, are you looking for anything specific or are you just researching?" Beth asked.

"We're trying to learn as much as we can about Joanna, specifically her life with Sterling," Luke told her. "We were hoping we might make contact with her during our investigation, but we only got through to Sterling."

"You really think it was him?" Beth asked.

"Oh, we're pretty positive," Luke remarked lightly.

"What did he say?"

Michael could have sworn he saw Luke cast a grim look up at Kate before he replied, "That he didn't like people in his house, and that he misses Joanna desperately. He's been hurting a lot this last century, but I'm hoping that maybe, if we can piece together a little bit more about what happened to Joanna, then we might be able to help him find some peace."

"Wow. That's just so cool what you do. Have you ever actually seen a ghost?"

"A couple of times," Luke said without tearing his eyes away from the computer screen.

"How about you?" Beth asked Michael.

He guessed she hadn't seen any of his interviews.

"Umm, I've seen a few," he said. Behind him, Brink scoffed. Fortunately, Michael was the only one who heard it.

"Hey, I think I may have found something," Luke announced. Sterling was hovering over his shoulder in an instant. Luke pointed to the screen. "Look at this. It's your marriage license."

"Whose marriage license?" Beth asked.

But Luke was too distracted to answer.

"*Sterling Samuel Hall and Joanna Elizabeth Stanton. Married January 21, 1834.*"

"You'll probably find some other records there, also," Beth said.

"A death certificate maybe?" Michael asked. "They could have written down the cause of death."

"It was an illness. Probably pneumonia," Beth said.

"If that's the case, and she was sick for a long time, then that could explain why we haven't found her," Luke said. "She may have felt that she'd made her peace with the world."

"No. I don't believe that," Sterling said. "She was too young. She had too much to live for. There was no reason for her to die."

214

Beth glanced at Kate – er, Sterling – with alarm. Michael didn't blame her. It must seem odd for a beautiful young woman to react so strongly to the passing of a woman who'd died years before even her great-grandparents were born.

"Kate, it's okay," he tried to assure Sterling.

"No. It's not okay. She didn't deserve this."

"No one deserves to die young but sometimes things *happen*," Luke muttered through clenched teeth, clearly hoping that Sterling would take the hint. "Now you need to calm down or I'm calling this whole thing off, because frankly, at this point, I don't know how much more there is to find."

Michael was beginning to think the same thing, when all of a sudden, the word *journals* jumped off the screen at him.

"Wait a minute," he said leaning forward. "Scroll down." Luke did. "*There have been reports that Joanna Stanton Hall chronicled her life through a series of journals, though no such artifact has ever been recovered from the extravagant home she shared with her husband, Sterling.*"

"Then that's where we'll find them," Luke announced, standing abruptly. "Beth, I want to thank you so much for your time and your assistance."

"Oh, it was my pleasure," she announced. Michael got the feeling that she suspected that there was a little more to their quest than simple research, and that was exactly why Luke was so forwardly dismissing her.

"Tell you what. When you get home, go to our website and shoot me an email to the address under our contact information. I'll send you something autographed."

Once Beth was gone, Michael asked Sterling, "Do you remember Joanna keeping a journal?"

"Not a journal. She was constantly writing, but she claimed that they were poems, sketches," Sterling responded.

"Did she ever let you see them?" Luke asked.

"No."

"Then they weren't poetry. Trust me, I've dated enough poets and would-be artists and there is nothing that they love more than showing off their work."

"Really?" Michael asked. He'd always figured that they'd be the exact opposite. In high school, he'd had a crush on a girl who enjoyed poetry and she never showed her work to anyone.

Maybe Luke just dated different kinds of poets.

"Oh yeah. If Joanna was writing poetry and drawing flowers, she'd at least show her husband. If she wasn't showing you, it was because she was writing things that she didn't want anybody to read."

"You think she had a secret?" Michael asked.

"No. We were always completely honest with one another," Sterling insisted.

"Sterling, I hate to tell you, but you answered that far too quickly and too adamantly for me to fully believe you," Luke said.

"What are you saying? That you doubt her?" Sterling demanded.

"No. I'm saying that you do."

Michael waited anxiously for Sterling to retaliate, to yell or lash out, but it never happened. He just stared at Luke with a strange mixture of insult and contempt. But there was something else there, too. Something that Michael had never before seen in Sterling's cold and bitter eyes.

Fear.

CHAPTER TWENTY-NINE

If there was one thing Luke had learned about great ideas, it was that they were just that: ideas. And just because the idea was great in theory, it in no way guaranteed that the execution of said idea would be great, or even feasible.

Scouring the entire mansion for one journal? *What were they thinking?*

Okay, maybe it was a series of journals. That didn't make it any less impossible to find in a building roughly the size of some of the smaller Texas towns. Even with Carolyn's assistance and Brink wandering through walls, they'd barely managed to search ten percent of the manor by nightfall. Even though they'd started with the most likely places, the master bedroom, the sitting room, the library, there was still no sign of any journal.

Exhausted, Luke slumped down onto the floor, amidst the debris of what at one point had been the second story sunroom, and rubbed his forehead with the heel of his hand.

"This... is going to take a while," he moaned.

"I think it's about time you call it a night," Carolyn advised. "You've been working hard. You're all exhausted. You can pick things up again in the morning. And besides, you've done so much research already. Not finding those journals... it wouldn't be the end of the world, would it?"

Michael cast a drained and defeated look over at Luke. They'd given Carolyn the same cover story that they'd given everyone else: that they were sticking around for additional research. But after having it repeated back to him so many times, even Luke had to admit it was beginning to sound pretty flimsy. Who busted their tails over an old journal anyway? A journal that, for all they knew, might not even exist?

217

No one.

There had to be another way to send Sterling packing. And by "packing," he meant all the way to the hereafter.

It was clear now that Sterling wasn't in his right mind, and probably hadn't been since his father died. Why else would he have developed such a sudden and unhealthy attachment to a woman he barely even knew? Hadn't anyone had the common sense back then to tell him that his obsession with Joanna was, quite frankly, creepy and unsettling? Or maybe the reason no one had told him as much was because he had no one else. If he'd had no one, no friends or family, then Luke could understand how easy it would have been for him to latch himself on to the first person to show him love and kindness. He guessed that person had been Joanna.

Sad as that was, however, it still didn't justify possessing and threatening to kill Kate.

"I think we need to have a pow-wow," Luke announced once Carolyn had left the room, leaving him alone with Michael and Sterling. "We've been at this all day. Now, we will be happy to continue helping in any way that we can, but Sterling, I know you've got to be feeling the strain now. Possessions take a lot of energy, and she's already gotten away from you once. You're not doing anyone any favors by holding onto her."

"What are you saying, Mr. Rainer?" Sterling asked, crossing Kate's arms.

"I'm saying that it's time to let her go. We've gone above and beyond what anyone else would have done in this case. I promise, we will still try our best to help you, but dude, I've got to be honest with you. There is a real chance that we won't find this book. And if we don't, I know you don't want to hurt her. None of this is her fault. It's not my fault, and it's not even Mikey's fault, even though for some reason, you're trying to make it his fault. You know what it's like to lose someone you love. You know how much it hurts. I know you're not going to do that to him. I don't think you could."

218

Sterling blinked. Then, without a word, he stooped down, picked up a stray piece of shattered glass, and dug a deep and jagged gash down Kate's inner arm.

"NO!" Michael and Luke dove for Sterling at the same time. Luke wrestled the bloody piece of glass out of Sterling's hand, cutting himself up in the process, while Michael grabbed the wound on Kate's arm with both hands and tried to stop the bleeding.

"HELP! Carolyn! Emily!" Luke yelled at the top of his lungs. Then he turned on Sterling. *"What the hell is the matter with you?!"*

"You were wrong," was all Sterling said before both Carolyn and Emily appeared, looking anxious.

"Luke, what's the mat - oh my God!" Carolyn exclaimed. "Emily, go and get the first aid kit." Emily obeyed. "Kate, sweetheart, what happened?"

"She tripped," Luke answered. He knew Sterling wasn't going to talk and Michael, he could tell, was too angry to speak. His face had gone absolutely white and his eyes were locked on his bloody hands, still clamped around Kate's arm. "Cut herself on some glass."

"Oh, dear. Well, we'll get some hydrogen peroxide and wrap that up straight away, and then I think you need to get to the hospital. I'm no nurse, but I'm sure she's going to need stitches."

"Right. We'll get her there," Luke assured her as Emily came scampering back in with the first aid kit. "Thank you, sweetheart."

"You're welcome," she murmured. "Do you need any help?"

"I might ask you to help me tape her up," Luke said. Then, he took Michael's shoulder and looked at him. "Mikey, I'm going to need you to let her go. She's going to be okay. Do you hear me? She's okay."

It took Michael a few moments to react, but slowly, he loosened his grip on her arm. Blood began to flow freely again but, with a hasty decision to forgo hydrogen peroxide, Luke pressed the gauze to the wound. It bled through almost immediately. Quickly, Carolyn handed him another piece while Emily stood by with the medical tape.

Finally, after what seemed like forever, they got the bleeding under control. Most of the color had drained from Kate's face by that point and Luke knew they needed to get her help as soon as possible. It was only then that he remembered they had no car, and he didn't want to wait for the time it would take a cab to get there. He figured they would just have to call an ambulance when Carolyn, bless her soul, offered to let them take her car.

As Michael escorted Kate, or Sterling, down the stairs to the car, Carolyn grabbed Luke by the shoulder.

"Your friend is all right, isn't she? She didn't seem quite herself," she said.

"She'll be fine. I think she just got a little queasy with all the blood," Luke explained. He wasn't about to drag anyone else into their mess. "Thanks again, Carolyn."

And with that, he followed his friends out of the manor and into the cool October air.

Seven hours and eighteen stitches later, Michael, Luke, and Sterling returned to the manor. Dawn's early shades were just beginning to streak across the sky and Michael realized that they'd all been awake for almost twenty-four hours. He didn't know about the others, but he wasn't sure how much more he had left in him. Luke seemed okay, but not as okay as Sterling, who still appeared ultimately unaffected by anything. Was that how possessions worked? Did the body somehow adapt to the habits of the spirit inhabiting it? Or would the spirit eventually succumb to the needs of the mortal body?

"Well, that was fun," Luke announced, sounding a lot angrier than Michael had ever heard him. "Did you have a good time, Sterling? Waiting all night in an emergency room for something that could have easily *not happened*?"

"Luke, calm down," Michael warned. He was exhausted, he had the world's worst headache, and most importantly, the last time Luke had decided to provoke Sterling, he'd run a shattered piece of glass down his girlfriend's arm.

"No, I'm not going to calm down," Luke snapped. "Sterling, we've been busting our asses trying to help you, but thanks to you, we just wasted seven hours on a senseless and stupid injury; seven hours that could have been spent resting, or at least preserving whatever remains of our energy to help track down Joanna. Now, I care about Kate and I want her safe and unharmed, so rest assured we're still going to help you. But I need you to know that I am done with you. And the moment we find Joanna and you leave Kate, I hope you go straight to hell."

Before Sterling or Michael could respond to any of that, Luke stormed up the stairs and vanished into the manor.

Brink appeared immediately.

"Well, someone's in a good mood," he noted darkly.

"Anything?" Michael asked. His friend had stayed behind at the manor to get in a few more hours of searching.

"Nothing. Sorry, man."

"It's not your fault," Michael sighed.

Meanwhile, Sterling had wandered across the yard over to the side of the manor, and stood staring into the distant woods.

"He still won't leave?" Brink asked.

"No," Michael murmured. "And I don't know what it's going to take, Brink. We're no closer than when we started out yesterday. I've... I've never felt this helpless before. If anything happens to her -"

"Hey," Brink cut him off. "You can't think like that, okay? She's going to be fine."

"Is everything all right?" A new voice interrupted their conversation.

Michael and Brink both turned to see Emily Drake, still dressed in her night shirt and pajama pants, standing on the porch.

"Oh yeah, everything's fine. I'm just... waiting for Kate." Even to his own ears, the lie was flimsy.

"I heard the door slam open and I thought something might be wrong," Emily said.

"Sorry about that. It was Luke. He's pretty tired. I'll go tell him to keep it down."

"No, it's all right," Emily said. "Is Kate going to be okay?"

Michael glanced over at Kate, still standing as Sterling with her back to them, the early morning sunlight casting shadows across her shoulders and hair.

"I hope so," he said.

Emily nodded and turned to go back inside, but then she stopped, turned around, and looked at him.

"Why do you need to find Joanna's journals?"

"Research," Michael answered automatically.

"Did he tell you to?"

"No. Luke's a good guy. Kate and I offered to stay and help him."

"Not Luke. Him," Emily said. "Mr. Hall."

"Why would you think that?" Michael asked.

Emily drew in a deep, shaky breath, and Michael realized with a start that she was trying not to cry.

"Does he have her?" she asked. "Kate... Is she...?"

Michael didn't know why he was so stunned by the young girl's perceptiveness. She'd known all along that there was a ghost in the house. She'd even been able to sense his presence in the kitchen that night. But to detect a possession?

Luke just might start coming around, begging her to join the team.

Michael swallowed the knot in his throat and croaked out, "She's fine. She's going to be fine."

Emily shivered and wrapped her arms around her slim shoulders as tears began to run down her cheeks. "He scares me," she said, keeping her eyes locked on Kate. "They all scare me, but not like he does. He's different."

Michael felt a rush of lightheadedness as he realized what Emily was trying to say.

"Emily... can you...?"

Finally, she looked him in the eye.

"I thought that I was the only one," she said. "Then I read about you online. And I thought maybe if I met you, if I could talk to you, then I wouldn't be scared anymore. But I never meant for this to happen."

By that point, she was openly crying, and Michael wasn't sure how to comfort her. Careful to keep Kate within his line of vision, he climbed the steps up to the trembling girl on the porch.

"Emily, it's not your fault," he told her. "It's not anyone's fault, except for his." It felt odd saying the words, especially since Michael had been blaming himself for Kate's misfortune for the past twenty-four hours.

"Wait a minute. Are you saying that you can see me too?" Brink asked.

Michael turned, incredulous, and stared at his friend.

"Really? You think now is the best time?"

"I'm sorry, man, but this is exciting! I mean, you're the only one who's acknowledged me for *years*. It's kind of exciting to have a fresh face to talk to!"

To Michael's relief, Emily managed a small smile.

"Kate talks to you," Michael reminded him.

"Yeah, but it's not the same. She still can't *see* me or actually carry on a real conversation," he argued. "Hi, Emily. I'm Brink."

"Hi," Emily replied.

"I don't scare you, do I? Although, if the answer is yes, I'll be totally flattered."

For the first time since Michael had met her, Emily laughed.

"No, you don't scare me."

"Drat. I've gotta work on that." Brink pouted.

"How can you possibly work on that? You're a blond pretty boy with a bad haircut and a cartilage piercing," Michael teased lightly.

"Shut up, nerd," Brink grinned. "You know, one day, this whole experience is going to make one hell of a story."

"A story?" Emily asked.

"Yeah, you know, like with the romance and the manor and you being able to see me and everything -"

"Of course!" Emily exclaimed.

Brink looked pretty proud of himself, but Michael got the feeling that she was no longer paying attention to him. Sure enough, she turned back to Michael, her eyes full of more hope than he had ever dreamt he'd find again.

"There's still one place they could be," she said

"Where what could be?" Brink asked. Really, Michael was glad to have Brink in his life, but sometimes, he could be thick as a post.

"The journals. I can't believe we didn't think of it before. It's where we stored all the old books that we found; the ones that were still preserved enough to be used for decoration."

"Where?" Michael asked.

"The Storybook Room."

CHAPTER THIRTY

For a guy who'd worked in a library for most of his adult life, Michael was amazed by the sheer quantity of books stored in a single room. The Storybook Room was truly a sight to behold, with books lining every shelf along every wall, the mantle, even nooks below the windowsill. The bed linens and the drapes were the color of old parchment and the only paintings on the walls were paintings of books or quotes.

"Wow," he marveled. "That's a lot of books."

"This is the room where Gavin stayed," Brink said. Both Michael and Emily turned to look at him. "I spy, remember?"

"I've got to be honest," Luke said, totally unaware of the comments Brink had just made. "I like our chances of finding the journals in here a lot more than I did in any of the other rooms."

"Sterling, are you sure you don't remember what her diaries looked like? Color, binding, anything?" Michael asked.

"She used several different ones, always a different color."

"So that means all of them could be in this room and scattered, or one of them could be in this room and the rest lost to either age or elements," Luke said.

"Or the garbage man," Brink muttered.

"Well," Michael said, rolling up his sleeves and feeling oddly encouraged. "There's only one way to find out."

Michael, Luke, and Emily each took a separate wall while Sterling lingered in the middle of the room, watching them. Honestly, Michael thought he could have helped a *little*. After all, he had a perfectly capable human body to work with

225

now. However, one glance at the fresh sutures in Kate's arm and he decided to keep his big mouth shut.

About thirty minutes into their endeavor, Carolyn appeared in the doorway and gasped.

"Wha - what do you think you're doing?"

"Mom, it's okay!" Emily piped up. "We think the journals are in here."

"The journals? You mean even after last night you're still looking for those darn journals?"

"Carolyn, we know how ridiculous this must seem to you, but we promise, we'll have this entire room picked up just as soon as we find them," Luke promised.

"Luke, I do appreciate what you and your friends are trying to do, but I think this has gone on long enough. You're welcome to stay here as long as you'd like, but it is time to -"

"I've got one!" Emily exclaimed.

Michael glanced up at her, his heart pounding with a strange combination of anxiety and relief.

"Oh no," Carolyn said sternly as she marched toward her daughter, her hand outreached. "Emily, I know you admire them, but I don't want you getting involved with this. Let me -"

But quicker than a flash, Sterling flew across the room and planted himself in between mother and daughter.

"You will not touch that journal," Sterling hissed.

Carolyn looked stunned, and then insulted.

"Young lady, what has gotten into you?" she asked, grabbing Kate by the forearm that wasn't stitched up.

Sterling glared at her, and Michael suddenly realized the ghost was seeing so much more than the woman who may have mildly offended him by seizing his host's arm. He was seeing the woman who had invaded his home, taken over his possessions, and who now tried to come between him and his beloved Joanna, and the loathing in his eyes reflected it.

"Mom, no! Don't touch her! She's possessed!" Emily cried.

226

"What?"

"Kate isn't Kate. Sterling has her. And he's not going to let her go unless we find Joanna," Emily explained.

"Emily, listen to yourself! Do you have any idea -"

"Carolyn, with all due respect, we really don't have time to argue. Now, you can either believe your daughter or not. Either way, we need those journals," Luke said.

Michael could see that Carolyn was still reluctant to accept what was being said.

"Mrs. Drake, please. We need you to trust us," he begged.

After what seemed like an eternity, Mrs. Drake finally relinquished her hold on Kate's arm.

"Very well," she murmured, her jaw tight.

Oh well. They didn't need her approval, just her permission.

Emily dove into the journal immediately and began scanning the pages.

"This must be one of the earlier ones," she announced. "Before they were married."

"What does it say?" Sterling asked.

"October 23, 1833 - Mr. Hall accompanied me on my walk today. He tells me not to call him that anymore, Mr. Hall, I mean, as we are to be married soon. Yet I still find it difficult to address him in such an informal way. Sterling. Somehow the word does not feel right on my lips. I say this not because I am not fond of Mr. Hall. Quite the contrary. I care for him a great deal and I know he will make a splendid husband. It is entirely a matter of respect. He and I come from different worlds. He is used to getting his way and I, as the daughter of a lowly fisherman, have been taught to never forget my place in this world. Mr. Hall could have anyone his heart desires. I still do not know why he chose me, nor am I entirely certain he will not change his mind about me..."

Michael looked over to Sterling for some sort of reaction, but there was none. Had he known this about his wife? Had she eventually learned to confide in him? Something inside told Michael that the answer was 'no.'

Emily skimmed ahead to another page and resumed reading.

"November 19, 1833 - As the wedding draws ever closer, I am beginning to realize that it may, in fact, happen. Perhaps I've been the fool to think otherwise. Sarah tells me that these feelings are natural and I will adapt to the idea of marriage soon enough. I have neither the heart to tell her nor Father nor especially dear Sterling the true nature of my reservation..."

Michael closed his eyes. Of course there was more. There was always more. Joanna couldn't just be like any other girl, thrilled to be marrying the richest guy in town. She just had to have second thoughts, thoughts that she'd apparently never confessed to anyone outside of her journal.

"You still want to hear this, Sterling?" Luke asked.

"Yes," Sterling answered with certainty.

Mrs. Drake eyed both of them like they were acting out some sort of bizarre script.

"Anything else, Emily?" Luke asked.

"Not really in this journal - oh wait! The last entry. January 17, 1834." She cleared her throat and began to read.

"My wedding is less than a week away, yet never before have I felt so alone, so confused, or so ungrateful. Sterling is wonderful. He is everything I could ever hope for in a husband: gentle, kind, loyal. He is a learned man, thoughtful, though not entirely patient. He knows what he wants and will stop at nothing until he has his way. A defect of being raised by the wealthy, I suppose. Aside from that minor flaw, he could very well be the man of my dreams. Although, I fear he has cast

all of his hope upon this marriage and that his capacity for happiness exists only with me. It is for that reason that I come to you.

"I fear I will let him down, and in a way, I fear I already have. If I am not perfect for him, the shining example of everything he believes me to be, he will be heartbroken. He is such a dear and, I am loathe to write it, fragile soul and I could not bear to hurt him.

"I have received word from John. Oh, how long has it been since I last wrote his name? After he departed on this most recent voyage, I was certain I would never hear from him again. Even Sarah advised me not to allow my heart to dwell on him. We are worlds apart, after all. And yet, when we were together, no matter how brief a time, I felt whole, complete, as though neither world existed at all, only he and I.

"Oh, I am a wicked woman for even daring to think such things, let alone entrust them to this meager diary, and only days away from my wedding vows. But I must get the words out lest I lose my heart and mind completely.

"Please, please know that I do love Sterling. I do. And in four days, I will gladly kneel beside him and pledge to him my fidelity and my honor. I only hope that one day, I can also pledge to him my heart. My whole heart."

Emily closed the book.

"That's where it cuts off," she said.

So there they had it. Joanna had been in love with another man. But that didn't mean that she hadn't loved Sterling. In fact, she'd even stated as much. Perhaps throughout their short marriage, Joanna had forgotten about John and learned to live happily ever after, just as madly in love with Sterling as he was with her.

But unless they found the other diaries, there was no way to know for sure.

"Sterling, if you want, we can keep looking -" Michael began to say, but when he turned to face him, Sterling - and Kate - had vanished. "Sterling?"

Journals forgotten, Michael, Luke, Brink, Emily, and even Carolyn went from door to door, calling out both Kate's name and Sterling's. Afraid that Sterling might try to pull the stunt with the window again, Michael and Brink bolted up the stairs toward the upper room only to find it empty and untouched.

Just as he was about to dart out again, an old painting of a ship at sea drew his eye.

Joanna feared the ocean, he suddenly remembered. Sterling had told him that during their conversation at his grave. The same conversation in which Michael had confessed that he would do anything for Kate.

Sterling had believed that Joanna's fear of the ocean had stemmed from a fear of losing her father, but now, Michael wondered if even that was a half-truth. John had clearly been a seafarer himself. Perhaps the ocean served as a reminder of the man she knew, deep down, she could never have.

"She turned to the forest," Sterling's voice echoed inside Michael's mind.

The forest. His gravesite. His and Joanna's favorite place.

Suddenly, Michael knew exactly where he'd find Kate.

For what he sincerely hoped was the last time, he raced down the flights of stairs, out the front door of the mansion, and finally, into the forest, back to Sterling Hall's grave.

Sure enough, she was there, kneeling in front of the headstone, her head bowed low, her blonde hair falling gracefully around her face. Michael approached cautiously, unsure of whether he was seeing Kate or Sterling. He prayed it was the former, but he had a feeling Sterling would hold on to her, at least until he'd said his peace.

Michael knew that Sterling heard him, but he still didn't look up. Instead, he clutched Kate's fists in her lap and stared, as if in a trance, at his own headstone. Michael was beginning to wonder what he should say, if anything, when Sterling finally broke the silence.

230

"She cried on our wedding day." Kate's voice was barely a whisper, the words heavy with heartbreak.

"What?" Michael asked. He knelt down beside Sterling, finally catching a better glimpse of Kate's face. He was stunned to see tears streaming down her face.

"She tried to hide it, but I knew. I saw the sadness in her smile, the tears through her laughter."

"Maybe she was happy," Michael suggested.

"No. She wasn't," Sterling replied with certainty. "I've been the fool in all of this. I mistook her compassion for love."

"She *did* love you, Sterling. She even said so."

"She pitied me," Sterling spat.

"Maybe she did, but that means that she cared about you. Sterling, she knew how much you loved her. And maybe if we find the other journals -"

"There is no need. I know what they will say." Sterling's tone had softened again. "She never mentioned him to me knowingly, but there were nights she would tremble and weep in her dreams, always calling out the same name. And it wasn't mine."

John, Michael thought.

"She tried to love me, and she did a very good job of it. But in the end, I was never what she wanted. I was never enough..." With that, Sterling lost all composure. He pressed the heel of Kate's hand to her forehead and dissolved into heart wrenching sobs.

Michael didn't know what to do or how to comfort him. Had he been with Kate, he would have taken her in his arms, kissed her, and assured her that everything would be all right. But with Sterling, he didn't even know where to begin, so he decided to go with the first thing that came to mind.

"Kate was engaged once," he said. He wasn't sure if that was what Sterling wanted to hear, but something inside told him to keep going. "His name was Trevor. But he died and she - she lost her memory of him." Sterling didn't say anything.

Michael continued. "Even though she doesn't have any conscious memories of him, I know that somewhere, deep inside, at least some part of her does remember. She has a scrapbook full of pictures of him. She's still in touch with his mom, and she even visits him in the graveyard. She loves him, even though she can't remember him. I know a part of her will always love him, and trust me, that is not an easy feeling to live with. But I know she loves me too, and the love she feels for Trevor doesn't in any way impact the way that she loves me." Michael hoped he was making at least a little sense. "Joanna did love you, Sterling, and she honored and respected you. You mattered to her. And I understand that may not be enough for you, but I don't want you thinking that she didn't care, or that she married you out of pity."

After a long moment, Sterling turned Kate's tearstained face up toward Michael.

"Do you truly believe that, young man?"

"I do."

"And you still believe that she has... crossed over?"

Michael knew that one had to be answered delicately.

"Deep down, yeah, I do believe that. I think her spirit is at peace. But I also think that when your time comes and you finally get there, she's going to be really happy to see you."

"You do?" Sterling asked, tears once again shimmering in Kate's bright hazel eyes.

"Yeah, I really do." Michael told him earnestly. "I think she's missed you."

"I miss her too," Sterling whispered.

Then, he closed Kate's eyes and took a deep breath. As he exhaled, a warm golden glow engulfed Kate. She turned her face up to the sky as the light grew brighter and brighter until it became a golden white flash, so bright that Michael had to shield his eyes.

And then, just like that, the light was gone, and Kate was falling back, straight into his arms. Anxious and far too hopeful, Michael held her and cupped her face in his hand.

"Kate?" he whispered.

Slowly, she opened her eyes and blinked up at him.

"Michael?" she asked, sounding confused and weary.

Michael couldn't contain himself. With a rush of joy and love and everything in between, he wrapped his arms around her and hugged her so tight that, he felt his muscles begin to strain.

"Oh, God, it is so good to see you," he told her. Then he loosened his embrace and looked her in the eye. "I love you, Kate."

"I love you too..." she replied, still quite visibly lost. "Why am I crying?"

Michael grinned and took both of her hands.

"It's kind of a long story," he said. It was only then that he realized that while her left hand held his, her right hand was still tightly balled in a fist. "What's wrong with your hand?"

At first, Kate didn't seem to understand what he meant. Then she glanced down to her hand and uncurled her fingers.

There, in the palm of her hand, sunlight danced and glittered off the dozens of blood-red gems of Joanna Stanton's garnet necklace.

CHAPTER THIRTY-ONE

"I still can't believe it," Kate said. She, Luke, and Michael were all camped out in their terminal, waiting for their flight, which had been delayed for at least another two hours. "I can't believe I was possessed, like full-blown *Exorcist* possessed, and *you didn't film it.*"

"Not my fault. Your boyfriend told me I wasn't allowed to," Luke tattled.

And as usual, it was back to Kate and Luke versus Michael.

"Sterling was threatening to hurt you! I didn't want Luke to do anything dumb, like *provoke him into cutting your arm open with a piece of glass,*" Michael said.

"Yeah, speaking of which, how am I supposed to explain this to Gavin? Or my parents? They're never going to let me go anywhere with you again," Kate teased lightly.

"Well, you could try telling them the truth," Luke suggested.

They all exchanged glances.

"Nah."

By that point, they'd all begun tearing into the snacks they'd bought at one of the terminal shops. Luke gnawed on a piece of beef jerky while simultaneously chugging mouthfuls of root beer, Kate scarfed down a bag of potato chips, and Michael treated himself to a bag of sour gummy worms. They'd been his favorite as a kid, and he hadn't had them in years. After the week they'd just had, he'd learned that one of the best ways to ruin a life was to take the good things for granted, whether that be a kiss from the girl he loved or a piece of his favorite candy.

"Oh, I forgot to tell y'all," Luke muttered through a mouthful of jerky.

"Swallow, then talk," Kate advised.

Luke did as she said.

"Anyway, I forgot to tell you, while we were cleaning up the mess in the Storybook Room, we found a few more of Joanna's journals."

"Really?" Kate asked. "Did they say anything interesting?"

"No. For the most part, she was really happy with Sterling. She loved him and she was looking forward to starting a family with him. They were trying to get pregnant when she got sick, just your typical cough and fever. But then," he paused to take a sip of root beer. "Then, she got a letter from John's brother over in Europe. John's ship had been lost at sea. She died only a few days after her last entry."

"It sounds like she just gave up," Kate said.

"Or died of a broken heart," Michael added.

"That's really sad. Poor Joanna."

"Hey, she's at peace now," Luke reminded her. "As is Sterling."

"Are you going to mention that in the episode? That Stanton Hall isn't haunted anymore?" Kate asked.

"No, I think I'll let them go on believing that it is. Give Carolyn and Emily a little extra business from all the folks wanting to stay in a haunted bed and breakfast. And who knows? The human brain is a fascinating little device. Sometimes when people go in expecting to find a ghost, the mind creates one for you."

"Mind over matter," Kate said.

"Exactly. By the way, did Emily tell her mom yet?" Luke asked.

"I don't think so," Michael said. He'd told Kate and Luke about Emily the night before, after they'd all eaten and washed up and had answered Kate's numerous questions about what

235

had gone on while she'd been, as Luke put it, "under the influence."

"I don't blame her. I think Carolyn still thinks I was faking," Kate said.

"At least she was nice enough to let us stay a few extra days," Luke said.

"That's true," Kate sighed and leaned into Michael, resting her head on his shoulder.

"You know, I just found out that we'll be heading down to Florida for our next investigation. You guys in?" Luke asked.

"No," Kate said.

"Absolutely not," Michael replied at the same time.

Luke chuckled and downed the rest of his root beer.

"I mean, if you want to take us to Florida, then yes, we're totally in. But if we have to go ghost hunting again, sorry, no way. We're out," Kate said.

"Oh, you'll change your minds. Sooner or later," Luke grinned.

"We'll see about that." Michael didn't share his friend's certainty or his enthusiasm. The only thing he wanted was to go home, eat, sleep for about twelve hours, and then live happily ever after with the girl of his dreams. Unfortunately, he'd also come to learn that life was rarely ever that simple. It wasn't like a movie where the credits rolled after all the conflicts had been resolved or a book wrapping up its story on the final page. The story of a human life never ended, not even in death.

But really, that was a good thing.

"So, you still think you'll take that job at the insurance company, Mikey?" Luke asked.

"Actually, I think they gave that job away after I told them I was going to be unavailable on the day they wanted me to start," Michael replied dryly.

"Oh well. Easy come, easy go."

Actually, no job was "easy come," but Michael didn't feel like arguing. Instead, he closed his eyes and breathed in the

236

scent of Kate's vanilla perfume. He'd almost dozed off when he heard a phone chime. Michael didn't open his eyes, but he felt Kate shifting around, like she was reaching into her pocket for her cell phone.

"Who is it?" Luke asked.

"Gavin. I texted him earlier to tell him our flight was delayed," Kate murmured as she typed out a response. "Listen Luke, I'm really sorry about him and Gail."

"How come?"

"Well, he's my brother so I feel like it was my responsibility to make sure he behaved himself, but he didn't, and he stirred up all that unnecessary drama," Kate said. "I'm also sorry that... that you had to see her with another guy."

Michael opened his eyes again. *Now* he was interested.

"What are you talking about?" Luke asked.

"The way you were acting whenever they were together, I mean, it seemed pretty obvious that it made you jealous."

Luke stared at her for a moment before he burst out laughing.

"Wait a minute. You thought I was *jealous*?"

"Well, yeah!" Kate said, clearly surprised by his reaction. "I mean, you always got after her whenever she'd hit on Gavin. You blew up at her for spending the afternoon with him. You always just seemed so angry whenever she was around him."

"Oh man, how do I explain this?" Luke asked, rubbing his face in his hands. "Gail is one of my best friends, but she and I... we clash. I get frustrated with her because she takes her stupid flings more seriously than she does her job. That's not to say she's not good at her job. I just wish she'd act a little more professional when these people invite us into their lives and homes and businesses. That and..." Luke trailed off. He seemed to be debating whether or not to elaborate any further. Of course, it was too late. He'd already sparked their curiosity.

"And...?" Kate asked, urging him to continue.

237

"That, and I know seeing her with other guys just about crushes poor JT."

Kate gasped. Michael still wasn't sure he knew what Luke was saying.

"JT likes her?" Kate asked.

"Oh, yeah. He's had it bad for her since the moment they met. But she's this loud, promiscuous hothead and he's probably one of the most chilled out, laid-back guys I've ever met. He's my best friend and I want him to be happy, and it kills me to see her continually hitting on all these guys right in front of him. Because I know, at least on some level, that she knows how he feels about her. But she just goes on flaunting it. That's what really gets me worked up."

"Wow," Kate said. "JT's such a nice guy. I don't know why she doesn't go for him."

"Well, maybe she will someday, when she gets tired of hooking up with random losers. No offense to your brother."

"Oh no, I fully agree. He's a huge loser," Kate told him as her phone chimed again. She read the message. "Make that a huge loser who is warning me not to bring you back to the apartment and that Mom is on the warpath because I decided to stay a few extra days without consulting her."

"You haven't called her at all?" Michael asked.

"Well, I couldn't! And then after I finally snapped out of the possession or whatever, I was so hung up on what had happened that I sort of just forgot I even had a phone," Kate explained. Her phone chimed again. "Oh, and now she's mad at Michael again. She thinks you're a bad influence on me and I never had an attitude problem until I met you." She turned to look at him. "Apparently, you really know how to bring out the rebel in me."

"Well, I've always wanted to be a badass..." Michael joked. If Brink had been there, he would have guffawed and made fun of him for being a nerd.

"Mikey, I've met kindergarteners who are more badass than you," Luke remarked. Okay, so when Brink wasn't there to make fun of him, Luke stepped up to get the job done. Good to know.

"Well... at least I'm tall." It was quite possibly the worst comeback of all time, but Kate still threw her head back and laughed.

"Oh come on. How much does height matter, really?" The barely-five-foot-nine Luke asked.

"Oh, it matters," Michael assured him.

"Not asking you, Mikey." Luke turned to look at Kate.

"Well personally, I like tall guys," she confessed.

"Oh, you're biased. Your opinion doesn't count."

It was a ridiculous conversation, Michael knew, and one that he might not even remember in the years to come. But in that moment, he tried his best to savor what it felt like to poke fun at the little things, to be with friends, and to not have a care in the world. It may not have seemed like much in the long run, but he knew there would come a time when he would long for those moments of lighthearted laughter and careless freedom.

And as he accidentally made eye contact with the ghost of a young stewardess halfway across the room, he knew that time would be coming sooner than he would like to think.

ACKNOWLEDGEMENTS

I'd like to thank God, my Lord and Savior, for all He has done and for all the blessings of this life.

I'd also like to thank...

My mother, Susan, for continuing to believe in me even when others didn't. I owe you everything, Mom, and I love you more than I can say.

My father, David, for his patience and constant encouragement. Thank you for being my wingman at my first book-signing event! I love you!

My three AMAZING editors, all of whom deserve their own dedication.

Nancy Lamb, thank you for your wisdom and kindness and your willingness to go through the entire book with me and talk about what needed to be done.

Hannah Alvarez, thank you for being basically the smartest person I know and one of the best friends I've ever had. You are a constant source of sunshine in my life.

Kathleen Farmer, thank you for your eager enthusiasm, your sharp eyes, and your beautiful and open mind. You are, without a doubt, one of the most genuine souls I've ever met.

My friend and amazing photographer, Kaylynn Krieg. Thank you for the beautiful headshots and for being such a joyful and wonderful person. Let's go on a photography adventure soon!

Finally, thank you to everyone who has read *Cemetery Tours* and now, *Between Worlds*. Thank you to all the new friends I've made over the past year, near and far. I can't tell you how much I appreciate you, your support, your books that you've shared with me, your kind words, and everything in between. I hope you've enjoyed the experience. I know I have.

I'd also like to add a special acknowledgement here. To my sweet Jasmine, my friend and constant reading companion for twenty years. I miss you every day and I love you forever.

JACQUELINE E. SMITH is the award-winning author of the CEMETERY TOURS series, the BOY BAND series, and TRASHY ROMANCE NOVEL. A longtime lover of words, stories, and characters, Jacqueline earned her Master's Degree in Humanities from the University of Texas at Dallas in 2012. She lives and writes in Dallas, Texas.

www.ingramcontent.com/pod-product-compliance
Lightning Source LLC
Chambersburg PA
CBHW011509170626
46810CB00009B/3298